Christmas
on
Union Street

Kathleen Cranidge

2019 White Bird 1st Edition

Published in the United States by White Bird Publication, LLC, Texas

ISBN 978-1-63363-408-4
eBook ISBN 978-1-63363-409-1
Library of Congress Control Number 2019909977

Cover design: E. Kusch

Printed in the United States of America

Dedication

In loving memory of my dear mother, Suzanne. Thank you for your strength and humor, for true love, and for getting me hooked on tea. You forever fill my heart.

Acknowledgements

The idea for this book came to me while sipping tea with my friend, Pam, at our favorite café. I am grateful for your insatiable chattiness and those wonderful details that come with not being able to leave anything out.

Thank you to Renée Bennett for your talent in editing, your candor, your humor. You made this book so much better, so much more, and so much less. Your edits were not only spot on, but I enjoyed laughing to tears from some good zingers.

I am lucky for the love of three older siblings—yackety-yak around the dinner table, squished into the car before the advent of minivans, and summers at the cottage, leading me to observe and yearn to tell my own stories. And I am inspired by the diabolical torture that comes from being the youngest—love to say it, laugh about it, and pull from it. My way of giving back. I love you always.

Thank you to readers of the draft, my sister and Christmas décor guru, Laurie, my Auntie M, and dear friend, Brigitte. And thank you to Victor Paul-Elias (friend and author)—for your support, your feedback, and for bringing Christmas with you to Europe in July.

I am forever grateful for my Aunt Madeleine, for your love, encouragement, and the best pep talks.

And of course, my love, Dave, for landing at the place I was serving tables at all those years ago. Thank you for your honesty with my writing, and everything else, and helping me reverse out of many a plot dead-end. Your bluntness is astounding, but I am grateful, but mostly for making me laugh, for your love of Christmas, and for dancing with me.

Thank you to White Bird Publications for making this happen.

Christmas
on
Union Street

White Bird
Publications

Chapter One

The day I answered Gina's ad for a room in a five-bedroom house close to campus, she invited me for lunch. The place was ancient. I wavered as I stared up at the four stories, but a flurry of snow nudged me along the path to the large covered porch. It was starting to come down with the momentum of a shaken snow globe. I smiled, thinking of Gran and all of her snow globes that she left out year-round. I looked down through clouds of my winter breath at my sneakers caught in a drift. Peaks of snow stood stiffly above my ankles. It reminded me of my mom's meringue pie. Not this year.

I hadn't hauled out my winter boots even though there was a snowfall warning for the next few days. The urge to flee my basement apartment, which felt more and more like a holding cell beneath Eric's place, was too intense. I couldn't bring myself to rummage for them with most of my things already packed.

Wind chimes jingled beside my head. An impulse to turn around gripped me as a gust created more of a clatter than a melody on the porch. I pulled my coat tighter. The vacancy rate was low, especially a few months into the semester and just before Christmas break. I needed a room. I looked down the street. Muted colored lights peeked through the blanketed boughs of many of the snow-covered pines. The street looked familiar. Had I walked by here?

Gina answered the door with a quick wide sweep as soon as I rang the bell. "Well, welcome," she boomed. I was startled by her presence. She towered over six feet tall. By far, the biggest welcome I'd ever had in every way.

"Oh, hi. I'm Ali. I'm here about the room?" Gina kind of looked like a thinner, hippie version of Julia Childs. I pulled my coat even tighter. I felt over-dressed, facing her. She was *flowy* in her layers and dangly jewelry. I looked beyond Gina into the warmth. I could feel it radiate against me. I followed the thick papered-walls, the rich oak staircase, and the vibrant runner I tried to see the end of as it led to the end of the hallway. Was that the kitchen—the aroma of something cooking reached the foyer and pulled me in.

"Yes." She gave me a once-over and looked to either side and beyond me, as though she didn't want to miss welcoming anyone else in. "Yes, yes, come on in before we have to shovel you out."

I couldn't help but check over my shoulder, to confirm I didn't have anyone to bring in with me. "Thank you. Wasn't expecting the snow to fall this quickly." I looked again at my sneakers, embarrassed I hadn't made the effort to get to my boots. Who wears sneakers with a winter coat?

The house was inching toward uncomfortably warm. I pulled off my hat, and my hair sparked and clung to the wool. As we walked in, I kept the faux-fur of my pompom cupped in my hand, like a pet I didn't want to put down. I peeked into the two rooms on either side of the foyer—so many things. A library with stuffed shelves, a living room of soft edges—I thought I saw a quilt on top of another quilt.

Gina turned to me, and I pulled my gaze away from all her knickknacks and layers. "Was surprised to get a call for the room a week before Christmas. It will be nice to have another tenant for the holidays. If you decide to take the room." Gina kept moving. "I like when we have a full house."

I looked up the staircase, then tried to take in the pictures that hung snug together on the wall down the hallway. They were all photos, mostly black and white in heavy frames. Did Gina have family that lived here, or were they all just black and white memories? Looking ahead, I got a glimpse of the window over the sink; it was fogged so I couldn't see the yard.

A huge pot bubbled and hissed on the stove, the aroma foreign but wonderfully sweet. The unusual blend of exotic spices filled the kitchen, which was smaller than one would expect for such a large house. A crystal hung above the sink, its gleaming intensity accentuated by the steam building on the window. I felt claustrophobic, but at the same time, so comfortable and strangely at home. Was it the warmth and hominess of the place, or of Gina? She looked and spoke to me as though I had lived here for a while already. Or was it relief from my escape of that cold tomb—no longer having to suffer his steps, treading above my hideout. Too dramatic, I know, but either way, I couldn't be warmer and happier even with an unknown yippie in her gurgling kitchen.

Opposite Gina, I squeezed into a chair, snug to the small table in the center of the kitchen. The tablecloth was a Provençal-style floral in rich amber, red, and green on a starched white background. Just a spoonful into the most amazing stew I'd ever tasted, Gina asked me what my sign was.

"My sign?" I lowered the heavy tarnished spoon and picked up a bright golden cloth napkin. I dabbed at the thick gravy at the corners of my mouth.

"Yes, your sign," Gina said. She looked puzzled. "Astrological sign?"

"Oh." I avoided her eyes and scanned the kitchen again. The crystal sparkled above the sink. "Aquarius?" *Was she kidding?*

"Water Bearer." She seemed pleased, but I had the sense she would have been pleased with any sign. "The water from the vessel washes away the past, leaving room for a fresh, new start."

What do we have here? I smiled, feeling wrapped in warmth, intrigue, and good food. I lifted my eyebrows, and my smile widened. I picked up my spoon. I didn't know what to say to that. I fiddled with the spoon, admiring it—it looked like an antique. By its weight, it had to be real silver. My gaze fell back into the steaming bowl. Spices wafted up and pulled me deeper.

"Aquarians need space and personal freedom. Any attempt to box them in will likely fail," Gina continued on this path. "Your room will be perfect."

I looked up and wondered where she was going with this. She looked excited, like she was anticipating me opening a gift. She was absently fiddling with a large purple stone that hung off a leather cord from her neck.

Her bulbous knuckles looked painful, but she seemed at ease as she moved the stone around. I wondered how old she was. Her hands that looked wracked by arthritis, pulled me one way, but her green eyes were clear. I didn't notice any wrinkles other than deep laugh lines. Her light brown hair pulled loosely into a bun sprung a few gray hairs from the roots and around her temples.

"Anyway, plenty of time for that later," Gina said. She reached across and picked up my bowl. "Some more?"

"Oh, no. That was wonderful. Thank you."

"Will you be here for Christmas, Ali?"

Here? I watched her move to the sink. She didn't look like she was into Christmas. Maybe she was being polite. I wanted to tell her I wasn't into Christmas, either. Not this year, anyway. Water surged out from the high faucet. She looked over her shoulder at me, waiting for my response as she rinsed our bowls.

"I hadn't really thought of it." It was a week away. I had thought of avoiding it, if I were to be honest. No one wants to hear that, though—not a week before Christmas. I was sure she would have been an ally.

"You're welcome here, of course." She turned off the tap and wiped her hands down the front of her dress, her smock? Is that what you called a muumuu?

I wanted to ask her what Christmas meant to someone whose first question had been, "What's your sign?" A Christmas Boho. Ho, ho. There was some theory or thought, someone famous had said—the greater the contrast, the greater the potential? Something like great energy only comes from the tension of opposites? I think it was Jung. Anyway, I felt that right there in Gina's wonderful clashing presence. I loved it. The nuttiness of it all made me feel at ease. A giggle rose and tickled my chest, but I kept it inside. My dad, who had the same giggle-reflex said some people don't get the giggles—it's not always a good first impression. Maybe I was more like Gina than I thought, or perhaps it was her presence that encouraged something I wanted to bring out.

"I'll show you the rest of the place," she said, saving me from answering. She led the way out of the kitchen.

I chewed on the question as I followed. Where would I be for Christmas this year? I didn't want to think about it.

We moved into the adjoining dining room. It dwarfed the kitchen with its long, mahogany table…buffet, sideboard, and hutch. Was she someone who couldn't let go of things, or did she just like to be surrounded by things? Lots of things. I quickly counted the place settings, each with a vintage looking silver plate with scrolled trim. Twelve. How many people lived here? It was an outstanding table. I kept wanting to peek at Gina. This table seemed too formal for her. I imagined the English royal family might have something just like it at a cottage—they would probably call a summer house. On top of the buffet was a blanket of cotton snow grounding a magnificent Christmas village. Warm lights glowed from the windows of the houses and shops. I stole a glance sideways at Gina, intrigued by this woman who seemed so opposite of Christmas. If I took the room, Christmas would be surround-sound.

Behind her, I glimpsed the living room. She motioned an arm in that direction, and we moved in. I could feel her studying me. A Douglas fir towered in the corner, encroaching on a bulky burgundy wingback chair with the beautiful complement of an ottoman in rich shades of gold and deep maroon paisley woven into the fabric. On the opposite wall, a huge brick fireplace extended to the ceiling. Large logs were neatly set in the hearth, which measured at least three feet by three feet. There were ample places to sit for a cozy dozen in that room, including a well-cushioned sofa in front of the window. Although it was the middle of the day, the December light coming in was minimal, but the lamps gave the room a warm glow.

We walked across the front hallway into the den. Books and books on thick wood cases ran from floor to ceiling on two of the walls. Next to a pecan-colored leather armchair, I noticed a tall side table with a pipe in a brass ashtray. Again, I wondered, who lived here? She caught me looking at the pipe.

"It was my dad's," she said. "After he died, I missed the smell of it. I started to light some of his tobacco and burn it, inhaling the sweet familiar aroma." She shook her head and paused. "After a few weeks, this little ritual satisfied me less and less." She gave me a funny look, as though she was sizing me up for the first time. "Then I savored some on my tongue for a few days. But I felt I was bordering on chewing the tobacco and I didn't think Dad would like *that*." She laughed. "One night, I filled the damn thing and took a few puffs." She shook her head then picked up the carved wood and inhaled deeply. "I know. It's the craziest thing. It's now a wretched habit." She said *wretched*, like my favorite great uncle used to say. Almost like it was something good. "Every evening, after the dishes are done, I come in here and have a little puff-puff." She laughed and brought it to her nose again then returned it to the ashtray and shrugged at me. She looked like she wanted more than a sniff. What a character. Everything about her was unique, easy-going…and intriguing. I knew then I would take the room.

Gina led the way up the stairs. Rich red runners softened our steps, but the wood beneath still creaked and groaned.

"Don't mind the noise. This house likes to talk." She smiled. "Your room is at the top. If you decide to take it." She paused on the large landing and pointed to two bedrooms on either side of the washroom at the head of the stairs.

"My room." One thumb jutted to the left. "And Harry's room." Her other thumb to the right. "Harry works a lot. Sometimes I think I could get away with having two tenants in there." She laughed. "It could be days before you meet. I know he'll be here Christmas Eve."

We continued up another flight of stairs. The next story held the same floor plan. She splayed her crooked thumbs to both sides again. "The door on the left is Nathalie's. Kiki's here on the right. You will hear her before you see her. A ball of energy, that one. She's visiting from South Korea to learn English. She's been here five months. She's determined to make every second count. Not even the cold Vermont weather can stop that one." She smiled at me. "I like to knit her things." She turned that smile to me. "Which reminds me. I love that sweater you have on. Such a lovely pink. Is it cashmere?"

I touched my neckline. "It is. My dad gave it to me last year for… Christmas." This time last year. I needed to get out of this subject. "How about Nathalie. Will I meet her soon?"

"Nathalie?" Gina looked surprised. Then the outer corners of her eyes turned down. "Oh, dear. Sorry." She raised an arm weakly toward the room that she said was

Nathalie's. "Nathalie died. Around this time last year." She leaned her hand on the doorframe and looked into the room. I wanted to inch closer to give form to the mass of shadows. I caught a sliver of a white duvet on a brass bed, a stack of suitcases facing the door, with a floppy hat on one and a stuffed lamb on top of another. "I haven't had the heart to clear it out. I guess I should. Well..." She sighed and touched my arm.

We continued up. I turned and stretched my gaze back to Nathalie's room. I pictured my mom's narrowed look she'd give me when we were invited to one of our new neighbor's house. I sometimes wandered off into the rooms and then asked too many questions. I liked empty rooms—I always made up a mystery. Maybe I wouldn't have to make one up here. Gina's breath filled the hallway, labored from the two flights of stairs. I thought back to the pipe in the brass ashtray. She held the banister and pointed upstairs. "That brings us to your room."

The runner on the oak stairs was almost plush, its deep reds more vibrant as we moved up, obviously less traffic to the fourth floor. She caught her breath and paused near the top. "Haven't had anyone up here in years."

I looked beyond Gina at the rich oak door. The final level, the attic, offered no landing. I pulled my sweater tighter. It was chillier up here. I hadn't signed a lease. As much as I already liked Gina, I wouldn't freeze for anyone or anything. And why hadn't there been anyone up here? I looked down the staircase—the rest of the house seemed to fall away…

"I put the heat on this morning," Gina said as if reading my mind. "I promise you one thing, I don't scrimp on heat."

I didn't doubt her. It was hard to forget the warmth the rest of the house held.

"Now." Gina hesitated. "As you can see, there is no bathroom on this level." She looked at me, apparently waiting for a protest. "You'll have to share the one below."

"Of course." An ensuite wasn't expected. I did want to see my potential room, though.

"And remember, there's no landing. So, if you do get up in the middle of the night, the stairs are right outside your door." Her hand held the doorknob, but she continued to pause. "It *is* an attic, but it's a pretty good size."

I smiled and nodded to encourage, my eyes on her crooked knuckles wrapped around the doorknob. Finally, she resumed the twist of the brass. She seemed to enjoy building suspense. She was good at it. It would be interesting for sure to hang out with her and that pipe. I imagined being curled up in the den some evenings after dinner. I'd even let her read my palm for fun. I felt that little giggle, wiggle in my chest.

"Oh." Gina slightly moved back.

I clung to the banister, leaning into her, my breath caught and held in my chest, giggle de-wiggled.

"Sorry, Ali."

I tried to see over her. But was she ever tall. I was pressed up against her, blocking the momentum of her reaction, but couldn't get my eyes around her. What was in there for God's sake?

"Huh," she said with subdued surprise, but she didn't move.

She *was* good. "What is it?" I asked, my voice a hoarse whisper.

"The tree." She finally fully opened the door and

moved in.

Now I could get my eyes on the room. There was a tree, about four feet tall, in one corner, aglow with colored lights. Straight ahead in line with the door was a window with heavy brocade panels gathered to each side, creating a bulky frame. Through those drapes, the sky was white, thick with snow. A king-sized bed with a substantial duvet and large pillows took position on an angle looking out at the room. I imagined my feet sinking into the luxurious shag rug beside the bed. The coolness from the stairway fell away. There was instant warmth from every slope and corner that lured me, starting right from its root of wide planked golden pine. As I took in the room, Gina continued to stare at the tree.

"Is there something wrong?" I asked. I had almost forgotten her lead up to this as I collided with magic. The beauty gripped me. The perfection of the room expanded my senses. I let go of my tour of the space and focused on the tree that had stopped her in her tracks. It didn't look like there was a bird or a mouse in the tree—I hadn't seen any of the branches move. I hoped there weren't any mice up here…I scanned the pine floors.

"No, no, it's just…the tree…um…" She looked over at me. Then she shook her head. "Oh, it's nothing. Sometimes I can be a bit forgetful." She shook her head again, but I saw her look at the tree and scan the room as if searching for something.

More intrigued than scared, I signed on.

I was able to move in the next day. Late afternoon, unpacked and making a tea in the kitchen, I heard a push against the front door, then a loud thump of it closing, and the *stomp, stomp, stomp* of feet shaking off excess snow. A *zip-zip* and then *clunk, clunk* of boots hitting the floor. It had to be Kiki. She entered the kitchen as I removed the screaming kettle from the front burner. She looked fourteen, but Gina had said she was eighteen.

"Oh." She gaped at me. She still had her coat on, which was a few sizes too big for her tiny frame. Thrust deeply over her ebony hair was a loose-knit pink hat. She started to pull it off as she walked toward me.

"Nice to meeting you." She removed her matching mittens and extended a small red hand. "Kiki. Um, it is Awli?"

"Yes, Ali." I smiled and shook her cold hand. "Tea?"

"Thank you, yes." She started to unwind a large cable-knit gray scarf. Although Kiki had done surprisingly well with English in a mere five months, the conversation was a bit stilted, but I enjoyed listening to her, and we got the gist of what each other said. We went through our names and our studies, and she told me about the snowball fight she had with a friend, and I told her about dropping a whole box of shoes on my way up the stairs and chasing down the first flight to get some of them. When she stopped laughing, she asked, "Natlie here?" She looked worried.

"Nathalie?"

"Oh." She looked down at her cup. "Natlie not here. Three days."

I squinted at her. I tried to pull something out of what she had said…was it miscommunication, a lack of grasp on the English language? Or was it a lack of grasp on reality? Her room was below mine. I looked into my mug. I felt too close to the table, too close to crazy.

Kiki gulped the hot tea—I guess she did everything fast. She then swirled the leaves on the bottom and frowned.

"You read?" she asked.

"Do I read?"

"Leaves. Like Gina?"

"Oh. No." But I leaned a bit closer to get a look inside her cup. Part of me thinking maybe I'd see something and part of me didn't want to look into her eyes…maybe I'd see something.

She stared intently at the specks scattered on the bottom of the pink and gold porcelain. A look of sincere concentration. But only for a moment. "Okay. See you later, Awli." Kiki stood abruptly. "Harry here?"

"No, I haven't met Harry yet." I'd ask Gina that night about Kiki. Gina would know if we were living with crazy. No. Gina would have cautioned me.

Kiki blushed. "He cute." She coiled the scarf back around her neck and covered her face. "But he never here." Just dark eyes peeked out.

She waved and tramped down the hall and then pounded up the stairs. The bathroom door slammed, and the house was quiet again. A few minutes later, I heard those little heavy feet bound down, boots zip, and she was off again. I later nicknamed her "Taz." I found an old Bugs Bunny episode online with the Tasmanian Devil so she would understand. She was delighted. The thumping persisted.

After the front door slammed the silence wrapped around me, rooting me into the chair. I examined the leaves in my cup, but they just looked like a wash of chewing tobacco. I thought of Gina and that pipe, of her reading tea leaves, her interest in signs—what was I in for with this wonderful eccentric? I squinted at the crystal over the sink. Was there a crystal ball hanging around somewhere? I looked around the kitchen as though I might see one shoved behind the toaster. I pushed through the quiet, poured some more tea, and moved into the dining room. The only sound was the gurgle of the radiator hissing as I continued further in. I had the urge to sit at the head of the table but turned and took my tea up to the attic to seek comfort in a smaller space.

Entering my room again, I was hit by the smell. I hadn't noticed it before. I set my tea on the writing desk to the right, just beside the tree. I took in a deep breath—it was furniture polish, a lemony scent, but there was something underneath. I looked at the desk and the wardrobe, then scanned to the large carved headboard. Old wood. It smelled like the cottage we rented when I was a kid. I loved that place. There were so many cupboards and drawers to find things left there from current owners, previous owners, and past tenants. There were thick quilts, wool blankets, and ancient newspapers. My favorites were the unique bottles in the bathroom half-full of mauve and pink liquids I wasn't supposed to use, but I often unscrewed or popped the crystal tops to steal a hint of the heavy scents. My mom said that they were probably too old. She always brought a pack of Ivory soap bars for the summer. She'd leave half of them in the big pine medicine cabinet when we left. Maybe everyone wanted to leave something behind—even a bar of soap. My least favorite find one summer was a doll with a cracked porcelain face. It frightened me so much my dad pushed it up into the attic. I shivered—attics were where things were stowed, memories buried. What was up here, what had made Gina jittery?

I walked over to the wardrobe and pulled on the cast iron handles, hoping there would be something in it.

Perhaps not a route to Narnia, but at least a quilt. I had to tug harder at the doors that hugged the wood within its frame. Inside the wardrobe were two shelves. The bottom one did have a quilt as well as two stacks of towels folded neatly on either side. Above there were a few novels. I scanned the titles on the spines. As I started to close the doors, I noticed a small box behind the books. I reached in and pulled out what looked like a man's jewelry box. I felt a bit of a snoop, but that didn't stop me. It never stopped me. Inside was a small key. I closed the lid to see if there was a lock on the box. I looked behind me to the right at the desk and spied one of those narrow drawers with a lock. I walked over and pulled on the drawer, and it rattled against my hand. I tried the key, but it wasn't a fit. A quick survey of the room for another spot for the key yielded disappointment. I rubbed the tarnished metal in my hand before returning it to what seemed like its hiding place. Who was hiding it? The last person who rented the room, years ago? Or was it Gina's—did she know about the key?

Shadows had started to lengthen and squeeze into the attic alongside me. It was dark, except for the lights from the Christmas tree and the sliver of light from the lampposts, which shone in creating a path to the door. I moved over to pull the heavy drapes closed but paused to watch the crystal flakes form on the mullioned glass. I knelt on the bench under the window and looked out onto Union Street. It was comforting, watching the snow coming down from my perch of the attic. A much nicer view than looking up from the foxhole of my old cellar. The only things I ever got a glimpse of from there were feet trudging by. It was definitely the right move—even though it took me away from him. But I hated just to see his boots, to hear him go up the metal stairs and a second later close his door, without pause. But then I thought of Kiki and her question about seeing Nathalie. I didn't want to have to leave this place to avoid Kiki the way I left my basement apartment to avoid Eric.

Dinner that evening was just Gina and me. I had gladly accepted the offer for the all-inclusive meal-plan added to my monthly rent. It would be well worth it not to have to shop and cook. As I wound down the stairs, my hand caressing the wood banister, I could hear Christmas music, soft and jazzy. I paused by the entrance to the living room, captivated by the Douglas fir lit up with its white lights, and the glorious fire casting warm shadows around the room. I wanted to curl up beside the tree to watch the flames reflect their dance on the ceiling and listen to the crackle. But the bouquet of spices wafting from the kitchen was too enticing.

"Wow, it smells amazing in here. How could anyone skip this?" I smiled awkwardly as I took in all the steaming dishes on the table. Just the two of us and so much food. Suddenly, I didn't feel that hungry. What would we talk about for a whole meal, with her so different from me? I thought of the "What's my sign?" question of just the day before. Ironically, that made me relax a little. She did seem to have a lot to say about a lot of things and was apparently comfortable with any topic. I did feel a bit of guilt as I looked down at all the dishes. When I had offered to help, it was an emphatic head shake and a wave of twisted hands. "You get yourself settled in, my dear," she had said, swooshing me along with those bent hands she seemed so at ease with—I wondered if they hurt, or were they like a callous—the pain gone, but the evidence of it always there.

"Harry and Kiki do get at the leftovers. Sometimes I get the chance to catch up with them when they get home late. It's so nice to have someone to sit down with at a normal dinnertime hour." She smiled at me.

"Kiki said something about she hasn't seen Nathalie in three days. What was she talking about?" I put that on the table right away. I had to know what I was dealing with. *Was* I living with crazy? Was crazy safe to live with?

"Ah. Kiki." Gina slowly shook her head. She sighed and gave me a look, a sizing me-up look. "Kiki thinks she sees Nathalie." She shook her head again. "Kiki *wants* to see Nathalie is what it is."

Tightness crept up and settled into the middle of my brow, leaving a weight in my chest along its way, binding me in place—even though I wanted to move more than ever. "Sees Nathalie?" *Well, there you have it: I'm living with crazy. And I'm already signed and sealed here.* I dug my thumbnail into my hand. I felt cornered in the middle of the kitchen. It was so warm, so hot. *Why is it so hot?* But at the same time, a layer of cold sweat tingled across my collarbone, down my ribs, and bled out my fingertips. "But…" I shook my head that felt too heavy. I sat down even though I wanted to leave. I looked at all the food. My hands lay in my lap as though they had been placed there. I wiggled my fingers.

"Are you okay?" Gina asked. "There's nothing to it, really. Just an overactive imagination on that Kiki…and me, well, just an old fool hanging on…" She nudged one of the bowls closer to the middle of the table.

What did that mean—was she including herself in this—did *she* see Nathalie? I didn't believe in the supernatural or anything, but I believed in crazy, and I didn't want to live with crazy. I waited, nodding to push the conversation forward, a nod of encouragement to hear something I wanted to hear.

Gina paused and mirrored my nod. "As I said, I'm still holding on, I guess. I can't seem to give up Nathalie's room. I'm getting close, I think." Gina nodded her head with conviction that time. "And Kiki, well, she was so intrigued by Nathalie. I talked about her so much. Too much, maybe, for a while. She wanted to know all about her. I don't know, it seems she's trying to keep her spirit alive. Pauvre petite bête." She waved her hand. "Sorry, my grandmother comes out of me sometimes. That means poor little thing. It literally means poor little beast, but don't tell Kiki." She laughed.

I liked the little French expressions she threw into the conversation. I stared at her across the blend of spices wafting up. I wanted to ask her about my room after all this talk. The attic. Why hadn't she rented *that* out for such a long time?

She smiled warmly at me, looked down and motioned toward the food. Steam hovered above the dishes like fog cover—that's how I was starting to feel about this place. What lay beneath?

"Now, what do you say we eat while it's hot?" Gina said. "You know, if Kiki ever really saw…" She waved a crooked hand and laughed. "She wouldn't be waltzing around mooning over it. I know she would let me know quickly. We'd all know."

I smiled and leaned back into the chair. Gina made everything seem like you should laugh at it. She started to serve herself and motioned for me to do the same. Some of the dishes looked familiar, or like something familiar, but there were a few I wasn't sure about.

Luckily, I wasn't a picky eater, because there were some weird looking things. That seemed about right for Gina's table—I would have been disappointed with a plain old pot roast. "What's this one?" I scooped a spoonful of meatballs from a heavy blue and cream-colored serving dish. An intense burst of hunger waved over me as the aroma streamed closer to my plate. The thick salty steam from boiled potatoes lay behind the surplus of the varied dishes. The combination was one I'd never experienced, yet there was a familiarity and comfort with each inhale.

"That one is called *Poutine Rapées*—it's a mixture of raw grated potato, cooked potato, and salt pork formed into balls, simmered, with brown sugar and molasses. It's one of my favorites. My grandmother was French. She made this better than any other I've ever tasted."

"She was from France?"

"Oh, no. She was born in this very house. She was Acadian."

Acadian? I knew Acadians were in Maine and Massachusetts, but Vermont? Gina may be an Acadian descendant, but she seemed more like a Cajun. I pictured her frying catfish with that pipe in her teeth. I smiled, and my senses swept all the dishes.

"I never found out her secret, but I've gotten close to it over the years. I'm pretty sure it had something to do with butter. Always more butter in her cooking—even if it wasn't in a recipe, there had to be butter. She used to say, it was too familiar to her to be classified as a recipe. And this here"—she ladled chunky looking stew in a golden broth onto her plate— "is *Fricot aux Coques*, translation: clam stew." She passed it over to me. "And of course, these are fiddleheads, simply with butter and sprinkled with plum balsamic vinegar.

Consider yourself lucky—not too many are serving fiddleheads this time of year. I froze some to steal out of the freezer from time-to-time. And those are *galettes à la morue sèche*—fancy name for dried cod fishcakes. Finally, *Chicken Fricot*, which is one of the most popular Acadian dishes, chicken and onions browned in butter, with diced potatoes and summer savory in lots of chicken broth. Bon appetit."

"Wow. There is a lot of food here. Thank you. Bon appetit."

After the dishes, I joined Gina in the den while she smoked her pipe. With a long wooden match, she set the room aglow, then packed the bowl of her pipe with tobacco. White, silvery, and gold candles flickered at different heights on the bookshelves, and a large crimson candle with three wicks glimmered beside the chair Gina sank into.

"I believe pipe smoking contributes to a somewhat calm and objective judgment in all human affairs." She struggled not to laugh. "My dad used to say that to defend the habit to my mom. He borrowed that line from Einstein."

"Hard to argue with Albert." I smiled and settled in. I liked the bonus of the pipe.

"Or my dad."

"Right." I laughed along with her.

It felt like I'd been there in that den every evening for a lifetime. I could get used to this, I thought. We never had this much stuff. I scanned the bookcases. We never had layers to get underneath and settle into, always moving every few years. Always having to start over.

Gina tapped her pipe. I checked my phone and jumped up. "I have to head to campus. I have a meeting tonight." I paused and took a small step toward her.

"Thanks for dinner. It was unbelievably good. See you tomorrow, I guess…"

"I'm a nighthawk, you might just see me right here, depending on when you get home."

I hurried to campus. Every Thursday night, I met with the CCCs— 'Cracking Cold Cases'—a group for criminology undergrads. It was only my third month with the CCCs. Not bad, the handle. But I thought it would have been funny if they had called it the CCOs— 'Cracking Cold Ones.' But they would have been flooded with applicants. They were anyway, so when I received my acceptance letter, it was like looking at winning numbers on a lottery ticket. I loved everything about the group—signing the confidentiality agreement, the windowless room below the library, the quirky people who never missed a meeting—but the cases drew me there every Thursday. It wasn't a secret, but it felt like one. We tried to solve cases the police hadn't been able to piece together. Only cold ones, though—the active ones were too confidential. We pored over case notes, hoping to find something overlooked, to tag on to. Sometimes we interviewed families of the victims, a weary witness, or a police officer or other field experts. We gave it our all to come up with theories for the crimes. Buried a floor under all those books, with nine other dedicated criminal minds, I felt I belonged—for the first time, there was a club where I fit in.

Gwen, the club president, started it for personal reasons. Lynn, a friend of hers, went missing about four years ago and she's never been found. Gwen was with her the night it happened. Lynn said good-night and left to walk home, and Gwen never saw her again. Gwen still hangs up posters of her friend. I went to a vigil in Lynn's honor Gwen organized when I joined the group. She holds one every year at the beginning of the semester. I held a candle as I squeezed into the crowd, squeezed into a sorrow I couldn't imagine, but it pushed against me. Pain pulsed through the circle connecting us to a past…and for the ten from our group, to a future seeking justice. Professor Vale, who teaches a crime scene investigation course, helps advise the club. He puts in a good word for our credibility, but still, we don't get too much the public doesn't already have access to. Most of our investigation is barebones, looking through old paperwork in hopes we might pick up on something that might have been missed, tucked away.

I was the last one there, which was unusual, a first. I squeezed in and shut the door, but no one cared about stragglers. I passed Michelle, her long hair, almost black, creating a curtain around her and her laptop. She was staring at a flowchart. She bobbed her head at me, and I waved. As I settled with my laptop, others eventually pulled away from their screens and gave a head bob, some smiles. Gwen touched my arm and gave it a squeeze, but she was focused, we were there for a reason. Some of us concentrate more on detailed notes and timelines, others try to visualize the scene by pulling up street views on maps. The group hasn't solved any crimes yet, but the cops appreciate us. They are so busy, therefore happy to offload lower priority cases to unpaid volunteers. Everyone in the bunker has an average of ninety percent or higher and was chosen because they demonstrated superior critical thinking skills and because all of us want to pursue something in the field of criminal justice. My mom had hoped that I'd choose law, but I've always been a fan of Nancy Drew.

We had two cases—Gwen's friend, which was ongoing, and another we started when I joined the group. A twenty-one-year-old woman, Leslie McAvoy, was working her third night-shift at a gas station when she was murdered. Her body was found two days later, ten miles away off the highway. The police thought it was two escaped prisoners from a minimum-security institution out of town, who had turned up in Burlington around that time, but the DNA was not a match, and the case went cold about three years ago. I was two years older than Leslie. And Gwen's friend Lynn had been eighteen. The McAvoy case for me was harder. We had pictures of the dump site. For Lynn there was hope…or we could pretend there was. We could still call her missing.

"How's it going?" Gwen whispered as I hovered over the images of the gas station and the apartment across the street.

"That apartment." I pointed at the screen. "I just keep coming back to that."

"Yeah." She chewed her lip. "I get that feeling, too." She mentioned a few things she was looking at, then moved around the room, whispering, pausing with the others.

When we left, it was late enough the porters had locked all the other doors. As we branched out across campus onto the empty streets, a creeping cold case thought sidled up to me—maybe I shouldn't be walking home this late at night. But as I headed back to Gina's, the snowstorm was a comfort, a blanket along the way. I got drawn into the Christmas lights.

I could see the glow in the front window and the outline

of Gina, right where I had left her a few hours earlier, as she had predicted—it was just after eleven. I was glad she was still awake. I was always ready to keep going on Thursday nights.

"It's so Christmassy in here," I said after I shook off the snow and moved into the den. Even though I wasn't drawn to the holidays this year, I couldn't avoid it—and I liked Gina, despite the fact she was like living with Christmas. And I was happy it was so warm. I was already acclimatized and couldn't imagine sitting down for the evening in my old draughty dungeon, the quiet dragon above. When I met Eric, he told me he was a dragon. He paused when he said it, for effect. He liked the handle of the Chinese zodiac sign. But when I looked up the weaknesses of a dragon, it seemed about right—elusive, often seeming to be in a daze. I typically look for the positive, but when leaving something…or someone behind, I opt for self-preservation.

"Nathalie loved Christmas." Gina smiled. She looked like she had been dozing or daydreaming. The smell of dried fruits and cedar hung in the room. "She brought Christmas back into my life after many years." She stared into the candle flames beside her.

I only nodded, not wanting to break the spell—curious to hear about Nathalie. I chose a large embroidered cushion in lieu of the chair in the other corner, pulled it in closer to Gina, and drew my legs underneath me.

"She moved in when she was only seventeen. The longest I've ever had a boarder stay on. Four years." She seemed to be pulling memories out of the flames flickering beside her. There was no sadness, just immense fondness in her green eyes.

I'd only known Gina just over twenty-four hours,

but it was obvious she wasn't prone to melancholy. I started to feel comfort there on that first night, at home in a strange house that felt more familiar than any had in years. Comforted, even though only mere hours away from sleeping two floors above a man I hadn't met and a floor above a young woman's room that still held her in its memory. I shifted, hugging my knees into my chest, relieved to be away from the small basement apartment I'd left behind just that morning. Away from the cold air creeping in through the single-paned windows and under the door. Away from the deafening stealth of Eric on the metal stairwell leading to the apartment above. And the shudder of the pipes and the footsteps overhead followed by the muffled voices on his TV.

"I'm glad you'll be here for Christmas, Ali." She looked pretty darn content with that pipe. "Oh, and before I forget, Nathalie introduced a tradition a few years ago, I will continue to honor. Everyone who lives here invites one guest to dinner Christmas Eve."

I looked at her, my brows knitted up onto my forehead. I hadn't said I'd be here for Christmas. I went over our conversation at dinner—no, I hadn't committed to that. How odd. I felt heat rise through my sweater. I didn't think I was ready for a head-on with Christmas.

"You will be at the house, won't you? You mentioned your mom being in Colorado, no? And your dad in New York?" she asked.

I hesitated, but pictured the mahogany table set for twelve and the village glowing alongside on the buffet. I loved it when people said things like "the house" as though it were the place to be, the only place to be. I loved the established familiarity. Where else would I be? "Thank you. I suppose I will. A guest? A guest for Christmas Eve?"

"Someone who has nowhere else to go, an acquaintance, or even a stranger." Gina looked more excited than I'd felt in years.

I thought of Caroline and Mags heading home for the holidays. Both had invited me to spend Christmas with their families. Mags had left a week earlier. She'd called me an hour before her bus left to make sure I hadn't changed my mind. Hearing the busy bus station in the background made me feel lonely. It was the first year I wasn't heading home for the holidays. She had begged me one more time to come with her. "Come on, what else are you going to do? Hunker down in that depressing basement apartment avoiding Eric?" I hadn't found Gina's place yet, and she knew the market was tough for rentals. I hated to think of her picturing me there, lying low—I'd have to call her to free her of that image.

I enjoyed my visits to her place in Boston. Such a contrast to being an only child. It was so lively with her brothers and her sister talking over one another, often sounding like they were on the cusp of an argument, but that never happened. Not in front of me, anyway. But with my move, it felt too hectic, or that was a good excuse. I looked at Gina as she tapped her pipe into the ashtray. I didn't have anyone I could think of to invite.

"No exceptions." She wagged her finger at me.

How did she do that? Always responding to my self-talk. I shifted on the cushion. I wasn't sure how I felt about her reading my mind or sensing what was on my mind. Maybe she was a witch. Would she classify herself as a witch? What was a modern-day witch, anyway? Mags would know, Mags would want to be one. I'd ask her when I called. I shut out those thoughts in case Gina was trying to access them. I stifled a smile. I didn't mind a witch.

"Everyone brings a guest," she continued.

If nothing else, at least I had started to feel something about Christmas. I was intrigued about the days ahead, but even more about Gina, so fantastically eccentric, who continued to offer up mysterious tidbits about herself, her boarders...her former residents.

"Well, looks like I'm leaning toward a stranger. Hmmm. How does one ask a stranger to dinner?"

"You'll find the right person. It will work itself out."

I was starting to feel tired. It had been a long day. I was looking forward to that king-sized bed. Kiki still wasn't home. I didn't expect Harry, but it would've been nice to meet him.

"Nathalie often brought a stranger. Harry too." She stared off. "Harry was very fond of Nathalie. I worry about him a bit."

I shifted. My foot was asleep, but I didn't want to move too much. I wanted to hear more about Nathalie. I leaned to the side and scrunched my toes together.

"Harry stopped by the diner the nights Nathalie closed, so he could walk her home. I know he stayed at work an extra hour to be able to time it right." The light from the candle lit her face. I noticed the deep lines around her eyes I hadn't spotted before. "It had been snowing heavily, a day much like today." Both our gazes shifted to the window. Big flakes spiraled down underneath the lamppost onto the sidewalk. I braced myself for details of a car sliding through an intersection on the slippery roads.

What she told me was not at all what I was expecting.

"I was surprised by the doorbell at midnight. Not just for the hour. It was rare someone rang at any time of the day. Most people who visit us just walk in. Usually a courtesy knock, but it's rare anyone waits for someone to open the door. But midnight? Never. I knew something was wrong." Gina paused, and our eyes met. She gave me an apologetic look before she continued. "She fell into Lake Champlain." She shook her head slowly. "They say she may have jumped." She looked up at me and paused. "I still have a hard time believing that. She had to have fallen…"

I was mesmerized as I listened to the brief account of what happened. Surrounding Gina's deep sadness after Nathalie's death was an unrelenting puzzlement over it. My mind reeled as I waited for her to continue. The Secret of the Champlain popped into my head. That was my weakness—always quick to jump into a mystery. I felt for Gina as I watched her eyes bounce with the memory, waver with the loss, but I also started to go somewhere…

"I knew her as well as if she were my own daughter. We spent so much time together. There were times I sensed a remote sadness in her, but she never lingered there. She loved being happy. But she worked at it, I guess. I never felt the sorrow I picked up on had been that deep, though. I hate that they say she may have jumped…but I guess…" She rubbed her forehead. It looked like she was trying to erase what she had just said. "It tortured me for some time. I was angry for not being more perceptive or not asking the right questions." She dipped a crooked finger into the pooling wax around the wicks. I had the urge to get up and join her. She peeled the cooled wax off her finger and continued. "We were close, but there was a wall of privacy around her. I respected that. There were certain things people normally talk about that she didn't. Like family." Gina pressed her lips together and pulled them up, an attempt at a smile.

Nathalie. I realized who she was talking about. It was *that* Nathalie. Nathalie had lived *here*. I knew the case, everyone did. I had devoured every article in the paper. They recovered her body almost a week later near Shelburne Point. The police concluded it was suicide. There had been drugs found nearby. I remember the reporters interviewing friends of Nathalie, the emphatic protests she had never done drugs. My mind traveled back to the news the year before, trying to picture the house—they would have at some point shown the house, mentioned Gina. I went back to standing outside, looking up at it just the day before. I had felt something, there had been something familiar, or something had made me hesitate, almost turn away. Now, it was the main draw. It nudged… no…it pulled…yanked me further in. But I tore myself out of the details. "I'm so sorry, Gina."

"Thank you." She nodded. "Anyway, I just wanted to let you know. I didn't want you to wonder about it."

We sat peacefully for a while. We turned again to the heavy snow coming down and had a moment. Gina, for the memory of a dear, loved one. For me, a subdued reverence for someone I would never know, a pull to know more about. The candlewicks flickered on the side table. We both gazed into the flames. A mystery blazed in my mind.

Going up the stairs, I absorbed every creak. I felt like I was intruding or something—every step an announcement…a warning. Nathalie had lived here. I paused on the first landing. There was a soft glow from Gina's room. Harry's room was dark. The warmth of the den and my time with Gina fell away with each step. Before reaching the second landing, I froze. A flash of

Gran in her coffin jumped into my mind. I tried to squeeze away the image. I hadn't had one of those shots jolt me since she passed away two years ago. The weeks after she died, I'd sit up in bed with damp pajamas, sweat beading across my chest, trying to shake those images. I picked up my pace, pulling myself out of my stupid fascination that kept creeping into the shadows in my mind.

The third floor was dark, except for the nightlight illuminating a path to the landing from the bathroom. I felt the empty rooms on either side, especially the left, Nathalie's room. Kiki's felt empty, empty for the moment, but Nathalie's emanated a void, an absence. Inside the bathroom, I leaned back against the door, waiting for my breath to slow. I brushed my teeth until they hurt, not wanting to go back out or up. I stared into the mirror and made a fake smile. Then a more exaggerated one. When the fake fell away, I thought fondly of my mom, remembering the first time we made those faces together and ended with a laughing fit. I had walked in on her making that face in their bedroom. The sight of her had startled me, but she was quick to get me in on it. I often wondered what had made her scared or sad that day when everything seemed so perfect to me.

Chapter Two

I walked to the diner well before dawn the next day. Up before the rest of the house, it felt strange to be in all that space by myself—like a forgotten visitor. The comfort created the night before with Gina had inched back when I woke that morning, like the night after a party, not wanting to bump into anyone in the kitchen. Although I wanted to escape the quiet, I paused outside Nathalie's door—always open, always dark. The floor creaked as I peeked into the dark space, taking in the outlines…the shadows that started to form and move in my mind. Another creak got me moving. I tiptoed down the stairs.

I closed the heavy front door, thinking of the sneaking of Eric. Despite the dull nag against my heart, I couldn't help but appreciate the sound of that— sounded like a book title—the Sneaking of Eric. After it ended between us, we crept at different times. I suspected it was easier for Eric—not a creep, but a creeper, he seemed chronically rootless, whereas I was more of a pattern seeker. I shook the thought away and pulled my hat down. The sidewalks weren't plowed, so it was slow going. Most of the houses slumbered and were dark except for rims of Christmas lights on eaves and on snow-laden boughs. It was still except for my steps crunching into the snow, rebounding against the edge of the morning. It was a stiff cold, even without a wind blowing. I welcomed the effort of the trek, warming up as I pulled in and out of the snow with each step. I rounded a bend in the road and saw the glow of the diner.

The heat from a vent above rushed at me as I entered the foyer. I lingered a moment between the two glass doors, enjoying the burst of warmth, taking in the red 50s-style barstools that lined the counter, the framed old-time movie posters, and the Christmas tree squeezed just inside the door. I slid into one of the booths along the window, caroling welcoming me from the speakers in the ceiling. It was early, but the diner felt like it had been opened for hours or maybe never closed. I wondered if it was one of those all-night spots. There was only one other customer starting his breakfast at the counter, a USPS Parka on the barstool beside him. A young woman topped up his coffee and headed over to my table. A bulky gray sweater hung to her knees, wrapping around her stick frame before belting loosely at her tiny waist. I thought of the paper dolls I found one summer at the cottage that held my attention for an afternoon as I folded edges in to keep their clothes in place. The server's dark hair was short and messy, the kind of messy that looked good. A few wisps of pink were barely noticeable underneath at the nape of her neck. Maybe if the dolls had hair like hers, they would have stuck around a little longer.

"Morning," she said cheerily. She poured coffee without asking, but I wanted some. "Menu?" She pulled one out from under her arm, on auto-pilot.

"I'll have a couple of scrambled eggs and wheat toast. Thank you."

"You got it," she said. Her porcelain skin was flawless with a small cluster of freckles across the bridge of her nose, but beneath her eyes bore a deep shade of purple. As I poured a second creamer into my coffee, I wondered how someone could be that tired at…eighteen? She couldn't have been much older. I felt a pang of guilt that I was only working the summers. It was my last year for that, though, full-time forever lay in wait for the spring. Would I stay in Burlington? I'd miss Caroline and Mags if I went back to New York.

Mom wouldn't be happy if I didn't go back home. How often was she even in the city anymore? I wouldn't be surprised if she moved to Colorado, where she was spending more and more time with Brad's family. She had been disappointed I didn't want to go skiing with them over the holidays. Dad would encourage me to stay where I was—he was never a fan of a big city. He had one year left before he would retire, and he was plenty tired of New York. After he retired from the military, he got a cyber-security analyst job there. He was having a hard time walking away from the pay, but with my mom moving on, he was going to, too. Maybe he would come north as he had hinted a few times. I missed them both, but I hadn't been ready to spend Christmas with just one of them.

A few more people came in out of the dark, bringing in snow on their wooly hats and hoods, tracking a path to a table or booth. The sky was just starting to lift the night. An older man stooped under the decorated tree on his way in and placed a bag there that looked heavy. When I arrived, I hadn't noticed all the canned goods underneath the slouching boughs—it was a real tree. The overhead lights were dim, easing early risers into the morning—an approach more than likely adopted by the tired server. But she looked cozy, like the diner. She looked like this was her living room. I scanned the tables and booths. Good-sized colorful mugs face-down snuggled together in pairs and fours. The cutlery seemed shinier than any place I'd ever seen. *I wouldn't mind a living room like this.*

"Morning, Mr. Brooks," the server called out from behind the bar. She was filling a metal teapot with boiling water.

"Morning, Sally." He took a booth facing me but closer to the door. I watched him remove his thick wool hat. Loose gray curls fell below his ears. He looked to be in his early seventies. His steel blue eyes lifted to take in the diner. I pulled my gaze away, so he wouldn't catch me staring.

The man at the bar took a last swig of coffee, drew a bill out of his wallet, and placed it beside his plate. He turned and lit up when he saw this Mr. Brooks.

"Hey, Brooks," he said as he zipped up his USPS Parka.

"Morning, Adam."

"Didn't realize the time." He pulled on his hat. "See ya, Sal. Thanks."

"Have a good one," Sally said as she walked the pot of tea over to Brooks' booth.

I looked out the window, my reflection bouncing back at me as I listened, well, eavesdropped on their conversation, which was slightly muffled by Bing

Crosby's *White Christmas*. Mr. Brooks was concerned about Sally because she looked tired from working double shifts for the past week and a half.

"It's only till Christmas," she said, summoning more enthusiasm than she seemed to have.

"Rick's hired someone? Not just a promise of someone?"

"That's right. He says her name is Andrea."

"Good."

"Good. Now, if the inquisition is over, I'll bring you your breakfast?"

"Actually, I'll just have a half grapefruit and one of those bran muffins."

"Joe has some gingerbread pancakes this morning." Sally raised an eyebrow. "You sure? I also noticed him whipping some cinnamon cream."

"Hmmm, tempting, but no. These Friday morning cakes are starting to catch up to me."

"Where is that?" Sally laughed.

Brooks patted his belly, but he didn't have one. "Just get a customer what he wants, okay?"

"One grumpy-man special, coming up."

"Very funny," he called after her as she headed to the bar.

"Just a warning. It's typical. A man of your age starts eating that and soon as you know it, he starts to get grumpy. I've seen it happen. Too many times," she called back, pulling the cellophane off half a pink grapefruit with a bright cherry at its center.

A group of four walked in, followed by a couple, and a few lone diners who looked like they were there to get in and out before heading to work. Within the next ten minutes, the diner was three-quarters full. After Sally had everyone's cup full and all the orders in, I caught her eye. She came over right away.

"Sorry, did you want your bill?"

"Yeah, sure." I paused. Without thinking it through, the next words started to race out of my mouth. "I couldn't help but overhear about you being short-staffed. If you need someone for a little while, I could pick up some shifts, if you like?" I paused again, folding the bill then smoothing it back onto the table. "Just temporary. Help you through the holidays. I'm a student so will be busy in the new year—but I could help out until then." A nervous laugh sputtered out, sounding kind of like a hiccup. After blurting my offer, I realized it sounded odd—I sounded odd, but I had started it, so I was going to keep going. "I've waited tables before." I attached my verbal resumé.

She stared at me with a frozen face. I wasn't surprised.

"I could use the tips," I added. "Christmas money, you know."

"Oh, ah…" It was her turn to sputter. Her dark brows knit together. "Well…" She sized me up. Was I legit? I think intense fatigue made her want to believe. She looked around the diner and twisted her lip. "I'd have to ask Rick." She did that twist of her mouth again, finishing with a bite down on her lower lip. "You sure?"

"Yeah, definitely. It'd be fun."

"Fun?" She squinted at me. "You sure you've done this before?" But she added a smile.

I laughed. "Anyway, you're busy. I'll leave my number on the table." I looked down at the crinkled bill. "I don't need any change. So, let me know. I can start anytime. I'm just a couple of blocks away." I pointed over my shoulder.

Sally moved around the diner, looking re-energized.

I headed out into the snowy morning to set to work—the search for my dinner guest.

I trekked along Main Street. I was in no rush to get anywhere, so I enjoyed moving through the tunnel of snowbanks, alongside the drifts pushed up against storefronts. A few windows waking, soft light edging around blinds with the closed signs. The sun started to reach my path. Crystals glistened ahead creating sparks in the snow. Although I couldn't imagine how I would find a guest, images of prospective tablemates popped into my head like one of those old slideshow projectors. I easily got caught up in the fantasy. But what took me more was the rush of excitement that surged within me after those past few months. It had been three years since my last real boyfriend. Since then, there had only been Eric. About one year of Eric.

But only Eric turned into more of Eric than I expected, more of a crush to the heart than I imagined. I never dreamed I'd have such a relationship, how it started, anyway. Mags and Caroline called it a booty-call, which made me cringe. It wasn't that at all, but they loved the idea. "We've never met him. And do you go out, do you have dates?" Mags had asked when I protested. It wasn't that, though. It wasn't that at all. We had been friends for about six months. It started with half hours here and there, chatting on the fire escape when we returned home around the same time on a Tuesday night, on a Friday night. The summer had been hotter than usual. I had started to sit out on the metal stairs, my only outdoor space, to get some air on those scorcher nights.

I saw my first cricket that summer. I always thought crickets looked like grasshoppers. But one evening, searching for a breeze on the escape, I noticed a beetle-looking bug on a step below. It chirped. I leaned down closer to it; unconvinced, I waited for proof. Sure enough, it gave another chirp.

Eric popped his head out of his door above me. "Hey."

I looked up and smiled, then down to the cricket. But it was gone. "Do you know what crickets look like?"

"Yeah," he said as he stepped onto the escape and closed the door behind him. "Sort of like a grasshopper."

"Sort of, but they're really ugly. They look like they have some beetle in them."

"Doing a project?" Eric sat down beside me. I started to like his shoulder against mine. Moving out of 'just friends' territory was my favorite part of a relationship.

"No. No project. Just saw one for the first time."

Those nights progressed to him following me down the steps into my apartment when the heat lifted. After five months of 'more than friends,' easily following those six months of 'just friends,' I started to love him. Everything about him. I loved his quick laugh, his quicker smile. But something happened—I began thinking. About what I would do after university, after that year with Eric. What would he be doing…? I realized we didn't have a lot in common. I tried and tried because I loved him. It was weird to be in love and want to leave. But I started to notice things, like when he'd ignore me for the television but would pout when I didn't put my homework aside when he immediately wanted my attention. Sometimes he'd just jump up and leave, seem cooler the next day. Then it wasn't as hard. Once you start to notice things, then it's easier—anyone can start to bug you. It took me a few more months.

It took my mom longer, but when she did get there, she couldn't stop talking *at* my dad, picking at him. The worst was when she stopped laughing at his jokes that she always found so funny. No, the worst was when he stopped laughing, stopped trying to make her laugh. He ran out of jokes. After the move to New York, things changed. It was harder for my mom, I think, without that support network of the military. She started to loathe it the last years before he retired, feeling trapped inside it, she had said, but I guess it was harder not having all those people who knew your name, even if it was only for a few years at a time. After the yelling stopped, it felt like it was over. A silence settled in. My dad started to walk around it, work even later.

For me, it was gradual, because I still loved Eric…loved the way he laughed, loved him touching my shoulder when he laughed. My dad hadn't been laughing anymore those days building up to the end, but that's not what my mom had been looking for, anyway. I think if he had laughed, she wouldn't have liked it.

Eric was so different from me, so different from anyone I had ever hung out with, but I didn't really know who that was—who he was. There was an odd excitement around the whole idea I attracted someone like him, but even more that I would entertain a guy like him. Nonetheless, it didn't take me long to fall for his shaggy hair, the tribal tattoo on his lean muscled bicep, to ignore that he wouldn't talk about himself.

So, on one of those nights when he was in my apartment joking and not talking about anything, avoiding everything, I ended it. "Eric, I really like you."

"I feel a *but* coming…" He nuzzled my neck and started to pretend to bite. "I don't like buts that come after 'I really like you'…" He laughed as he kept nibbling.

His joking bugged me, too. I had liked that he laughed at everything when he was on the fire escape, but it bugged me more and more inside my apartment. I think it bugged me because I loved him and didn't want to have to miss it when he left, when I asked him to leave. "Stop it." I kept my back rigid. "Seriously. I think we should cool things. I think we're too different and I don't want to…" I had cringed when I said 'cool things' because it's not what I had meant.

"But I'm crazy about you." He moved his hands up my waist. I wanted to let go, to not care, to not always think, but I pulled back.

"Please, Eric." I turned to him, bowed my head, and leaned into his chest. He held me for a long time, and that was it.

I endured three more months of hearing him but never seeing him. Both of us adjusted our schedules, him coming home later in the evenings, me making sure I was home earlier. There were times I thought I heard him pause and my heart would ache, part of me wanting to meet him on the fire escape, sit and feel his shoulder against mine.

I brought myself back to Main Street, happy to have the distraction of who would be my dinner guest. But as I walked along, part of me wished Eric could be my guest. I felt the urge to go see him more than I had in weeks. As much as I wanted to get away, it was harder being away from him. When he was still a flight of stairs above me, there was a small comfort in the sheer discomfort. There was a possibility. But I had come that far, seeing him again would make it worse. I feared he'd always be someone I wished I could've had more of. I didn't want to be married ten years to a substitute and still think of Eric. Eric, who probably *was* a booty-call. I cringed into the bright snow.

Caroline had said I should have let it play out. She was convinced I would've ended up not liking him on my own without having to force the end. She said I always drove an outcome, analyzed too much, including her. She had made a face but laughed. She was emphatic that relationships should fall apart on their own, as they always did…always the case with her. She unequivocally found something that irritated her with her men after a few months. Her pessimism in this one area depressed Mags and me. She believed men and women could only last six months, tops, otherwise someone was either desperate or depressed.

"What do you suggest for the evolution of the human race, then?" I had asked, going along with her because she was always fun to watch.

"Artificial insemination," she had said with her fake-serious face that she was so good at delivering.

It was busy on the main drag with less than a week left until Christmas. It made me think of Gramps. After dinner on Saturday nights, he used to ask Gran if she wanted to drive the drag. She never said no. It was nice being in a small city. Gramps would have liked it here. He liked small cities. I missed him. He loved this time of year. I smiled as I took in all the snow-covered decorations. But as I passed by people on the street, I started to feel self-conscious. I'd never been out on the prowl looking for someone. It was different than strolling along. It would be ludicrous to pick up a stranger. Weird. Maybe it was all just weird. Most people had somewhere to go Christmas Eve, anyway. I focused on the shop windows and the white-blanketed sidewalk a few steps ahead.

I passed a young woman who was just off the sidewalk, huddled up on a curb. She was so young. I could see the little girl in her eyes, but her cheeks were collapsed and blanched. Her gloves were worn thin, as were her leggings. I noticed her drawing her fingers inside to pull away from the holes at the frayed tips. I couldn't imagine how cold she must be. My breakfast sat full in my stomach, like an obstruction surrounded by the emptiness I felt.

Did I have any cash on me? Yes, I had a ten. I passed her, pushed the bill into one of my mitts, and dropped the pair. I picked up my pace and prayed she'd pluck my mitts off the sidewalk. I shoved my hands into my pockets and fought the urge to look back at her. The last thing I wanted was her to feel like I had baited her. I should have just given them to her, but there was something about her that made it hard to just give, toss and walk by. Mostly, I didn't want to embarrass her, but it was also her age, too close to mine. She was too similar to dodge, to walk on the other side of the street from, to dismiss. Is that what I usually did, too unrelatable to take in?

The cold bit through my pockets at my fingers. I thought of how easily, how, without thought, I could walk into any store and replace my mitts. How many pairs did I already have? I rubbed my fingers together and balled them into fists. No, I could go an afternoon without a new pair of mitts. Shops were opening for the day. Blinds lifted, closed signs flipped over to open, and lights brightened the windows. I ducked into the more Christmassy ones—maybe I would bump into someone…a guest. I felt a rush of excitement, but how could I ask someone, even if I wanted to? It'd come off weird, stalker-like. Caroline would be all over it. She didn't have a shy bone in her body. I wished she were there to help with my project. But Gina's soothing voice rang in my ears: "It will work itself out. You will know when you find the right person. You'll just know." She also had said something surprisingly like what Eric had often said: "When we let go, everything we need comes forth." I know neither had coined the thought, but it made me smile coming from someone like Eric. For Gina, it seemed about right, something she would say. As I lifted a candle to my nose in a perfectly claustrophobic Christmas store, the familiar smells of home came to me. I smiled and relaxed.

"That's my favorite. It smells like Christmas."

I turned to the vaguely familiar voice. Mr. Brooks from the diner was coming down from a stepladder with a large hardcover book in his hands. I must've looked shocked. My mouth hung open the way it always did when I was caught off-guard. One of those things I've tried desperately to put an end to, but in the moment, can't seem to. Small town that it was, I didn't expect to see Mr. Brooks outside of the diner, especially on the same day. Nor did I expect he would work in such a place. He looked like an ex-Navy Seal or someone who worked on the docks. Probably could still pull his weight down at the harbor.

"New in town? Never seen you. Now twice in one day." He stepped off the ladder.

"Oh, hi. No, but new to the neighborhood. Just moved to Union Street."

"Gina's place?"

I stared at him but pressed my lips together to anchor my mouth shut.

"I only know as vacancy is low these days. And Gina had posted a sign in a few of the coffee shops. I noticed it wasn't on the board at the diner any longer."

"Yes, just moved into Gina's."

"And do you have your guest for Christmas Eve? Don't look at me like that again." His smile reached his blue eyes. "It's the nature of the beast—living in the inner city. I was once a guest at Gina's. Gina's guest." He looked down at the book in his hands and rubbed the dust off the colorful jacket.

"No. Not yet. What's the book you have there? It looks wonderfully illustrated from here."

He turned it to face me. It was a beautiful version of *The Night Before Christmas*. "My wife…she used to read this, every Christmas to our kids. When she opened this store, she would read it Christmas Eve to whoever wanted to come by for the reading and hot chocolate before she closed for the day. I was thinking it was time to pick up her tradition again. I didn't have the heart to get it down until now. She passed away ten years ago. I think it's time."

"I'm sorry, Mr. Brooks." He gave me an odd look. "Now you're looking at me funny. I heard Sally talking to you. I'm Ali, by the way." I moved to the middle of the store amongst all the books and reached out my hand. "What time do you plan to read Christmas Eve? I'd love to come by for that."

"I was thinking around three o'clock."

"I will look forward to that. My dad used to read it, Christmas Eve, as well." Despite my resistance to the Yuletide, I felt a pull to be part of Mr. Brooks' story time—it was just a story…

"Good. So, if I get misty-eyed, you can be second in command?"

Although I wanted to stay and talk more to Mr. Brooks, I knew I should let him get back to the big mess of books on the counter. And I was supposed to be finding a guest. "Well. I will get back to my little project and leave you to all *that*." I raised my eyebrows at the clutter around him.

He made a guilty face and shrugged. "Righto. And hopefully, we will see you at the diner tomorrow."

Before I moved back into the snow, I heard a book drop. It sounded like someone had thrown it down. It made me jump. When I looked back over my shoulder, Mr. Brooks was looking to the back of the store. There were a lot of books, but when he turned around, I felt self-conscious. I whipped my gaze forward, headed out.

Chapter Three

Late that afternoon, I heard from Sally. She was thrilled I could pick up the breakfast shift. She gave me the option of shifts and was happy I preferred the early one. She could use a little sleeping in for a few days, she said. "I can never seem to get to bed early enough, but given the opportunity, I can always stay in bed a little longer." She went over a few things, but there wasn't much to worry about. She'd pre-fill the coffee machines. All I'd have to do is press the button. Joe, the cook, would be in an hour before me for prep. Really, the only thing to do was put out the dishes of creamers and ketchup bottles on the tables. Make sure the menus were clean, shine the cutlery. "If you sell coffee, everyone's happy," she said. "And if you can laugh at them joking about hooking the pot to an IV line, you're a saint."

Yes! It would be nice to have a little extra cash—some walking around money as Gramps used to say. It was tight just working the summers. My dad always topped off my bank account in the early spring when I was starting to plough for pennies, checking and rechecking every coat and turning my purse inside out, hoping I had a zipped section I forgot about it, excavating the couch and counting stamps on my coffee card, anything to find that extra dollar. Mostly, it was a gum wrapper or something worse—a Kleenex, or getting a stab from a bobby pin. With some shifts at the diner, I could pick up a gift for Gina, maybe a little something for my guest.

First, I had to find that guest. Walking up and down Main didn't seem to be working. I passed the young woman I had seen earlier curled onto the curb. Despite my resistance, our eyes met—but like a flash, we pulled away from one another, but the image stuck to me as I headed back to Union. But I noticed my red mitts on her hands.

No one seemed to be home when I arrived back at Gina's. There were two teacups on the kitchen table, both half-drunk. I wondered if Kiki had flown in and out with a friend. It didn't seem like Gina to leave anything out. I didn't know Kiki well, but it was easy to imagine she could have gotten distracted and hauled off in a hurry. It felt weird again to be alone in the house. I wasn't used to all that space. Alone in a small space was much different than alone in a big house. I listened to the quiet house, with the intermittent creaks and the hiss and hum of the radiator, the…muffled voices?

I followed the murmurs to the front of the house— but there was no one in the den or the living room. The voices were clearest by the staircase. My gaze travelled up through the banister and spindles. The voices were too near… I looked back down and noticed there was a door, its frame blended into the wood on the stairs. It was a smaller version of a regular door—I thought of Alice in Wonderland—but only five feet high and narrower than a standard door. Big enough to squeeze through without a shrinking drink, at least.

I recognized Gina's voice—that didn't surprise me, but what was she doing? Who was down there with her? I tried to hear something more than the mumbles I couldn't make out. I leaned up against the door, I couldn't help it. The words started to form, Gina's voice became louder, maybe the end of the meeting or whatever it was. Maybe she was giving someone a reading or whatever you call it. My heart started to thump. Gina said, "Just make sure your luggage is tagged and confirm your flight before you go." Then I heard the other person, a woman's voice. "That's it?" She sounded disappointed. So was I, that was kind of boring for a psychic. Or maybe she was lending a suitcase stored in a crawl space.

Gina spoke again, "That's it. Three times a year, the planet Mercury is in retrograde—lots of travel snafus, delays, cancellations, luggage mix-ups, but nothing to worry about." I pulled my ear away from the door and stared at the wood. *What?* A chair scraped against the floor. "But I can't shake you turning over the death card, Gina," the woman said. I froze. It *was* a reading. I had to get out of there, but I couldn't move, and I wanted more… "Honestly, that's it," Gina said. "I wish they would take that card out of the mix, it's the 21st century. People are scared enough." She laughed, but the other woman didn't. "It just means change. That's it, that's all." I heard more movement, I looked toward the front door and turned to the kitchen. How fast would they be up? I decided to make a run for it—quietly. I moved as fast as I could on my toes, down the hall, and up the stairs. I took two at a time, listening for the door, but just hearing *creak, creak, creak* with my every step.

I made it to the attic without hearing anything from below. Maybe the woman needed more convincing. As much as I didn't believe in that stuff, I hadn't liked the sound of the death card. I moved to my window and stared down at the snow that continued to build. I felt a little claustrophobic, trapped, looking down from all those floors. A death card in the house. I pulled my sweater tighter even though I felt hot. I wanted a glimpse of the woman—what does someone look like who comes to someone's house in the afternoon for what, what was that—a reading? What does someone look like who had that delivery—how do you convince someone it just means a change, someone who believes.

I heard the front door and leaned right up to the window to get the full view. I could see the back of her as she moved down the path away from the house. A normal coat—camel colored—but I couldn't determine her age as she had the hood up. I felt a little disappointed. I didn't know what I was expecting, what I wanted to see. I followed her to the end of the path. She turned and looked straight up at the attic. I froze, caught by her placid eyes, which looked colorless, maybe gray? The snow was bright around her, such a contrast to those eyes. I ducked. She was young, I wasn't expecting that. I couldn't tell, exactly, but she looked close to my age. I was expecting, I don't know, someone older, maybe bored one morning, circling an ad while staring through the paper at the kitchen table. Curiosity pushing her to call the number…wanting to escape or trawling for drama. That's what my mom said about New Agey stuff—people were trying to stir the pot. Did the woman sense me staring down at her? I shuddered and fought the urge to peek down again. She looked like the reaper, with her large hood. Like an attempt to fool him.

I heard a thump, but it sounded like it had come from the wardrobe. I stared up at it from my squat under the window. I hadn't seen any mice. I prayed I didn't live with rodents. I pushed myself up, paused, then moved over and put my ear against one of the doors. I felt a wave of hysteria as I gave a couple of raps and listened for movement. Nothing. I looked down at the floor, gripped the cast iron handles, and swooshed both doors open, jumping out of the way. I sat back on the edge of my bed and waited. The only thump came from me—*thump, thump, thump*. How ridiculous. I was going to drive myself crazy…eavesdropping on people and listening for mice that better not be there. I finally walked over and looked in. The second row of books had fallen, making visible that jewelry box I'd seen the first day, with that single key inside. Was that a hiding spot? Not a very good one, but was it? I scanned the room again, wondering where that key fit.

"How was your day, Ali?" Gina lit her pipe, and her shoulders sank into the soft-cushioned wingchair. She looked tired, but content.

Did it take a lot out of her to foresee things? Or to pretend. I imagine pretending would be worse, but no, I couldn't conceive Gina forging anything, which meant she believed. I watched her as she fiddled with her pipe. Did she have people come by the house often for this fortune telling, or do they call it that? That sounds too amusement parky. I wanted to ask her about it, but I didn't want to admit I had listened by the door. What was down there—a card table, candles, a crystal ball…a curtain of hanging beads to pass through. I would have to find the chance to go through the door into Gina's wonderland. There was something about it. I thought there was something important down there, or maybe the people led down there were key. Key suspects floated into my mind, which gave me a little jolt.

I had to find a way. And I couldn't let on I knew, maybe it was secret. I brought my energy back to my day—it had been a good one. "Great. I have a job for a week or so at the diner."

"A week or so? How does that happen?"

"I overheard the server, Sally, talking to Mr. Brooks, they're short-staffed, I offered to help for a bit, starting tomorrow morning. I guess you know Mr. Brooks? I saw him again at his bookstore, small town." I took a breath after spilling out everything I could with one exhale. I hadn't realized how excited I was to tell someone, to tell Gina.

Gina bobbed her head in a half-nod and looked out the window. It continued to snow—the whiteout nudging up and bonding to the glass. It seemed as though she had missed my question.

"He said he was your guest once for Christmas Eve?" I made it specific.

"That was a long time ago." She looked back at me and shrugged. I couldn't imagine any falling out between the two.

"Oh?" I hung a question mark in hopes to keep some momentum even though there wasn't any—it was me pushing her.

"Small town." She shook her head at me. "We *are* a city, you know. Largest city in Vermont, in fact." But she winked and continued. "It was five years ago. That's eons ago." She waved her hand, seeming to snap out of it. "That's okay. Don't look so glum. I have a full life here. I don't think there's room for a man, anyway. You know, there has to be *lots* of room to fit one in." She made a face, but her eyes flickered, and then a shift of the conversation…onto me. "What about you? Anyone special in your life?"

I shook my head and looked down. I didn't want to think about Eric. I was relaxed and had enjoyed a day full of distraction. I breathed in the smell of her pipe that now reminded me of Christmas. With Gina, everything was reminding me of Christmas. She was making it hard to walk around, hard to dodge. I played with replacing *Rockin' Around the Christmas Tree* with my version of *Walkin' Around the Christmas Spree*. No, spree sounded awkward… I don't think it would be a hit with too many others. I watched the silvery gray wisps of pipe smoke curl and float up and past me, melding with the undertones of molasses, cinnamon, cider, and the rich oaky smell of the fire always a layer. The house was like a Christmas quilt—every day a new patch added.

"Hint taken. But if you do ever want to talk about it." She smiled, stretched her legs, and wiggled her thick-socked feet. "Would you like me to knit you a pair? I would love to. Knitting is my meditation. The hardwood floors get to you after a while." She continued to move her feet as though actively displaying her work.

"I would love a pair. Thank you." I put my hands around my toes as I drew my knees in closer to my chest. I gave her a sidelong look. She did make me feel comfortable. I'd never felt so at ease with anyone this quickly. "His name is Eric. It's been three months, and I can't seem to shake him." I felt her compassion, even though she didn't say a word. "We were too different. I knew we wouldn't end up anywhere, so I ended it. I sometimes regret it because I miss him so much. But I know it would hurt more in the long run."

"Let me see your palm." Gina reached out her hands, her long fingers like the prominent front legs of a praying mantis, bent and held together at an angle.

I hesitated a moment, then got to my knees and scooted the few feet over to her chair. I offered my right hand. But if she pulled out a deck of cards, I didn't know what I'd do.

"No, no, your left." She seemed to settle right into it. "The left hand shows potential and what could be…"

Her hands were calloused and warm. I looked at her as her expressions went from raised brows to puckered lips. I didn't think too much of palm reading. Maybe there was a crash course that had a facial expression volume—the right amount of brow raising, etc. But I felt a bit of anticipation as I waited and watched her. She was immediately into something on my palm. It was a few more moments until she spoke.

"The top line is your love line. Yes, just as I thought. It's straight and parallel to your headline. This means you have a good handle on your emotions." She seemed to be about to push my hand away but paused and peered at it further.

General, that could be a standard, I thought. But her pause created a push inside that surprised me. I didn't believe in any of this, but I couldn't help but want her to continue. "And?"

"Well, it looks to me like you shouldn't think with your head so much. I don't know if it's this Eric that's supposed to be in your life?" She paused, and I wondered—is she seeking validation like the ones at the local fair in their gauzy tents. But she continued, "It seems someone is supposed to be in your life around now and last for an indefinite amount of time. Hmmm." She smiled, and I got the impression she wasn't much of a palm reader. Maybe a romantic. Embellishing or blurring the lines.

She was big on astrology, though, and much what she said did seem fitting. She reminded me of how Aquarians are very protective of their freedom. She wondered if this could have something to do with my pulling away from "this Eric," she called him. As much as I wanted him to be just "this Eric," unfortunately, I wasn't there yet.

"Is he a Libra or a Gemini?"

"His birthday is October 26th—I don't know what sign that is…" I just knew he was a dragon. I stared at Gina. I hated the hope that pulled across my chest.

"Oh." She scrunched her nose.

I noticed her shift. She shrugged and looked out the window, searching for another topic it seemed.

"And?" I tried not to sound too anxious. There were no cards on the table.

"And what?" she said.

"You know what. Not a match I guess, huh?"

"It's not a science."

"Well, let's have it, anyway. You can't leave me hanging," I said. I tried to sound light, but my shoulders felt like someone was pushing down on them, driving me into the floor.

"No, not a match." She looked serious. "Scorpios are moody."

"So, are a lot of people, no?" There had to be a little

more than that for her to react so coolly.

"When matched with an Aquarius, a Scorpio can become very jealous and possessive."

Eric? He was more aloof than anything, but I didn't say anything.

"It can be great at first. But once a relationship starts to evolve, when you put other people…life into the mix, it doesn't usually end well."

It had been just the two of us always. Hmmm. The right decision, maybe? But the pain of that thought pulled at my throat. I continued to stare at her. I was disappointed by her assessment. But it was validating even though it didn't feel very good. I settled back into the cushion and shifted the conversation. "Harry really is never home. I've heard him come in a few times, I think."

"I know. If you want to catch him, you have to be a nighthawk like me. He usually leaves the house around seven and gets home around eleven-thirty. And you were out of the house before the crack of dawn this morning, well, before, I think. He was hoping to meet you, too."

"Well, it looks like I might have to wait until Christmas Eve to meet him. I'll be up and out before six for the next few mornings. Hi ho, hi ho."

"Good for you. Nice of you to help Sally out. Lots of wonderful people gravitate to that little diner. Not just the people who work there. It has a good energy to it— it seems to pull people in."

Like here, I thought. I was getting more and more used to Gina. I loved the way she talked about energy, good souls, and her astrology tidbits intrigued me. I felt I was getting to know more about myself by hanging out with her, and it wasn't through astrology. But I found her "star-speak" interesting and sometimes spot on, which was kind of fun.

"Yeah, I got a good vibe from the place." I giggled. She gave me a wry look but smiled. "Do you ever go?" I asked.

She shook her head. "To the diner? No. I don't find the time these days."

We sat for a few quiet minutes with our own thoughts. I had a lot, mostly about what she did with her time or was she avoiding the diner, Mr. Brooks.

I brought my mug back to the kitchen. As I walked in, I was surprised to see a door leading out to the backyard I hadn't noticed before. I almost missed the counter as I put my mug down and moved to look out the window on the door. I cupped my hands and peered out, feeling the cold from the outside immediately. Condensation fogged the glass. I covered my hand with my sweater and cleared a spot to regain the view. There was a large evergreen strung with white lights near the back of the property. Only a soft glow emanated from the boughs laden with the heavy snow. Enough to cast light on a set of footprints from the fence tracked to the door. I looked back and forth across the yard, but it was too dark to see much more. Going back to the tree, I noticed a bird feeder hung from the fence along the property. Gina must have been out earlier to fill it.

I waved to Gina as I walked by the den, but her head was back against the chair—the crook of her neck confirmed a nod toward sleep. Heading up to the third floor, I noticed a light coming from the left side of the hallway. Nathalie's room. Gina must have been in there and left it on. Maybe she was thinking of another renter. When I reached the landing, the light went off. I gripped the banister and froze. The front door pushed open. I flew down the two flights of stairs into Kiki's arms. I must have looked crazed. But it was Kiki who surprised me—she wasn't surprised one bit by me.

"You saw her?" she whispered. "It okay."

"Saw who? I didn't see anyone." I was gripping Kiki's forearms tightly. Luckily, she had her oversized-parka on. "Sorry." I let go of her.

"No? What is then, Awli?"

"The light was on. It was off when I got to the top of the stairs."

"She didn't mean scare you. Here, let me get things off. Where Gina?"

What was she talking about? Gina scaring me? Gina. I couldn't believe she wasn't in the foyer with me after my bounding down the stairs like that. I moved over to peek into the den, and her head was still back against the cushioning. She must have been exhausted.

"Sleeping? She sound at sleeping." But despite that, Kiki brought her finger to her lips and pointed up the stairs for her and me to go up.

I kind of wanted to grab my coat and haul out of there, to be honest. Even though I didn't believe in spirits or whatever Kiki believed in, I didn't like that I lived with someone who did. I thought of my old bunker—at least I knew the devil above me—hell, I'd even stay with that devil tonight.

"It ok, Awli. Come. We go up."

I searched Kiki's eyes for fear—or crazy. But she didn't seem frightened, and I didn't know what crazy looked like. I'd never met crazy. "Come," she said again with her arm reached out.

As we walked up the stairs, I kept looking ahead over Kiki. I'd try the light. It had probably burned out in that room…in Nathalie's room. But I felt a little prickle at the back of my neck and felt every muscle in my legs with each step. As much as I didn't believe in anything supernatural, my mind kept racing. A light bulb had expired, or it was a coincidence—I believed in crazy coincidences. I was the first to dismiss any ghost sighting or ghost story I had ever heard and easily found reasons for what had happened. I often fell back on must haves— the person who saw the ghost must have been sleeping, or must have been on drugs, or a light bulb must have burnt out at the perfect time.

When Kiki turned right and switched on her bedroom light, it felt as though I took my first breath since I saw the light go off in Nathalie's room. Maybe if we didn't call it Nathalie's room… Kiki motioned me into her room and gently shut the door. I was surprised at her stealth. Why did she seem to want to keep this from Gina? But I was also amazed by her ability to *be* stealthy, to be quiet. I'd already gotten used to her pounding up and down stairs.

Kiki's room was a total clutter box. This confused me as she had only been in Vermont for a short time and didn't seem like she was ever in the house long enough to clutter it. A Christmas tree like the one in my room was nestled in one corner. She went over and switched on its small lights, turned on a lamp on the desk, then a pink bedside lamp. Finally, a swipe to the wall to extinguish the bright overhead light—Gina's flare for a welcoming atmosphere had obviously rubbed off on her. She stood for a moment and took in the room with her hands together. I smiled down at her. It was the first time I'd seen her stand still.

That stillness was fleeting. She moved to her closet and pulled a box from amongst more clutter. The clothes barely swayed, so snug together on their hangers. The top of the box brushed through the clothes to the front.

She pushed other boxes and shoes out of the way. My God, she had a lot of stuff. She plunked down with her legs around the box and motioned me over.

"These Natlie's." She picked up an envelope that hovered on top of books, dropped it, tunneled through more books, maybe an old photo album.

"Kiki!" I looked back over my shoulder, but took a step toward the box. I had never seen someone so brazenly invade someone else's privacy. Well, other than myself, but only when necessary for the sake of a case, of course. Even though Nathalie had passed away, it didn't seem right to sift through her things. But I strained to glimpse inside the box.

"She wanted me to have it."

"What?" I didn't want to hear about her seeing things or imagining things…but I did want to see concrete things…

"A month after I am here, I found it. I know she want me have it. I saw her same day I find box. She want me to know something. Hard for me to read. Getting better. She sent you to read. She want your help."

"Oh, for God's sake, Kiki." I stared at her with my mouth open. But I was dying to see what she had.

The front door creaked. We looked at one another.

"Okay. Not now. Harry home. Goodnight, Awli."

I stared at her, surprised by her brush-off. My feet felt stuck to the floor, my eyes to the box.

"Okay. It okay. She good. No worry. We talk again." She looked at her bedroom door—her further attempt to shoo me out.

I brushed my teeth and tiptoed up to the attic. It was already later than I wanted to be getting to bed. As much as I wanted to meet Harry, tonight was not a good night. Five a.m. would come too quickly as it was.

When I opened my door, I had the same reaction Gina had only a few days earlier. The lights on my tree were on. I must have put them on before dinner. But as I got under my thick duvet, I allowed myself to wonder. No, there was no ghost. A ghost—that was crazy. I did believe there was something with Kiki, though. I believed she believed there was something, anyway. Maybe Kiki was overtired. She was out all the time. I didn't know her, maybe she was on something. She didn't seem like it, though. Maybe she took something to keep her awake. She did seem over-stimulated. Too many energy drinks, I don't know.

I pulled my blanket up over my chin and peered into the room. Shadows roused my imagination. I resisted turning the light on. I remember my mom saying you had to train your mind not to take you for a ride—imagination is for the daytime, she had always said. At night, put it to sleep. I concentrated on not thinking, but that accelerated my thoughts—a montage of images swarming my mind—Kiki's belief in Nathalie's ghost, the light going off in Nathalie's room. But Gina had said there hadn't been anyone staying in the attic for years…

Chapter Four

I woke early after struggling most of the night with my sheets, not finding comfort or much sleep. The glow from the nightlight in the bathroom shed a soft radiance on the landing below. I was used to tiptoeing around, but Gina's house felt like it listened to every step. And it always talked, as Gina said. I wanted to find out what it had to say. I had to try the light in Nathalie's room. I looked behind me, then flipped on the switch. The overhead light came on—no burnt-out bulb—revealing a neat, square room with the brass bed I had caught a glimpse of and a desk with a row of books across the back. Perfectly ordinary. But the suitcases that were near the door were no longer there. I wanted to look at the book titles on the desk, but I heard a creak from the hallway. I tiptoed down the stairs.

Joe was plugging in the lights on the tree when I arrived at the diner. I knew he was the cook by the white coat and small white cap most of them wear. I was happy he had the lights dimmed as they were yesterday, but my senses lit up to the smell of the coffee, the sound of it perking.

His head brushed against boughs on the way up and a few of the bulbs clinked together. "Ali, I hope? I haven't had my coffee. I'm not ready to take down someone who wants eggs before coffee." He smiled and extended his hand.

I pulled off my mitten. "Hi. Joe?" I squinted at the pine needles sprinkled on him and looked for a switch on the wall. Weird.

He nodded and shook my hand. "I know." He put his hand up. "No switch. That'd be nice first thing in the morning, wouldn't it?" He had a smile that teetered on a laugh. Did he always smile like that? I kind of hoped so. I liked those smiles. "You're freezing. The coffee should be ready in about five. Nice of you to help out. You new in town? Haven't seen you around."

"Just new to the area." I pulled off my hat and coat, looked around for a coat rack.

"You can hang it in the back." He guided me through the kitchen to a small room without a door. There was an old couch and armchair with a low square table in the middle. Once a nice dark wood, but it was full of white coffee mug rings, etchings, and carved initials. There were six hooks along the far wall with one coat and a lone metal folding chair with salt stains around its legs. I hung my parka at the other end and took a seat on the oh-so-cold metal chair. I pulled off my heavy boots in exchange for sneakers. There were some cheaply framed pictures on the paneling—most of them were fishing shots.

"Rick's obsessed with fishing. I added this one last

year." Joe walked over to the wall. "I wanted to see if he'd notice." His smiled teetered. My smile pushed in that direction, too. A little teeter goes a long way. Joe straightened the plastic frame. The image was of a river with tall golden grass swaying along its shore, in the background, a house with a red roof. It honored the theme of water, so it blended with the montage of fishing pictures.

"Nice."

"Yeah, I guess Rick's okay with it, or he hasn't noticed. He probably imagines there's some good fish in that river." He laughed. "You good? Gotta get back to my prep."

I nodded. "Thanks."

"Holler if you need anything."

After I had all the tables set, I poured myself a coffee, leaned against the counter, and waited for my first customer. Maybe today I would meet my guest. I only had less than a week. I stared out through the large windows at the heavy snow coming down. It was dark, but there was a streetlamp emitting a yellow glow outside the diner—an ancient back-in-time one with the round globe and intricate cast-iron details. If the snow continued for another day, we would hit a record. I hoped we would. Might as well keep it coming and go for it. If you're gonna have it, then have it, is what my dad always said.

Next to Sally's notes for me was a worn black apron with the straps wrapped around it. I unfolded it and tied it around my waist. Above the Christmas tree, the clock on the wall indicated five minutes after six. It *was* Saturday, I guess there wouldn't be a before work crowd. I hoped there would be a rush at some point—it would be nice to make a bit of money and pass the time with possible candidates for Christmas Eve dinner. Joe came through the swinging doors, and I jumped.

"You good? We usually get busy around eight on Saturdays, but we'll get some regulars trickling in any minute." He switched on the Christmas music and poured a coffee.

"Smells good back there. How long have you been working here?"

"Since Rick took over and re-opened the place. 'Bout five years now."

"Wow. That's a pretty long time." As far as restaurant jobs go, it was.

"I guess. Doesn't seem that long. When you get to be my age, time doesn't seem as long." He made a face. I had the feeling if I knew him longer, it'd be a wink.

"Yeah, you're ancient." He looked about thirty, which was kind of bordering on ancient to me at the time.

"Thanks."

His hat covered most of his hair, but some dark curls crept out behind his ears and around the back of his neck. I noticed he was taller than I thought as he stood beside me. Also, pretty cute, even with the scruffy beard. I felt a little self-conscious suddenly. A flat-faced look from my mom came to mind. My last year in high school, I brought home a guy who always seemed to have his pizza shirt on from his delivery job. She had said I was attracted to guys in the wrong uniform. She had laughed when she said it. But he turned out not to be my type, anyway. I had still hated it when she said that. My face rushed with heat—what would she think if I brought home Joe? He was too old for me, anyway.

"Hey, Ali?" He waved his hand in front of my face. "You still here?"

Oops. I have a problem when I meet a cute guy. I

fought a blush that I could feel starting to creep up to my face. *Oh, no.* "Yeah. I'm back," I said. "Is this an all-Christmas station?" It was all I could think of.

"Yep. That time of year. Looks like you leaped ahead of us to spring." He grinned and swigged his coffee back and pushed through the doors, leaving me alone with Frank Sinatra: *I've Got My Love to Keep Me Warm*.

I checked my phone, scrolled to Eric's last text. *Need help with the move?* And then my, *I'm good, thanks.* I couldn't have borne watching him carry my things away from him. I hovered over delete. But I couldn't. I still needed a last line. Would there ever be another line, another text, another call? No. I didn't want that.

I opened a drawer under the coffee machine. It was crammed with yellow post-it notes with the top of each pad curling in at the corners, pens that looked like they were out of ink, rubber bands, a pair of scissors, and some Scotch tape. I absently sifted through but withdrew my hand when I saw loose birthday candles. I didn't want to feel the wax crumbling and sticking to my fingers. I continued to stare at the mess. My eyes combed the contents, amazed at all the stuff in there. A fishing hook for God's sake. I was glad the candles had been deterrent enough. I could have been dealing with much more than irritating wax on my hands. Rushed to Emergency, just my first shift at the diner with a fishing hook stuck in my finger. I rembember reading about a paramedic crew, busting a gut carrying a patient on a stretcher down a flight of winding stairs. One of them slipped, and they dropped the poor guy, who ended up with a broken back to go with his scorched genitals he'd given himself trying to kill a cockroach. I don't think any names were named. But still, I could imagine a few laughs if I showed up...maybe there would even be a blurb in the paper—server catches worker's comp with a fishing hook.

I had the urge to organize the drawer but thought I should keep out of it. As I was about to close the drawer, I saw something gold and shiny. I picked up a pen and used it to shift the items on top out of the way. It was much larger than a fishing hook. I looked up, feeling like I was going through someone's personal items. I thought of Kiki and paused. No, this wasn't personal, this was a mishmash of stuff that obviously hadn't been looked at in a long while. I was surprised to see it was a watch. A nice one. Funny seeing it buried underneath all that rubble. I put the pen through the band and lured it up. It was old-fashioned looking. What was it doing there amongst all that junk? I don't know what possessed me, but I wanted to see it on my wrist. It was so unique. The thin straps were twined to the face, so delicate. The door to the diner jingled as I secured the clasp. I guiltily closed the drawer but didn't have time to remove the watch.

"Good morning!" I called, walking over to a booth where a couple was landing. He was late twenties, neat hair, open expression, but a bit wilted around the edges. She was about the same age, her hair twisted high as though trying to lift fatigue, her red coat, too bright against her pale face. The watch felt tight around my wrist. It was obvious they weren't regulars by the way they hesitated for the perfect booth, skimmed over the other tables, taking in the diner. I remembered doing the same just the day before. I could tell they were having a favorable first impression as I had—it was an ideal little spot.

"Morning," they both said and simultaneously

turned over their mugs.

I poured coffee as they watched. "You're up early on this snowy Saturday," I said.

"Got in late last night after a long delay. Snuck out of my parents' condo this morning—it's just around the corner." The guy pointed over his shoulder and looked back as though amazed they made it through the snow. "It's a pretty small place, didn't want to start looking for coffee and clanging mugs a few feet away from their bedroom. Plus, we're kind of jetlagged."

"Surprised you were able to land. Must have been stressful this close to Christmas. Guess you're lucky there was even a flight." I stared out the window, and they did the same for a moment. "Where are you visiting from?"

"Colorado. My parents moved here about six months ago. Dad retired from the military. Jenna and I surprised them for the holidays." He picked up Jenna's hand. A gleaming diamond shone from Jenna's ring finger. I guessed they had another surprise for his parents. It had the look of being new by the way she kept drawing her left thumb underneath her palm to wiggle the band.

"I'm a military brat, too." I rested the coffee pot on the edge of their table. *And my mom's in Colorado right now*—but I didn't want to go there.

"So, this a hometown for you now?" He smiled. "We brats are always homeless until we move out on our own. I like Colorado. It was my dad's last post. I'm staying put." He laughed.

"Going to school here. But after…it might be." Maybe it would. Gone were the days when I finally fit in at a new school, and my dad would be quieter than usual around the dinner table…I knew another move was coming. Maybe I would settle in here.

"Graham…this brat here…" Jenna tapped his hand, "was supposed to be working straight through Christmas. It was a nice surprise for me, too." Jenna scanned the diner as though looking for something. "Love this place." But her words fell off like arriving at the end of a trail.

"Yeah." I looked around. It was still new to me.

"These spots are great. They're almost becoming extinct, aren't they? I was relieved we couldn't find a chain along the way. You get so used to them—so used to pointing at the big plates on the menu, hey?" She jabbed a finger down. "I want this."

We both laughed. Graham shook his head at her with a smile you couldn't take away from him. Jenna also had one of those newly-engaged grins.

I left them, taking the menus without pictures, rang in their orders, and started to fill coffee filters. Sally had said, as long as there was enough coffee, nothing else mattered in a diner. I kept thinking back to the box in Kiki's room. Nathalie's things. What was it that wouldn't allow her to rest? Not in the sense of her roaming Gina's house. I still didn't believe that. But there *was* something about Nathalie that seemed awake, a restless remnant of her in the lives she touched or barely touched. Kiki didn't even know her, yet she was hell bent on finding out more about her. She even believed she saw her. She had said she saw her. I shuddered. I didn't believe it, but I didn't like to think of it, either. And look at me—even I wanted more of Nathalie.

The bell jingled again. I was happy to welcome more customers. A man around Joe's age stomped his feet and pulled off a Bruins wool hat as he took a seat at the bar. Right behind him, another couple came in, older than Jenna and her fiancé, but not much. They gave me a funny look, and I heard the woman whisper, "Guess Sally's off." They slid into one of the booths by the window. The energy livened. Both parties seemed comfortable here, obviously regulars. Bruins guy surprised me with his heavy Boston accent, not only a fan of the team. He mentioned the weather, then ordered a rare steak with fries with a fried egg on top of the fries. Sunnyside up.

I went into the kitchen. "Hey Joe, I have an order for a rare steak..."

"I'm on it. Bern's a regular. Don't make that face. You never know until you try it." He slapped the steak on the grill. I think he made a bit of a grimace.

"Also, for those two omelets I rang in with fries—I assume I get my side of mayo from one of these fridges?" I pointed at the two refrigerators behind me. Joe motioned to the one on the left. "No home fries here?" I said as I grabbed two small plastic containers with mayonnaise pressed up against the little plastic lids. "I can't wait to see what they do with the mayo." I remember working at a spot where a regular always wanted a side of peanut butter for his Clubhouse sandwich.

"You'll wanna grab four of those for them." He pointed to the fries, then flipped the steak. "That couple went to Europe last year or somewhere, and now they always want lots of mayo. Guess it's a delicacy over there. Just weird here." But he laughed. "We do have home fries, but the fries are just that good. Most of the regulars opt for them no matter what time of the day it is."

More people came in. I poured a round of coffees

and took orders, the diner now in full swing. The dessert case housed the syrup as well as the grapefruits. I pulled out a glass container—the spout was clean, no drips or crystallized sugar, and looked freshly filled—and deposited it on a table full of giggling teenagers. The bell jingled. Mr. Brooks came in covered in snow. I filled a pot of water and looked at the five different assortments of tea. I was sure he was a regular, orange pekoe tea guy. If I was wrong, I'd buy his breakfast.

He pulled off his hat and sighed, a good happy to be here sigh. "How goes the battle? Joe helping you out?" He looked around at the other customers then back at me. He had done that same sweep the day before, as though taking inventory. He opened the paper sleeve and removed the tea bag. *Yes! Too easy.*

"Joe's been great."

"Good. Now, Joe's going to think he knows what I want. But this morning I have a craving for something." He paused and gave me a firm look. "I want some of that chili he made yesterday. And don't let him tell you it's too early for that. He just has to pull it out of the fridge and heat it up. I don't want any of that garlicky toast, though. He can throw me a few fries instead. Just a few. A handful."

"Must be a full moon or something." I smiled.

"Just don't let him give you a hard time." He squeezed the tea bag with his spoon against the pot a few times but left it in to steep longer.

As soon as I rang in Mr. Brooks' order, Joe called out to me.

I hated to annoy a cook, even if I wasn't eating their food. "Mr. Brooks said you just needed to heat it up." I wrinkled my nose and shrugged my shoulders up.

Joe raised his eyebrows and went to the fridge,

shaking his head. "Taking advantage, that man."

But beyond his gruff, there wasn't a hint of irritation. I noticed he had one of those faces naturally set on the happy side, even when his face was neutral. Not like some who looked like they were frowning even when they smiled at you. Mags admitted she had that bitch face. Those who didn't know her, sometimes thought she was a snob. She definitely wasn't, but I had to agree—if you didn't know her and saw her on the street, she didn't come across approachable. But funnily enough, she was the one who struck up conversations with anyone who interested her. She was a grumpy-looking people person.

After I topped off coffees, I went back to Mr. Brooks' table. He gave the impression he was a people person. I liked his way of taking everything in, the way he looked at the other customers. Maybe he had been a Navy Seal or something—he had this way of sweeping the place that seemed like he was searching or on guard.

"Joe give you a hard time?"

"Nah."

"Good stuff. Now, tell me, how are you settling into Gina's place?"

"Almost feels like home. Gina's so interesting and the most amazing cook." It felt natural to chat with Mr. Brooks, but it was only our second conversation. I felt a little self-conscious—it was a little too familiar. Small town. I smiled, thinking of Gina's reaction the night before. It did seem like a wee small town compared to New York.

"She is both of those things." Mr. Brooks finally removed the teabag from the pot. What was it between those two? Gina had the same look of regret, I think, when I mentioned Mr. Brooks. "And how are your other roomies?"

"I haven't met Harry yet. Kiki, she's sweet. She…" I stopped myself. TMI? I didn't know what I was about to say, but I thought I shouldn't say anything at all. The bell sounded from the kitchen. Saved.

When I placed the chili before Mr. Brooks, I wondered if he regretted his order.

"Thanks for making it happen," he said and looked at the chili with anticipation.

"I'll leave you to your…ah…breakfast?" I joked. "Should I bring some Tums over?"

"Very funny, but I've been blessed with a gut of steel." Mr. Brooks unfolded his napkin on his lap. "Hold up a sec. An old guy can't eat something this hot." He put his hands on either side of the hot dish, testing to see if he could touch it, then moved it an inch away from him. "You were about to say something about Kiki. You had a funny look on your face. As a matter of fact, you had a bit of a face on you when I walked in. You looked at me like you hadn't seen me in a long time."

I stared at him for a moment. Why so interested? — shot hot through my mind, but I released it pretty fast. In fact, if I had been working at the diner longer and knew him more than a day, I would have slid into the booth for a few minutes. I scanned the diner, making sure everyone's eyes were set on the food in front of them, not looking for coffee or condiments.

"Do you open the store on Saturdays?" He looked like someone who knew a lot of people. Everyone seemed to know him. I wanted to know him. He looked like he might have answers. I liked people who had answers.

"This time of year? Sundays, too. No rest for the wicked."

"Do you think I could drop by after my shift? Just after 3:00 p.m.?"

"Of course." He gave me a funny look but smiled. "Okay, did I order this chili, really?"

It started to pick up. The couple from Colorado piled their winter clothes back on around 8:00 a.m. They waited at the door to catch my eye before heading back into the storm. They kind of had the same smile. It would be neat to see them after twenty years of marriage. Boston moved on—he left me a more than generous tip. I hadn't talked to him that much. He was content to be buried in the sports section. I got into a rhythm of filling his coffee. He liked it topped off when it was half-full. Not like some who cup their hand over their mugs if you even pass by their table, like you are part of a conspiracy to force more caffeine on them. This was better money than the fine Italian restaurant I had worked at one summer. Plus, I hated opening bottles of wine at a table, watching people sniff corks. I preferred the quick pace of the diner. And the company. Most people were happy with the smell of coffee and the presentation of their eggs on a plate. It was a comfort having so many regulars coming in even though I didn't know them as regulars. Sally would know these people. She wouldn't have to ask much of them. And Nathalie would have been the same when she worked here.

With only two tables left, both looking content to linger over their last coffee, I prepped for the lunch rush. It was nice to have a bit of a reprieve. Joe ducked his head out of the kitchen. After giving the dining room a scan, he came behind the counter to pour himself a coffee.

"Good idea," I said and paused to join him.

"Hey, not bad. Almost seemed like you've worked

this scene before."

"Thanks for your help. I've worked in a few restaurants, never one like this, though. It was a lot busier than I'm used to. I kind of like it better this way."

"Does make the time fly, for sure."

We leaned against the counter and stared out at the weather. The coffee tasted better than I remembered it to be earlier. "Is it just as busy for lunch on Saturdays?" I said, comfortable shoulder-to-shoulder with Joe.

"It can be. Probably will be as it's the last Saturday before Christmas."

Joe headed back to the kitchen. The bell jingled, and the young woman I saw on the street the day before came in and made a beeline to the pay phone beside the Christmas tree. She didn't look around, so she didn't see me. Would she recognize me? It was odd to see someone using a payphone. They already looked like antiques with only a few sprinkled at the odd old gas station, or outside a relic convenience store, or at diners like this one. Was it still twenty-five cents to make a call? Her bony knees shook as she dialed a number. A beat-up pair of army boots climbed halfway up her calves, engulfing her skinny legs, frozen underneath her thin black leggings. The hood of her light blue bomber jacket rimmed with faux-fur had a few stains on it that looked like coffee. Although she tried to push it off her head when she came in, it was still high on the back of her head, keeping her raggedy looking blond hair stuck beneath it at the back. Underneath all that mess, she was striking. Too thin, too unkempt, but beautiful.

I tried not to stare at her. I moved my way along the counter, pretending to be busy, straightening out the teas, lining up the mugs that were already in line. I finally neared the end of the speckled Formica and inspected the menus, running a rag over the already clean plastic covers. I couldn't hear anything from her, but she moved a lot and nodded and shook her head. I know I'm a snoop. It can't be helped. Maybe I would be sifting through Nathalie's things soon. No, that wouldn't be right. But if it were needed…

The girl moved to the side, and I caught a glimpse of the flashing green on the phone. It was the message: Please insert twenty-five cents. Huh, it still was twenty-five cents. Oh. I instinctively looked around for allies, then back to the kitchen to where Joe was a call away. She was pretending to be on the phone. But why? I looked at her legs in constant motion. She was cold. It was an excuse to come in to warm up. I knew my mouth was open, to what extent I wasn't sure. Caught with my nose in her business, she turned abruptly, hung up the phone, and whipped up her hood. I wanted to call out to her, but what would I say, I'd already made her uncomfortable. My red mitts on her hands pushed against the door, like stop signs reflecting back at me.

As she dashed away from the diner, from me, I caught her profile one last time. I felt the loss in my throat, the pain pulling down to the pit of my stomach. The warmth I had been enjoying now made me dizzy. I walked to the window, my eyes following her as she bobbed through the snow. I thought of my old pogo stick, one of my favorite Christmas presents. How long had it been since she had a gift under a Christmas tree?

Lunch was steady, not as busy as breakfast, but I was still glad to see Sally when she arrived at twenty minutes to three. She folded her coat and pushed it under the counter. I wondered why she didn't bring it to the back room. "You can transfer that one over if you want," she mumbled, her head nodding toward my last table, then she leaned closer to me. "He stays at least two hours and always leaves one dollar. But your choice." She shrugged, but she still had that good-natured smile.

Joe wasn't in the kitchen when I walked through. He was in the back room putting on his coat about to head out a side door. He turned and looked over his shoulder at me. "Caught."

"Making a run for it?"

"No, honoring a bad habit." He looked embarrassed.

I admitted to my own brief encounter with cigarettes. "I guess it can be pretty tough to quit." *God, what an idiot,* I thought. Just assuming he wants to quit. Well, doesn't everyone? No one's trying to hang on to that one.

He looked at me funny. "You guess? You did, didn't you? Quit?"

"Yeah, but I only smoked for a season—barely a summer, so it wasn't all that hard. I couldn't wait to quit, actually. Stupid to start." I struggled with the foot in my mouth and made a face. "It didn't take for me." I rolled my eyes, wanting him to know I was an idiot for running down smoking. That gave me a rise. I know I had a lopsided smile on my face, trying to hold in a laugh. I wished I had known him longer so I could share the joke—that was too much—'An idiot for running down smoking.' I trapped a giggle and looked down to untie my apron. Mags had been chain smoking like Bette Davis that summer I picked it up. She was into the old movies. She had even set out boxes of cigarettes in her living room and her bedroom. "Those were the days," she had said, "when they had boxes you flipped open in every room with unlimited cigarettes and decanters with port or sherry on the buffet…when did we get so uptight?" She got over it, too, realizing the glamour wasn't really there. She started to stare at her face in every mirror, finding a wrinkle that she made me examine.

Joe grinned. "Never heard of it not taking. You're an odd duck, Ali, but we'll keep you. For the season. Huh. A pattern."

He opened the heavy exit door, and I got a glimpse of white, and a gust whirled in with a puff of snow, like the diner breathed him out and the weather was breathing snowy exhales back in. He pushed the door closed quickly behind him. Immediately I was in a vacuum of silence. I sank into the old couch and paused before I started to cash out. My feet pulsed, and my thighs felt tingly, like pins and needles. I wanted to curl up right there. If I did, I was sure I'd fall asleep. But I couldn't help but close my eyes—just for a moment. Not long after, my head jerked up as I heard running water. I jumped up in a panic expecting to see a flood pooling around me from a burst pipe. It was so loud. Like rapids. It stopped as quickly as it came, like a needle being ripped off a record album. The painting Joe had brought in caught my eye as my mind played tricks on me. It looked for a second like the water was swishing up onto the shore. I must have nodded off for a second and fell into one of those lucid dreams. Yes, I must have, as I was still in the same position, settled deep into the cushioning. My eyes adjusted to the room again.

I faced a "Closed" sign when I reached Mr. Brooks' shop. I looked at my phone and at the store hours, my heart sinking when I saw 10:00 a.m. to 3:00 p.m. for

Saturday. It was twenty minutes past, maybe he forgot. With my hands cupped around my eyes, I balanced on my toes to get a full view inside. I saw the glow of a lamp at the back beyond the counter that was now free of all the clutter. It was like looking onto a theater set with the warm lighting, the books, candles, and other knickknacks. It came to life when Mr. Brooks surfaced and made his way to the front door waving at me.

"Perfect timing," he said as he closed the door behind me and locked it again. "I made hot chocolate."

"I hope I'm not holding you hostage?"

"No, no. I haven't sat after-hours at the shop in a while. I'm glad you wanted to meet here."

We settled into comfy chairs behind the bookcases. There was a large round table about a foot off the ground, like ones you see in kindergarten classrooms. Vibrant cushions lined one of the walls, and on another wall was a table with a hotplate, a kettle, and a mishmash of mugs, one upturned filled with spoons. Beside the table was a small bar fridge. I felt at home as I looked down at my gooey marshmallows.

"That watch?" Mr. Brooks said.

I put my mug down and slapped my hand over my wrist. "I forgot…"

"Where did you get it?" He sat up beside me. We both stared down at it.

"At the diner…it was in the drawer. I don't know why, but I put it on…I forgot. Why? You recognize it, I guess?"

"It looks like…Nathalie's."

"Oh." It felt hot around my wrist. I started to undo the clasp. "I can't believe I forgot it."

"Well…" He tapped my hand. "It's a nice watch." He looked upset, and I looked like a thief.

I caught a glimpse of an engraving on the back of the face and looked at it, then Mr. Brooks. "I guess it was hers…" There was a heart and an N as an inscription. "Wonder what it was doing there?" I frowned and put it in my pocket.

"I never saw her without that watch."

We sat in silence for a moment. I tried to settle in again, but the watch felt like a weight in my pocket and the light last night flashed on and off in my head. I looked sideways at Mr. Brooks. "Have you ever seen an apparition?" I blurted out. "You know, someone who's moved on…passed away?"

"Like a ghost? No." He seemed a little relieved or something. I don't know what he could have been expecting. I know I wouldn't have been relieved if someone threw that at me.

"I didn't think so," I said, and sat up a little straighter, again. "I don't believe in them."

"No?" Mr. Brooks stood and grabbed a couple of spoons and handed me one.

"Do you?" I said as I mirrored him and scooped up a few marshmallows before they disintegrated completely. "Believe in them?" I prayed he didn't.

"I didn't until Ella left me. At first, I thought I just missed her so much that I was creating little 'occurrences' to ease my pain. But I don't know, Ali. I think it's possible." His blue eyes gleamed as he looked into his mug.

"Like what? If you don't mind me asking? What type of 'occurrences'?" My voice sounded louder.

"Just little things. Only a handful of times. Like a tap on the shoulder. Once her bedside lamp was on when I walked into the bedroom. Something subtle, her letting me know she's with me. Things I could dismiss, I suppose. But those few taps on the shoulder were hard to ignore." He tilted his mug back, then leaned forward to place it down on the table. "So, I'm guessing something's happened at the house?"

"Do you know Kiki?"

"Not really, no. I know who she is."

"She says she sees Nathalie. Last night she said she needed my help. Something about Nathalie needing to communicate something. She even has a box of her belongings. Some books and stuff. I think Kiki may be experiencing some form of delusion. Maybe a hallucination from exhaustion."

"A box?" He looked at me, and his eyes looked a little darker, not as blue as I remembered. "Have you experienced anything yourself?" He seemed anxious to know. A moment earlier, he had been light on the ghost thing, as though it was fun when it was happening to him. Maybe he had been pulling my leg. He didn't believe.

"No," I said a little abruptly.

He leaned closer to me and smiled. "Tell me now, was it a tap on the shoulder?" His eyes looked bluer again. Was he teasing me?

I tried to smile. "I don't believe in this stuff." I looked through the bookcases, I wanted to see the door. I shouldn't have brought it up.

"Sounds like you're having your doubts."

I was having doubts about a few things. But, I was there. I did want to tell someone, someone I hoped would dismiss it along with me, we could chuckle, even. "The light in Nathalie's room was on when I went up the stairs last night. When I approached the landing, it went off."

"Hmmm, the old light trick. I guess that's a popular one." He smiled at me.

"But I didn't even know her. Kiki didn't know her

for that matter. Why me? Why us?" Why wasn't he dismissing it, laughing and moving on to something else?

"I don't know. Her death was so tragic. It didn't make sense to anyone. There must be something there she needs to... I don't know. I don't think they should have closed the case…"

Maybe there was something. I would go to the station and see Detective McCool. He was my group's contact for cold cases, so I knew him well enough. He was used to me popping in. I'd ask him about the case, about Nathalie.

Mr. Brooks was still on my question about the ghosts. "I still have a hard time with this stuff, too, to be honest. But after my experiences with Ella, I'm more open, I guess."

"The Christmas tree lights in my room…" I said half-heartedly, but it felt good to say it. Get it out there.

"I'm sorry?"

"When I go into my room, the lights are always on. The Christmas tree lights. I think Gina might… I don't know. She seemed surprised by the tree lights when I moved in…"

"She did love Christmas." Mr. Brooks shook his head. "That seems like something she would do."

"Gina?'

He looked at me funny. "No, Nathalie."

We sat for a while without saying anything. I was tongue-tied. I felt like I had upset Mr. Brooks.

"What was she like?" I finally said.

"Thoughtful and full of thoughts." He laughed. "She had a deep-set wrinkle between her brows, and she was only twenty…or twenty-one." He paused. "She liked to help everyone, maybe too much." He looked down at his thumbs he was tapping together. "She liked to laugh even though she was quiet. It was a funny combination. I think she was sad, but it was hard to know. She was always in a good mood, but there was something. Obviously." He gave me a look like he wanted to tell me something more.

The shop had darkened with the setting sun. I felt a little cool and pulled my coat up around my shoulders. Mr. Brooks' face was warmly lit by the lamp beside him. He had such a kind face, but there was something beneath, that made me want to look away. At the same time, I wished I could read it. "If only we could gauge a person's true feelings…" I said, half to him, half to myself. I thought of the FBI counterintelligence officer we had in for a guest lecturer. He was an expert on nonverbal behavior. Surprising to most of us, the face is the least likely place to gauge a person's true feelings. Now I always look for things like that thumb tapping, what people did with their hands. If they touched their throat, it's a giveaway. Shows they're nervous or worried.

"Right." He looked at me with lips pressed into a sad smile. "But for whatever reason…" He stood up. "You're freezing. I have the thermostat programmed to drop down outside of store hours."

"No, that's okay. I should go. I've kept you long enough. Thank you. That was the perfect amount of chocolate." I raised my empty mug and stood.

I hurried along the snow-packed sidewalk. After a busy day in town, the streets were much easier to manage than they had been that morning. The snow had tapered off. I walked the festive colored blocks to the station. I was pretty sure Detective McCool worked until 5:00 p.m. My mind raced through those last couple of days.

So much had happened, so much had changed in my life in such a short time. I was drawn to Mr. Brooks and his little bookstore, which was much larger than I had noticed the first time I was in it. How could he maintain that these days? When was the last time I bought a novel from a bookstore? I pictured the candles and the little knickknacks on the front table, but still. I hadn't seen anyone in there the first day, and it was Christmastime.

Detective Harris was in McCool's office when I arrived. McCool looked over Harris' shoulder at me and waved me in. Harris turned and smiled, got up from her seat on the edge of the desk. "You look like you have a lead in your mouth," she said, teasing me. I liked her. We chatted a minute, but she got it, she knew I was there for McCool.

"What's going on?" McCool motioned for me to have a seat.

He smirked as I was already halfway into the chair. I knew he would have told me if he didn't have time for me. He would have held his hands up like he had done a few times when I barged in with a quick question or an idea I thought couldn't wait…that I couldn't let wait, to be honest. Cold cases can always wait, though. Unfortunately, most cold cases are unresolved homicides, so there's not usually any urgency.

I asked him about Nathalie. If he had worked on the case and why the case was closed.

There was a pause before he answered. I think I had surprised him. "There was no case, there, Ali." But there was something more than a pause in his response. It was a hesitation. I was sure of it.

"It's just people seem to think she wouldn't have jumped. There was no note, right?"

"There was nothing. That's the problem," he said.

Did he think there was more to the case by the way he said 'that's the problem'?

"What do you think happened?" I asked.

"Don't know." He shook his head. "When someone drowns and there's nothing—no witness, no note, well…what can you do? There's nothing you can do." He looked at me. Tapped his pen against the desk a few times. "It nagged me for months, to be honest. As you mentioned, her friends were emphatic she wouldn't have jumped. But she could have fallen. There was nothing to investigate. No one to investigate. I can tell where your mind's going, but there's nothing there."

And I could tell he wanted me to let it go. Maybe because he had to let it go after those months that it had nagged at him. Maybe because there was nothing to hold onto and that was frustrating to a cop. I got that. And maybe there was nothing. I was known to look for things when I shouldn't.

I called out to Gina, but the house felt empty. I paused on the staircase, wondering about the door underneath. Did I hear any voices? No, only the creaks of the house. Up in the attic, I pulled out my apron and felt a bump through the material. I ran my fingers along both pockets, feeling through all the loose threads, maybe I had missed some change. I felt something sharp. I turned it inside out. Buried half into the seam was a small key. Maybe it was Sally's. She had left the apron for me. It was probably a spare of hers.

I set the key on the table, smoothed out the apron and started to roll it back up. I noticed an 'N' drawn on the inside of one of the straps in white material crayon. I stared down at it in my hands. I could feel a pulse in the tips of my fingers. It must have been Nathalie's apron. I picked up the small key. And Nathalie's key. Maybe there was a spot at the diner it fit. Or maybe in her room.

Chapter Five

After I washed up, I went down to see if I could give Gina a hand with dinner. On the way to the kitchen, I passed the door on the stairs and ran my hand along it. I wondered if Gina had been down there again. Like a dare, I touched the brass doorknob. But hearing Gina and kitchen noises made me pull away. I moved into the warmth, steam, and spices.

"So, how was your first day?" Gina asked as she strained a pot of potatoes.

"Good. Excellent."

She looked over her shoulder at me, waiting for details.

"Such a great spot, great people."

"It is a little gem."

I poured out details about the customers as I helped bring serving dishes over to the table. It felt like the days I used to talk my mother's ear off in the kitchen after a day at school. I blushed as I realized my outpour was of little interest to Gina. But like my mom, she made it seem more stimulating than it was. Before we sat down, bolstered by our exchange, I bit my lip and stared at her. "A bit of a funny question for you, Gina?" I had a lot of them, but one, in particular, was on my mind, or I think I was squeezing it ahead of the others. It was the least personal question of the lot.

"Shoot." She put down a tea towel and wiped her hands along the front of her apron, turning to give me all her attention.

"Do you believe the dead can communicate with the living?" I wanted to know what I was dealing with—how many people in the house believed in nonsense. There was no way to ease into it, but it sounded silly tossing it out over the potatoes. I'd already tossed it out over marshmallows earlier—it didn't get any easier or sound any saner.

"Like a ghost? No," she said, like a strike. Was it a defensive strike?

"Oh," I said. I wasn't expecting that response, but I was happy for it—but honestly, I would have thought she'd be all over ghosts.

"I believe in energy, though." She smiled and placed a bowl of what looked like some sort of stew on the table. "I only believe in good, so ghosts don't appeal to Gigi." She laughed.

"Gigi?"

"My grandmother used to call me Gigi. She had a pet name for everyone. I don't know, it just came to me. Maybe because she was one for ghosts. She had a few stories." She served herself some stew and passed it to me. "Did you have a pet name growing up?"

"My dad calls me Gator."

"Gator!"

"He used to tease that my name wasn't Allison, but Alligator. He still does, sometimes."

Later snuggled into our spots in the den, we were comfortably quiet for a while. Gina happy with her pipe, me enjoying the smell of it as I sipped on the mulled cider she had made. It was easy to study her as she smoked. She put a lot of her attention on it when we weren't talking. At that moment, I was picturing her as a teacher. She would have been a favorite for many kids.

"Do you miss teaching?"

"Sometimes I do, a little. I missed it a lot at first. Thought I might have to go back. Can you imagine?" She tapped her pipe. "I did it for a long, long time. Thirty-one years."

"That is a long time. How long have you lived here?"

"My whole life."

"In this house?"

"This very one."

"That's incredible. We moved a lot." It would have been nice to have a home base, a group of friends who knew you, really knew you. I always had to fit into something that was already there. Gina made it easy to fit in. I asked her more about her family, her childhood, those years of teaching. As she reminisced, she hooked me. I imagined years in a house like this, all the things added, never tossed away, or maybe left behind by a guest, a relative who came to visit. I'd never seen so many knickknacks and books—wonderful clutter my family never knew at our temporary posts. "But your grandmother was Acadian? I didn't realize there was a community in Vermont?"

"My mother's side settled in Maine—Madawaska.

There is still a large Acadian population there today." Gina looked out the window. "Sometimes I wish they would've kept going down to Louisiana. I could have been a Cajun, imagine that!"

I could.

She shook her head and looked back at me. "No. I'd miss the winter. Anyway, so many questions." She smiled and blinked into the candle beside her.

I had more. This was just a preliminary. Easing into it…I wanted to talk more about Nathalie. "Sorry."

"No. I like it. I like that there always seems to be a question on your mind."

"Well then," I laughed and continued, "what's up with Kiki?"

"You must wonder what you got yourself into here, heh?"

So, there was something… Gina, too. Christmas and Nathalie were all around me. I started out wanting to avoid Christmas, now I had Christmas *and* a ghost in my face. I felt a giggle. Or I lived with people who wanted a ghost.

"I thought Kiki had let it go, but she is so stubborn, that one," Gina said.

In the kitchen, Gina had said she wasn't into ghosts. That included Nathalie, didn't it? I wanted to laugh, but she looked serious. "What do you mean?" I asked. I wanted to know more about Nathalie as a person. And Gina had hinted that Nathalie wouldn't have jumped. I wanted to know more about that.

"I don't know, Ali. It's strange. I don't know what it is with Kiki, I think she needs more rest is what it is. I know she's not bored." She chuckled and shrugged.

"What about you?" I watched her eyes flicker, or maybe it was the candlelight. But I had felt a pull since I arrived, not a supernatural one, but I think there was something about Nathalie's death. "You mentioned you didn't think Nathalie would have jumped." I couldn't help myself. I was bubbling with curiosity. "Sorry, I just feel there's something there, maybe I'm too enmeshed in criminology, my cold cases, I hope you don't mind?"

"I don't mind…" She stood. "But I think a cider would be nice. Would you like another?"

I followed her out to the kitchen. Gina rubbed the sides of her arms and looked around, frowning, then walked over to the back door and turned the latch to lock it. "Did you go outside earlier?"

I shook my head. My eyes slowly scanned the dimly lit kitchen, and then I focused on the crystal shimmering above the sink. Gina moved over to the counter and lightly patted the Christmas cakes she had made that afternoon. She pulled out aluminum foil from a drawer, to wrap the loaves. She turned to me. "Nathalie used to come in through the back door when she first arrived here. She's the only one who ever used it. I don't know why she did that. Maybe she was importing a bit of familiarity from home. A lot of people use their back doors. We never did here. There's not much room in this kitchen." Gina looked around, as though searching for something or someone…

Back in the den, Gina continued. "I thought she had maybe moved on. But now…"

My legs felt heavy, like they weren't attached to me. I rubbed the inside arches of my feet to ground myself. I didn't know what to say to that—I couldn't validate a ghost. I pulled away from that and continued where I wanted to go. "So, you think she fell?"

Gina shrugged, then shook her head.

"I'm sorry," I said. "I have to stop doing that. I don't

make many friends being such a snoop." I studied her face, gauging if she accepted my apology. I thought I better ease up. "You know, the only cookies I ever wanted to make were in a Nancy Drew cookbook." I laughed. "They were really good, actually. They were chewy, easy to fold in half, kind of like a turnover that you stuffed a paper message inside. I loved writing out the fortunes and watching my mom and dad consider their future I had thought up—I snuck in a few trips to Disney World, but mostly I tried to keep them authentic. You know, like: *He who throws mud loses ground.* Oh, and my favorite: *The fortune you seek is in another cookie…*" I laughed harder.

"I love it." She pulled on her fingers, like she was trying to take off rings on all of them at once. She sat up straight and rubbed the armrests. "I knew you had it in you." She laughed. "You put fun into your vocation. You started early!"

Gina's comment kind of felt like a reminder. I don't know that I still put fun into it so much. It wasn't cookies and fortunes, anymore. Well, maybe for her. I held a giggle. We sat for a few moments. I tried to let go of where I wanted to go, listening to the fire, the Christmas music in the background. I stared out into the snow, doing my best to hold on to all I wanted to ask Gina. Before I opened my mouth again, I stretched out my legs and prepared to get up.

"What's on your mind?" She stopped me.

"I guess that's going to be a problem with you?" I laughed. "You sense things, I suppose." The image of the hooded woman looking up at me from the road flashed at me. Could Gina really 'sense' things? I wondered if she knew I knew about her selling futures under the staircase.

She leaned forward. "Nothing will shock me. Too old for that."

I didn't doubt her. She didn't look shockable. "I am curious about the attic. Why hasn't there been anyone up there for years?"

"Oh," Gina said. She sounded disappointed.

Oh? I waited for her to move out of a pause that was hanging on too long. I felt a little pulse against the side of my neck.

Finally, she spoke again. "Did something happen?"

I hated the hesitation in her words, in her eyes. "No."

She looked relieved, which didn't help. "It's nothing, really. Well, it's something, but... I guess I should have mentioned it."

I was surprised I had stood up. "What is it?"

"It's really nothing." She reached for my hand, and I let her take it. She gave a small tug to pull me back down. I wanted to feel some comfort back from her. She continued, "Years ago, I had a young woman who rented your room, and she left after only a few days." She paused, looking uncomfortable. "She said she heard things. I thought nothing of it, just felt bad she had been frightened. You know, it's an old house. There are lots of creaks, I'm sure you've noticed. And another woman who rented it a few months later had the same reaction." Gina put her hand up. "It was nothing." She pointed to the ceiling. "A loose tile." She sat back.

"So, why no other renters after the loose tile was fixed." I held my hands down so I wouldn't put quotes around loose tile.

"I listed it a few times, but the rental market had turned." She shrugged. "And after Nathalie moved in, she asked if she could use the writing desk." She smiled into the flames beside her, as though watching a distant memory in the glow—I could see it dance across her face. "She loved it up there."

"Oh," I said. My mind moved slowly around what Gina had shared. I couldn't help but search for something in what she had said—was there something more? Was she holding on to a piece? I looked at her, studying her eyes in the glowing light.

Gina smiled. "You're looking at me like I am not telling you something."

"You're not holding out on me?"

"No, that's the long and short of it, my dear."

Was there a pause? Maybe it was just me, unnerved by this whole business with Kiki and Nathalie's things and the light. I pictured the attic. Nathalie had spent time there. "Okay," I finally said. I was making more out of this than was there. I pushed myself off the floor and placed my cushion back in the corner of the room.

"Night, Gator," she said.

"Night, Gigi." I scooted out. Gina's giggles receded as I moved into the kitchen.

I placed my mug in the sink and turned to head up to my room. But I heard something in the backyard. I think I did. Earlier, Gina had asked me if I had been out there. I rested my hand on the doorknob. Did it feel warm? I stared out at the snow glistening along the path lit by the light of the big fir tree. I stood on my toes. It looked like the back gate was open. I turned back into the warmth of the kitchen, then heard a click again in the yard. I bumped my forehead into the glass, trying to see farther along the perimeter. The gate was closed. My mind and my gaze zipped around the yard. Kiki was rubbing off on me. The gate was closed when I first looked. I turned away.

The kitchen smelled like a bakery. Beside the loaves were a few cookie tins. I thought of my dad, who I often used to find around this time of year eating cookies before bed or sneaking them in the middle of the night. I hoped he had some cookies. Maybe I could Fed-Ex some. I leaned on the counter, my back to the outside and bit into a ginger cookie. I realized I was delaying heading up to the attic. I didn't want to see anything. I didn't want to hear anything. My mind wanted to hold on to a reason. A short-circuit somewhere or something. I thought of Mr. Brooks and the lamp at Ella's bedside.

As curious as I was about Nathalie, I didn't want any shenanigans, as Gran would say. I would like to know if there was anything in that box Kiki had though. I thought of Caroline and Mags. They would already be into Nathalie's things if they were here. Mags would be looking, hoping for lights to go on and off. Caroline's mom had a Ouija board, and Mags always bugged Caroline to get it from her mom's closet when we were over. I never wanted anything to do with it. I had said it was ridiculous. But I also didn't like the idea of it. Did Gina have a Ouija board? Probably.

On the third landing, all was quiet—no lights were on. Just the warm glow of the Christmas tree night light shone on a patch of the white tiles on the bathroom floor ahead. Continuing up after brushing my teeth, I paused when I heard what sounded like a piece of paper sliding across the floor. I flicked on the hall light and froze, scanning the wood floors. Nothing. My mind was playing tricks on me. But when I reached the bottom step on the way to my room, there was an envelope. I stared down at it, then looked behind me. Kiki. But she wasn't home. I creaked back across the hall and peered into her room. It was pitch dark compared to the dimly lit hall. I waited for my eyes to adjust to the shadows in her room. My eyes strained. Did I hear something? No. I turned toward the envelope on the floor and bent down to make out what was written on it. *To whomever.* I paused, then placed the ball of my foot on it and slid it back toward Kiki's room. A draught. The heat. It must have been pushed out of Kiki's room when the heat came on.

"Hey, Joe," I said as I came in out of another snowy morning. It seemed like he had been at the diner for a while. The tree lights glowed, the Christmas music was playing softly, and it felt much warmer than yesterday. He smiled at me from behind the counter and lifted his coffee mug.

"How are ya today?" he asked.

"I'm good. It's so warm in here this morning." I rubbed my hands together. "How's it going?" I looked at him funny. He seemed different—more animated or something.

"Good. A bit wired. I think this is my third, if I were to be honest." He lifted his mug, and his eyes widened. They were kind and frank, more gray than blue. "I woke up an hour before my alarm and couldn't fall back to sleep. Good thing is I'm already prepped for the day. But I might crash, so you may need to take over." He smiled and tipped his mug back.

"That won't be good."

"Pour you a coffee before it's all gone?"

"Thanks. Back in a sec." I moved through the doors to the kitchen to hang my coat and change into sneakers. Sitting on the couch had been a mistake. I sank into the cushions, and every inch of me wanted to lay my head back and close my eyes. It was comfortable. The room was comfortable. I looked around. It made me think of a handful of friends' basements I had grown up watching TV in after school and later sneaking a first taste of alcohol someone had smuggled in on a Friday night. My first kiss. I thought of Eric. I missed his kisses. A rush ran through my body as I thought of the last time he was on my futon. I shuddered. He was on my mind more than usual. When Joe smiled at me that morning, I realized he had a similar smile to Eric. Just slightly. Maybe better. But that's just a crazy thought. He had to be close to five years older than me or more than that, maybe. I shook my head and sat up to remove my boots. How old was he, anyway? Lacing up my sneakers, I gazed down at the carvings in the old table. My eyes scanned freely at the names and doodles. I stopped on a small N&H with a lopsided heart carved around it. I thought of the N on my apron. Nathalie.

"Hey," I said, coming out for my coffee. I brought it up to my nose and inhaled deeply before adding the cream. "Mmmm. You can't beat it. Thanks."

"Within moderation." Joe smiled.

I blushed, the memory of Eric still pulsing through my body. Damn Joe's smile, I thought. I grabbed his near-empty mug, turned from him, and poured it down the sink to move away so he wouldn't notice my glow. "You are cut off."

"Agreed." He moved beside me, so I could see him, gave me a mock salute then headed to the kitchen.

I set all the tables, then sipped my coffee, and enjoyed the warmth of the diner. I savored the calm before the rush. There was still about twenty minutes until we opened. My fingers moved on the counter, tapping to the beat of *Santa Baby*. The watch. I looked over my shoulder toward the kitchen, then out into the snow. I felt for the watch in the deep pocket of my apron and eased open the drawer. Why would she have tossed such a nice watch underneath all that mess? Although it looked new, it was an old-fashioned style. I turned it over and ran my fingertips over the engraving. I finally let go of it and buried it underneath as I had found it the day before, careful not to spear myself with a fishing hook.

As I closed the drawer, I heard a muffled crunching on the snow outside. I looked up, surprised to see Jenna, the woman visiting from Colorado who had come in yesterday. She was bouncing up and down on her toes outside the door. I hurried over. It was still dark out, and there was no sign of Graham with her. I turned the lock and stepped back to let her into the vestibule.

She looked pale and as though she'd been crying. "Thank you," she said, as she moved in with me. She looked around the diner. "I know you're not open. Can I come in?" She stretched out each word as though a rubber band pulled at them.

"Of course," I said. I couldn't imagine why, though. I had just met the woman, and not really—I had served her one breakfast. "Coffee?" I asked. Even in the diner, it felt like a stupid offer. I walked behind the bar, my mind starting to race. It was weird having her there, alone and obviously upset. I took my time with the coffee as I waited for her to say something. Then I heard her cry as she started to hiccup some words out. She held out a paper. We both stared down at the front page. It was a picture of a young woman—her hair was a rich brown, long, with a short straight fringe of bangs highlighting large brown eyes. Her smile was slight. There was something familiar.

I pulled myself away from the image. There was something that drew me. I looked closer and read the caption—it was Nathalie. "I don't understand?" It came out as a whisper.

"What do you mean? You don't know her?" Jenna's face was mottled, and she looked shocked, irritated, and devastated at the same time.

I shook my head and looked again at the paper and searched the headline. Nathalie. It was weird to see her on the page like that—her image rippled through me, like a shock. I'd been hearing so much about her, my curiosity building, then to see her, dead, her image somewhat alive, a beautiful smile shining out of the paper. It was wrenching. Her name was so familiar, but her face unknown to me…until now.

I watched Jenna cup the mug and look down at it. Tears spilled down her face. A few drops shimmered on the counter. I waited for her to speak—I had nothing to say. Why was she at the diner? And what was she doing with that old paper?

"I couldn't sleep last night." She hesitated and seemed to have a tight grip around the coffee that she looked at but never tasted. "I went into the living room and started to read some magazines…" She tried to smile, but didn't make it, then took a gulping breath that shook.

Whoa. It was beyond uncomfortable, the quiet of the diner, the sound of a stranger sobbing, and the image of Nathalie, pulling me to look back at her, like a nudge. I didn't know what to do as Jenna tried to get out what she wanted to tell me. I picked at a chip of Formica on the counter and quickly stopped when I felt it expanding. I pushed at it, in an attempt to smooth it back in place.

"Then, I found this old paper." We both looked at it. "It's from what, a year ago?" She looked down, her eyes vacant, scanning. "I was about to fold it again, but the woman on the front page looked familiar." Her hands trembled, and she gripped the mug tighter. Her eyes were so red. "I know her. I knew her." Her shoulders started to shake, and she put her head down on the counter and whimpered.

I looked out into the dark morning and moved around and sat beside her, twisting in the stool to get closer. I put my hand on her back. It felt like I had dropped it on a stranger—but her grief hit me, and I was with her. Suddenly, I was with a friend. I held on to the pain in my throat so it wouldn't rush out. "I'm sorry," I whispered.

After a few moments, she pushed herself up, her chin still resting on her forearms and turned her face toward me. "You must think—I don't know what you must think…you just seemed so nice and with the watch…I was sure you would have known her, I wanted to know more…" She straightened and swiveled in her stool toward me. "She was my friend." She lifted the paper and stared at Nathalie, as though searching for the image to speak. "I still can't believe it." She rubbed her red face and reached for a napkin. The cutlery echoed as it fell onto the counter. "She worked here. Nathalie. It says that here." She pointed at the page. "But you didn't know her?"

I stared at her and shook my head.

"No?" She dabbed at her red nose. "That watch…" She looked at my wrist. "That watch you had on. I swear…" She looked at me again, then she asked again, "But you didn't know Nathalie?"

My hand slid down Jenna's back and fell into my lap like a weight. I looked down at it, following its path with that same sense that it wasn't attached to me—I wiggled my fingers. "No," I said. "Just picking up a few shifts over the holidays. It's my second day, actually."

"Oh." Jenna looked kind of confused, definitely disappointed.

I felt disappointed as well for not knowing Nathalie.

"I hadn't seen her since she left over five years ago. But..." She trailed off, staring into a memory, or avoiding one. She took in the diner again. "This looks like a place she would love."

We both looked around, as though touring with the spirit of Nathalie. Our eyes settled on the Christmas tree for a moment. I felt a warmth come over me as I glanced across the empty tables out the window. Our reflections bounced back as the dawn leaned lightly on the other side of the glass.

"That watch you had on..." Jenna paused. She looked at my wrist. "It looked like a watch, exactly like a watch Nathalie had, exactly. That's why I came back. I thought maybe she had given it to you. I wanted to talk to someone who knew her..."

"I found it in the drawer." I lifted my hand and pointed over the counter, hoping proximity justified my behavior. "I'm so embarrassed. I saw it in the drawer yesterday, and I don't know, I wanted to try it on and then..." I put my hand over my face. "...well, you arrived, and I didn't have time to remove it." I looked up at her and cringed through my hand.

She put her hand on my arm and shook her head. "It's okay, I would've done the same."

She reminded me of Gran at that moment. That's something she would have said to make me feel better.

"I just hoped you knew her..." She looked back at the paper and picked up the top edge and stared at Nathalie's image.

I hesitated only a moment. "I know someone who

was close to Nathalie. You could meet her? I rent a room at the house Nathalie lived in. Would you like to meet her—Gina? She owns the house… I know she would be happy to meet you. She loved Nathalie." I punched out the words, not able to throw my offer fast enough. I felt my heart rate pick up. Would Jenna want this? Would meeting Gina help?

"Oh, I..." Jenna looked at me and searched my eyes as though checking for the truth.

"Yes. Of course. Gina would love to meet you. I can bring you by the house after my shift. Today, if you like?"

"Well…okay then, yes, thank you, that would be great."

She didn't look like she was going anywhere soon. I didn't mind. Everything was ready for the morning, and it was still early for a Sunday. She started to talk about Nathalie. I got more of a glimpse into her life, further satisfying my intrigue with this woman who seemed to have affected so many. I leaned on the counter and listened.

Chapter Six
Jenna

I saw my best friend's first kiss. It was weird. Mark Flynn had a party, five days before Christmas. The basement smelled like homeroom—feet, sweat, cheap body spray, and lip-gloss. Any of those smells still bring me back to tenth grade. Nathalie's first kiss was to *I Don't Want to Miss a Thing.* I remember being jealous her first kiss was with Rod Jenkins, but more jealous it was to the perfect song. Head Pom-pom was already deep kissing with Head Hockey-stick in a corner. Everyone snuck peeks when they could, but their kiss wasn't new, just a different basement. I had been sitting on a hollowed-out plaid couch beside Marnie Dodd when Frank Peters squeezed between us. I felt his sweaty arm against mine and attempted to get up, but the deep scoop of the cushions and his thick rugby-thigh held me in place. Before my second attempt, I looked up to see where I would propel myself. That's when I saw Nathalie. A damp heat started to rise through my stupid blouse with the frills—the top button digging into my throat—a dressed-up infant stuck in a basket. I shifted, more like squirmed to move away from Frank. I didn't want him to feel my reaction—jealousy mixed with a whopping awakening deep within.

"What was it like?" I asked Nathalie later, as we crunched along the path back to her place.

"It kind of made me dizzy," she said.

I waited for more. But we walked in silence for a while. *Crunch, crunch, crunch.*

"Jenna?" Nathalie stopped and turned to me.

It was so cold, I wanted to keep moving. "What is it?"

"Do you think this means I have to kiss him again? Like I'm his girlfriend or something?"

"Well, don't you want to be?" She sounded like she didn't want that at all.

"No."

"If not him, who?" I couldn't believe there was someone else she'd rather kiss. Or call her boyfriend. I felt that pang again, I felt when I saw it happening. What a waste of a kiss and song.

"No one."

We came to the end of the path and turned onto her street. She lived in the middle of a long crescent, so we still had a way to go. My toes were numb. We both stared at opposite sides of the street at all the Christmas lights.

"Mr. Lahey," she said with an exhale. I stared at her purge of her breath, like watching a comet with its two tails jet out her mouth.

"What about him?" He was our English teacher.

"I'd like to kiss him."

"Oh, God. Please don't." I mirrored her rush of foggy breath and felt a surge of laughter coming on.

We gulped for air as we kept walking and didn't stop our fit until we got to her house. We turned off our lamps well after two in the morning. In the dark, I thought about Mr. Lahey. Did she really want to kiss him? I pictured him sitting on the desk at the front of the room. He was the youngest teacher at school, but still. I started to think of him, the way I thought of Rod Jenkins, and my face burned.

The following Tuesday, the last day of school before the holidays, Nathalie lingered after English class to talk to Mr. Lahey. He was in his preferred position, sitting on his desk. I took my time organizing my books. Now I looked at him differently, his jeans, tight around his thighs, his five o'clock shadow, making him look not so much like a teacher, but one of the guys on True Blood, and his plaid shirt open at the collar with a bit of chest hair creeping out—eeeww. Nathalie wasn't flirting with him. She wasn't like that. She stood with her back straight, and her book pulled tight to her chest. But *he* looked like he was flirting with *her*. I knew what flirting looked like. Unfortunately, by watching my dad at parties, he and my mom had around the holidays. He liked to serve the drinks, a little heavier handed with Mrs. Davis and Mrs. Roberts. I remember once overhearing my mom pissed at him when they were getting ready for bed after one of those parties.

I hated the way Mr. Lahey looked at Nathalie. Kind of like how my dad looked at the server at the Olive Garden. I dropped my book on the floor. It was louder than I expected. It sounded like I had thrown it down. Both heads bobbed up and stared at me.

"Oops," I mumbled. I leaned down to pick it up and

felt the blood rushing to my head.

"Well, have a good holiday, Mr. Lahey," Nathalie said.

"You too, and you have a good one too, Jenna." Mr. Lahey smiled at us both, his smile more appropriate than a moment earlier.

"Wanna walk downtown and get a hot chocolate?" Nathalie asked me as she deliberated over which texts to stuff into her backpack.

"Of course," I said as I closed my locker. We had started the tradition in grade five. I wish I would have known it would be our last time. I would have savored being with Nathalie more than the whipped cream. Something terrible happened over Christmas break.

I stood at the window and waited for Nathalie to arrive. I could hear my parents in their bedroom, discussing something in hushed voices. I pictured my mom sitting on the edge of their bed, putting on a sparkling pair of nylons, while my dad fixed his tie in front of their dresser mirror. They always had a big New Year's party. My mom had spent the day preparing appetizers, rimming glasses with salt, mugs with sugar. This year instead of me going to Nathalie's, she was coming here, and we were walking over to Marnie Dodd's.

"Knock, knock." My mom startled me. Right behind her was my dad. They were still in jeans and sweatshirts. I stared at my dad. I remember feeling the shag beneath my feet and seeing the walls around me all at once. I had the urge to rip my posters down—they were too close. My gaze moved from my dad, and I stared at my mom.

"Honey." My mom sat at the edge of my bed and took my hand, her grip too tight. My dad moved closer behind my mom and put his hand on her shoulder. My head spun. "There's been an accident." Her voice was choked. "Mia…"

My dad jumped in. "Mia fell into the river." He cleared his throat. "There's a search happening right now, but…"

"But what?" I whipped my hand out of my mom's clutch.

"It's so cold." My dad moved over to me and held my shoulders.

"Nathalie?"

"Nathalie was with her," my mom whispered.

"Nathalie's okay?" I could barely hear myself. My dad's hands felt heavy on my shoulders.

"She's fine. Well, she's home. We thought we would take you over."

I started to shake. Mia was like a little sister to me, too. I felt my skin cold and tight around my arms.

On the way over, I sat in the backseat and stared out at the lights lit earlier than usual, the extra cars building on the street, guests already arriving. We passed the Dodd's house. There were four cars in the drive and two on either side of the snowbanks. They always had family in from out of town. Marnie's dad was probably out back getting the rink ready for skating. Every light in the house was on. Nathalie and I were supposed to be heading over around 6:00. I felt guilty, as I wished Dad would stop the car and let me out.

Were my parents still having *their* party? Either way, I would be disappointed. If they did, I'd be mad they were being insensitive. If they didn't, I'd have to come home to an empty house. I wanted the lights to stay on until well after midnight, and not be able to sleep because of the noise. I didn't want to wake up the next morning and open the cupboard and see all the glasses still waiting, with their sugary and salty rims.

"Don't worry about what you say, Honey." My mom turned in her seat and reached her hand out for mine. "It's okay to just say nothing."

"We'll pick you up whenever," my dad said.

"You're not coming in?"

"We are, but we won't stay long. It's different for adults. Nathalie will appreciate you there."

Did that mean they were having their party?

My mom took a deep breath when she closed the car door. She had a loaf in foil in her hands. I hadn't noticed her take it with her when we left home. My dad sighed as he closed his door. My mom took my hand, and I grasped it, not caring I was almost sixteen. Their Christmas lights weren't on. We stood at the door for what seemed like half a minute before my mom reached for the doorbell then thought better of it and gave a weak knock. I guess she felt a bell was inappropriate under the circumstances. I wondered who would open the door.

My mom folded Mrs. Howard into her arms, the loaf in her hand, stuck out behind Mrs. Howard's back. My dad took Mr. Howard's hand, then pulled him in for a hug. I stood between them and looked down the hall into the kitchen. Out of the corners of my eyes, I could see everyone shaking, but no one made any noise. Mrs. Howard looked down at me and cupped my chin. "Nat will be happy to see you." I removed my boots but kept my coat on and headed upstairs.

"Hey," I whispered as I pushed on her door. She was sitting on the edge of her bed with a stuffed giraffe in her hand. Mia's favorite.

She looked up and stared at me. "I told her to shut up. That was the last thing I said to her." Her eyes dropped down to the giraffe, and she tugged on one of the ears.

"You didn't mean it." I moved to sit beside her on the bed.

"It was my fault." She sounded weird.

"Nattie, it wasn't your fault." I put my arm around her. But she was stiff. I hadn't known what to expect, but not that. Tears would've been much better than the rigid shell she sat in.

They found Mia's body that spring. We all grieved again. I am not sure about Nathalie—she and I had drifted apart. I tried to be a good friend to her, but she pushed me away. When I saw her in the hall before Christmas break almost a year later, she even looked different. Older. She had cut her hair in layers, it was feathery, and it looked lighter. And make-up. Her eyes were dull but lit with bright blue. Her lips were droopy, but always full of gloss whenever I caught a glimpse of her. That's all that was left for us. A glimpse in the hall. Her legs were skinnier and shot out from short skirts.

The last time I saw her, well, the last time I spoke with her, we'd bumped into each other at the Co-Op. I had been picking up butter for my mom. On my way in, Nathalie was walking out. She shifted from foot-to-foot with a paper bag in her arms. A carton of cigarettes jutted out the top. A year ago, we were walking home from Mark Flynn's party. Nathalie had just had her first kiss.

"How are you?" I asked, trying to avoid looking at the cigarettes.

"Good, good, you?" Her eyes darted around the parking lot.

I missed her. I tried to think of something else to say. She was so thin. A car pulled up, and she looked at me uneasily. "Well, great seeing you."

"Yeah, you too." She zipped off and jumped into the car. The driver took off without me getting a glimpse of who was in the car. I craned. Was that Rod Jenkins' car? She hadn't even liked his kiss a year ago. That was the last time I spoke to her, but I saw her two more times.

Once at the pharmacy downtown. I had turned out of the magazine aisle and saw her talking to Mr. Phillips, the pharmacist. Nathalie wound her legs in and out of a twist, then she bounced like she had to pee. Was she sick? It was weird to see her there by herself, at the prescription counter. I had only ever stood there beside my mom when she had picked up something for a cold one of us couldn't beat. I felt hot with my coat on, but more so from the shame of creeping into the conversation, but I couldn't pull away. I inched another small step closer but stayed hidden from Mr. Phillips. I pulled his words out of sentences and realized what was happening. She wasn't sick. She was having sex. Was it Rod, who just a year ago she had said she didn't want to kiss again? I felt lonelier than I had ever felt as I stood there, watching my best friend walk out.

The last time, she was walking out of a coffee shop with two take-away-cups. I slowed my pace as much as I could without stopping. She ran to the side alley and jumped into an old powder-blue Camaro. I couldn't see the driver through the tint on the windshield.

Nathalie disappeared. About a year after Mia drowned, there were more photos of the Howard family in the paper. A beautiful picture of Nathalie on the front page, then posted at the library, on the tack board at the grocery store—all over town for a long time. It was a school photo from the year before when she still had round cheeks and a crush on Mr. Lahey.

Another year passed, and Nathalie's parents moved away. My mom had said they must have sold their house for a dollar how quickly they got out of town without any good-byes. I hated seeing Nathalie's picture recede into the paper, no longer front-page news, a smaller and smaller image of her fading out of our lives. I started to think of her less, but from time-to-time, I fantasized about running into her, yearning to replace the last images I had of her that bore into my mind.

Unfortunately, her picture over her obituary was the replacement.

Chapter Seven

I stood at the door with my hand resting against the glass and watched Jenna until even the bright shine of her hair disappeared into the pre-dawn darkness. Joe came out of the kitchen.

"Thought I heard someone?" He frowned as I turned toward him. "Everything okay?"

I nodded.

"You sure?" His attention flickered around the diner and out the window. "Were you talking to someone?"

I nodded and walked toward him.

"Yeah." I looked at the clock above the kitchen door. Ten minutes to open. Did I have time to ask? Why did they open so early on a Sunday? "Did you know Nathalie very well?"

He frowned at me and nodded. "You knew her?"

"No." I poured a coffee and looked at him, holding up the cup in offer.

"What's going on?"

I stirred my two creams in and watched the spiral, the whirlpool. I felt like I was spinning into a current I couldn't get out of or let go of. "I don't know. It seems Nathalie has come into my life…" I paused, deciding how to put it, "…from the other side."

"Whoa." Joe shook his head.

"I know." I poked at one of the boxes of tea, put a tea bag in my apron, pulled it out, and tossed it on the counter. "Do you know Kiki?"

He looked at the tea bag, then back at me. "No."

"She has a room at Gina's," I said. "She's talking about Nathalie all the time, saying she sees her. It's giving me the creeps. But I think there's something more… I don't know."

His eyebrows lifted. Why was I telling him this? "Why all this about Nathalie, now?" he asked.

"I know. It's crazy." I wanted him to know I agreed with him. "It's making me crazy." I hoped he thought I was sane. I liked to think I was, anyway, until I got into this. I was into this, wasn't I?

Joe's voice was calm. "That's quite a lot of crazy." He paused, folded the edge of a napkin inward, then straightened the knife and fork underneath. "Weird." He shook his head and folded the edge of the napkin the other way to smooth out the crease.

"What is it?" I asked.

He looked at me as though he was about to pull away from the conversation. Nobody likes being intimate with crazy. It's fun to toss around, but not when it starts to stick. Crazy Glue. But I needed to know. "What?" I asked again.

"The other day, when you were in the break room…" He shook his head. "And then you were gone…when I came back in…"

I waited, nodding my head.

"When I came back in from outside, it was weird."

"What was weird?"

"The room. It felt weird. Quiet, but like someone was there." His shoulders moved up and down and sideways, shaking it off.

Here too, I thought. Great. But I stared at him as I processed the loss of a prospective ally. I had wanted someone who didn't believe, who would laugh and punch my arm to make me feel better.

He shrugged and wrinkled his nose, dismissing it, but it was too late. To be honest, I had felt something in that room, but I like facts, I'm not a vibe type. I hunt for a hunch on any given day, but a vibe? My hunches have legs, ones that stand and aren't see-through…

The door opened behind me, and I jumped. Joe tapped the table, then my hand and rolled his eyes at me. "Maybe a little work will be good for us, hey?"

"Good morning." I sounded like I meant it. I wanted to talk to a stranger who didn't know, who didn't believe.

"Morning." A man in jeans and sportscoat took a seat by the window and looked down at the paper he had set on the table. "Same, same."

I walked over with the coffee pot to catch his eye. Where did he come from—I hadn't seen him remove a coat, a hat, or brush off snow.

He looked up. "Oh, sorry. Thought you were Sally." He smiled. I realized he wasn't as old as I thought. When he came in, he looked to be about my dad's age, but up-close, he was more like Joe's age. No older. How old was Joe, anyway?

"Just giving Sally a bit of a break." I smiled at his open face, but there was something quick about his expression. His eyes seemed to snap a shot and move away.

"Yeah, some of that, thanks." He pointed at the coffee. "And two scrambled, no meat, fried tomatoes, and rye." He unfolded the paper. There was something about him…something that seemed hidden. "Working for the holidays?" he asked.

"Yeah. Here for the week." I paused, but I could tell he wanted to get at his paper and enjoy his coffee. He looked like someone who wanted to be there before the crowd.

I went to the kitchen and watched Joe fry tomatoes. He turned and squinted at me. "You going to ring the order in?"

"Oh." I looked at the tomatoes on the grill. "Never gets anything but that?"

"Not ever."

I went back to place the order. Joe hit the bell.

"Very funny," I said and picked up the plate. The butter melting on the rye and the smell of the herbs sprinkled over the tomatoes made my stomach come to life. I paused with the plate in my hand.

"What's up?" Joe peered under the lamps at me.

"He seems like an undercover cop or something?" I had gotten that impression, maybe too much criminology.

"You only happy when there's trouble?" He looked like he was about to wink at me.

It was steady all morning. Not as busy as it had been the day before, but a good pace. I was distracted as I poured coffees and cleared plates. I thought of my other roommate, Harry, whom I hadn't met. I wondered what he was like. But beneath my meandering thoughts, there was something gnawing at me. Just after lunch, it hit me.

Was the 'H' for Harry that was carved into the coffee table in the break room? He picked her up at the diner and walked her home. Maybe he knew more about Nathalie. What had really happened to Nathalie.

Postie guy came in and took a seat at the bar. He wasn't wearing his USPS coat, but I recognized him from Friday. "Hey," he said. "Sally okay?"

"For sure. I'm picking up a few shifts to help out."

"Cool." He folded his coat on the stool beside him and piled his hat and gloves on top. "Adam." He threw the Shaka sign at me.

I giggled. I loved that Hawaiian greeting, the hang loose gesture. "Hi. I'm Ali. Nice to meet you." I 'Shaka'd' back.

He grinned. "Yeah, I'll have coffee, please." He nodded at the pot I had in a hover close to his cup. "And a mushroom and cheese omelet with wheat toast."

"You got it." I moved to ring it in.

"Oh and no home fries, but some fries, please."

"You too?" I smiled up at him. "I gotta try those fries."

I looked around the diner. I liked feeling part of it—it would be fun not to have to ask so-and-so what they wanted, for them to be more than so-and-so. Where everybody knows your name competed with the Christmas music playing outside my thoughts. The tree glowed, and reflections bounced around the diner and off the windows. *It's beginning to look a lot like Christmas* became clearer, bringing me back to the present. It sure did, it had for a while. What a start to the winter. Start? It was the first day. Four days until Christmas. And I had no guest. No idea. Who was free Christmas Eve? I thought of the young woman I had seen on the street, who had come in for warmth the day before.

The door jingled.

"Hey, Mr. Brooks. This is a *real* surprise." I smiled.

He chuckled and moved to his usual booth by the window. I watched him scan the diner as he did on the other mornings. I poured his tea. Adam swiveled around.

"Hey, Brooks."

"Morning, Adam. Not used to seeing you here on a Sunday."

"Christmas shopping. I'll see you at your shop later. I want to get a Christmas book for my niece."

"I have a few of those." Mr. Brooks smiled and settled in. His shuttered eyes lingered on the man that kept his head in the paper. He was the opposite of Mr. Brooks. He didn't look at anyone or anything. Maybe he was an undercover cop.

I topped up Adam's coffee on the way to Mr. Brooks' table. The ding of the bell from the kitchen startled me.

"You good?" Joe bent down and peeked out at me under the heating lamps.

"Yeah, sure." I smiled at him.

I got Adam settled with ketchup and coffee and returned to Mr. Brooks.

"What are we going for today?" I asked with a little anticipation.

"Wait a second. We're not at the order part yet."

I wanted to sit. Settle in with him and take in the diner from a different angle, but I straightened, scanned the tables, and then gave him a quick account of my earlier meeting with Jenna.

He shook his head. "What a shame Nathalie didn't keep in touch with friends and family." I watched him struggle with that. Would it have been different if she did? He looked out into the snowbanks and then back at me, as though he was shaking himself out of something or somewhere.

I noticed a scar on his forearm, creeping out from his sweater—it looked like a deep cut. I shot my eyes back up to meet his.

"So, what do you think?" He gave a few taps to the table and looked toward the kitchen.

"I'm guessing not chili."

He squinted at me. "Hmmm." He pretended to consider that option.

"Yeah, I'm not buying it. I see a grapefruit or something in that category."

He tapped his fingers on the table and looked around. "It's Sunday." He pulled his sweater down over the scar.

"That's right."

"What's Joe got in those pancakes today?"

I hesitated only a moment, remembering the unmistakable aroma of the batter. "Apple-cinnamon."

"Perfect. No grapefruit."

After the morning rush, all the tables set for lunch, and the coffee set to perk for the fourth time, the bells on the door to the diner more than jingled. My head shot up. Kiki. Surprise, surprise—she even made bells jingle louder. She should be in a parade or something. I didn't have to ask her why she was there. She was there. She got right into it.

"So stress, so stress. This crazy, this guest thing. Who do I know? Ask a stranger? Crazy ask a stranger. Love Gina in bits. But…" After her rant, she scanned the diner, and her shoulders relaxed a little. I tried not to laugh, but I don't think she'd care or notice. I loved that she said 'Love Gina in bits.' She must have picked up the expression 'love to bits' from Gina—I think I had heard her say it.

Kiki ran her hand over the counter, absently fiddled with one of the mugs, and peeked at the guests at a corner booth. I'd never seen her so still. The diner had this effect. Or was it the music? I smiled, thinking of the cartoon. Wasn't that the Tasmanian Devil's one weakness—music? The only thing that could calm him down? I'd have to remember that in a pinch. I looked over at the lingering table. They hadn't even noticed the little devil come in. I tapped my hand on the bar counter. "Have a seat. Would you like something? Tea? Hot chocolate?"

She looked around again. Her eyes rested on the tree for a moment and then did another full sweep of the diner. "Nice in here." She took a seat on a stool. "So warm. I should make more visits." She continued to look around, taking everything in and forgetting about her guest, it seemed.

"Would you like something?"

She looked at me funny.

"A tea?"

"Oh. No. Too busy. You have guest?"

I shook my head. "No. Haven't a clue, either." I smiled at Kiki. "We'll figure it out. There's still time."

"Time? Three days Christmas Eve!" Kiki started to fidget and get that Taz look in her eyes. "Okay," she said as though I had spoken. She pushed herself away from the bar and jumped down. "Keep at it." She hurried out with a wave.

I stared out into the snow, watching Kiki recede away from the diner.

Joe came out the swinging door from the kitchen. I didn't mind the interruption. I smiled up at him.

"What's with you? Were you talking to yourself,

again?" He raised his brow and grabbed a mug.

I reached over and poured the freshly brewed coffee. His forearm leaned against mine as I tipped the pot into his mug. He was warm. I looked at his forearm and wanted to keep pouring. Keep touching. *Damn*, I liked him. Caroline was right. I was always too quick to fall for someone. But if I switched it up every six months as per her plan, who cares? I smiled. No, that wasn't me.

"You just missed Kiki," I said.

"Kiki?"

"You know, the one who sees Nathalie?"

"Oh, right, right. That's too bad. I would've had some questions." He rolled his eyes, but looked like he was about to laugh, then leaned back. We stood shoulder-to-shoulder, looking out at the people bustling along.

"I don't have a clue who to invite to Gina's, you know, this guest thing. Or I have too many people I'd like to ask, maybe." I thought of the girl. I thought of Mr. Brooks. I thought of Joe. My heart picked up speed at the thought of him sitting beside me at Gina's.

"Well, you can't ask me." Joe looked down at me and smiled. He nudged my elbow.

"Get over yourself," I said, trying to sound light, trying not to blush—that always works.

"Ouch. I meant I'm already on the guest list."

I tried not to smile. "Oh yeah? Who invited you?"

"I know people." He poured the remainder of his coffee out as the door jingled. He winked at me and pushed through the door back into the kitchen. I knew he'd wink at me sooner or later. It was too soon, I thought, but of course, I liked it.

I hadn't recognized it was Sally who came in. She was disguised with an oversized parka and scarf wrapped close to her face. She waved, stomped, and leaned down to place a bag under the tree.

"Heard it from a little bird you may want to head out early today."

"Oh?"

She pointed at the kitchen and smiled. "It's all good. I kinda miss the rush of the day. I am happy for it, so…" She looked around at the lingering table. "What you got? Want to transfer or settle up?"

"They already paid. You sure?" I noticed the purple had faded under her eyes. Proof she was getting some much-needed rest.

"Absolutely."

I paused. What had Joe said to her? I felt guilty.

"What is it?" She wavered a second and folded her coat into her little cubby hole.

We hadn't had much of an exchange beyond diner stuff, weather, and other light topics. We were always passing the baton. "Oh, it's nothing."

She looked at me as she jumped into lunch prep. I wanted to ask her why she didn't bring her coat to the back room. I wanted to ask her a lot of things. Did she share an apartment with anyone? Was she friends with Nathalie? I looked at her small red hands separating coffee filters. They were chapped with eczema and looked cold. What was her life like? Did she have a mother to tell her to put Vaseline on her hands or a doctor to give her a prescription for something that might work?

When I got out onto the street, I remembered I was meeting Jenna at the diner after my shift. I gave Gina a quick call to check in…of course, she was happy to have any guest drop by, but one who knew Nathalie…she couldn't wait. I could go home and come back, I had time, but I didn't feel like it. What I felt like was sitting in the diner, sipping a hot chocolate. I looked back at the fogged windows, and the warm glow inside and pulled my scarf tighter around my neck. Sally was talking to my leftovers—a couple lingering over coffee. She looked happy in there. I looked up Main Street and started to pull in and out of the snow. Maybe I could find my guest. I was running out of time. There was small comfort in knowing none of us had a guest yet. Well, someone did, probably Harry had invited Joe. Joe. Joe would be there. With Harry. It was odd to live in a house with someone I hadn't even met. Sometimes if I was still lying awake when he got home late at night, I strained for the faint sounds of him in our shared bathroom, brushing his teeth. He and I kept our toothbrushes on opposite sides of the medicine cabinet over the sink. Kiki's was in a glass right on the counter, a quick easy-access for her *brush, brush, brush,* then *snap, snap, snap* against the sink. A few times, I found it laying half on the porcelain basin, half on the counter, toothpaste caking around the bristles. I didn't mind. Mags would have whipped it into the trash bin. No second chances. I smiled, thinking of her. I hadn't had time to miss her and Caroline.

When I turned around a bend, I saw that girl from the street. She pushed up off a corner, one limb then another, like a deer's first attempt to stand. She pocketed change from a gray wool hat she scooped from the curb. I slowed my pace. She was shivering—her arms dangled at her sides with my red mitts on her hands. As she looked at the ground, she tapped her coat pocket, and then pressed against the outline of something on its inside, then her eyes darted in both directions. I pulled at my hat, and my breath billowed out in a big waft from my sigh. She turned and moved in a jerky stride; stiff from sitting in a mound of snow, but her long stick-y legs looked stuck in a bend she couldn't get out of. I flashed to my old Barbie days, yanking their legs and arms in and out of poses to satisfy what I wanted them to do—one time wrenching so hard I dislocated an elbow. Not mine. I never threw that Barbie out. Just picked over her as she lay disjointed at the bottom of the case, a bikini top, or tiny sunglasses covering her face or getting caught in her tattered hair.

It wasn't as cold as it had been, but sitting out in it would be a different story. I trod over the imprint she had left behind in the snow. I felt a chill stiffen up my spine as the icy mold crunched beneath my feet. A homeless ice sculpture no one wanted to look at or pay to see. I hadn't noticed any bills when she picked up her hat. As I followed her through the snowy flakes, I felt like I lived in a snow globe. That was *my* story. I shuddered at the possibility this was it for her—stuck in a broken-down snow globe. I couldn't bear to think of her sleeping outside, people walking by pulling at their hoods, crossing the street to the comfort of the lamppost.

After trailing her for a block, she ducked into the European coffee shop, Kaffee Brik. I slowed to a shuffle. I bowed my head and peeked through the shop window, took another step toward the door and stared into the café. Both my hands rested on the door—I wished someone would push me. Would she notice me or remember me from the diner? I didn't want to scare her off. But I was so drawn to her. I had such a helpless ache. How could I get her to Gina's, to be my guest for Christmas Eve? I'd have to make a connection, but I only had a few days. I suspected she didn't have anywhere to go. The thought of her alone shot a searing cold through me, but also emboldened me, I would go in. I'd have that hot chocolate. Sit at one of those snug booths, only big enough for one person per side that lined the perimeter of the coffee shop—they looked like tiny cubicles to hold guests on a magical ride. Even before the holidays, when I had passed the café, I had been captivated by its dangling décor and cuckoo clock—clearly an authentic import, eye-catching from the street. It was large and hung on the wood panel wall, centered above the bar counter.

I pulled on the heavy door and was greeted by intense heat. A rush of warm air from a vent above surged upon me. I wanted to stay under its umbrella, but my eyes scanned the café, and I moved on in. My first sweep of the place kind of made me dizzy. Suddenly, I felt hot, too bundled up in my parka. I pulled at my zipper and loosened my scarf as I continued with a slower scan, starting with the tables. More than half of them were full, and there was a queue of three people waiting to order at the counter.

I searched for a pay phone, remembering the girl pretending to use the one at the diner, but there wasn't one. She must have gone to the washroom. I joined the line, anticipating the hot chocolate. My priorities shifted for a moment. I hovered over the glass display case full of European-style Christmas cookies—more understated than the typical sugar cookies with their vibrant icing and gingerbread men with their currant eyes and noses. I scanned the thick shortbreads, the dense almond squares, sweet buns, and butter cookies in the shapes of wreaths. I thought of my tips from the diner and started to pick out an assortment I would bring back to Gina's.

It was my turn to order and still no sign of the girl. Not really a girl, I suppose, but she looked like one, for sure. I don't know what I had planned, anyway. I was lost in thought with bad attempts to establish a dialogue with her…the snow princess. I scoffed—how disgusting—I should just go get a Barbie and pull at her arms. That's the only conversation I could handle.

"May I help?" A woman in a crisp, white embroidered smock asked, with a…was it a Swiss accent? I guess German accent. She must be Swiss with all the décor.

She had cornflower blue eyes with smile lines that crinkled outward and crept down her ruddy cheeks.

"May I have a hot chocolate? And I'd like to order some desserts to take away."

She followed my eyes to the display case and gave me a conspiring look. "Of course. Is your hot chocolate to stay?"

I looked around again. "Yes, to stay."

She reached for a medium-sized mug and held it up to me. I nodded. She moved to a thick silver pot, warming on a hotplate, and ladled a generous amount of dark chocolate into the mug. I was lit with anticipation— my only regret, not opting for a large mug. She looked at me, like my mom used to look at me when I opened a Christmas present she was excited to give me.

"I can see you never have this here?"

I shook my head and stared at her as she poured milk into a stainless-steel frothing pitcher.

"It's real Swiss chocolate. You will like. I promise."

I didn't doubt it. I watched her continue the process, the machine frothing the milk. My eyes fixed upon her every move. She proceeded to spiral a generous portion of thick whipping cream around, up and over the rim until it peaked a few inches above. She finished with a heavy-handed sprinkle of shaved chocolate. Oh my. Before she handed it over, the bird came out to announce one o'clock. I yelped, and the woman stared at me and then smiled as my cheeks puffed out and I started to laugh.

"I'm sorry," I said and looked around at the other tables. If anyone had noticed they had forgotten me quickly and were back to their own hot chocolates and conversations. I looked up at the clock. "It's beautiful."

"And scary, no?" She laughed and handed me my mug. "You can pay later, when you pick up your treats, yes?"

"Okay, thank you."

"Enjoy." She winked at me.

There was a booth free at the front. I positioned myself with my eye on the door to make sure I wouldn't miss the snow princess. I did want her to be a princess. As I settled in and took my first sip, I wondered if she was okay. Only a little bit of the hot chocolate made it passed the barrier of thick cream. It was good. I looked around at the other patrons sipping, nibbling, and chatting, many with colored paper bags tucked beside them or on the edge of the tables. A break from Christmas shopping or perhaps a final stop on the way home. Maybe I could find a little something for Gina today. I finally broke through the wall of cream as it started to melt, and I greedily took a few sips in a row.

I paused to savor it a little longer, and when I looked up, there she was. Her eyes darted around the café without looking at anything or anyone, and she lifted her hood over her head. Her hair looked damp. She must have washed it in the sink. I shot a look over at the woman behind the bar to see if she noticed and she caught my eye and smiled. She didn't seem to care her washroom was being used without service. Extensively used. Now was my chance to pull away from my hot chocolate and introduce myself to her, or say hello, or I don't know… Maybe invite her to join me. If I had only thought of buying her one in a take-out cup—at least I could hand it off like a coward. Before I could come up with the perfect scenario or at least move, she scurried out onto the street. I thought of her wet hair and her shivering earlier. I looked down at the melting remainder of cream floating in my mug that no longer appealed to me. I pushed the mug a few inches forward and then pushed myself out of the booth. Only moments behind her, but her light blue hood bobbed up and down through the snow away from me.

I looked back at the café and rushed back in. The woman behind the counter looked up from her work and smiled warmly at me.

"I am sorry. I ran out of here without paying."

She laughed. "And I think you forgot something, no?" She fanned her hands above the display of desserts.

"Yes." I bent down to get a better look at all the options. I stared through them at first, catching my breath and thinking of the young woman and our unparallel lives that I wanted to bridge.

When I approached the diner, I slowed my pace. It was too early to meet Jenna, plus, I liked looking in through the windows. I liked the diner from all angles. There was something about a glimpse from the outside that gave me a rush. Maybe it was the anticipation of comfort—I knew what was inside: the warmth, the aroma, the music, even though it was full-on Christmas. The regulars were so friendly…and the cook. I felt a wave flush through me. And then it was as though rocks hit the window, thrown at me from inside the diner to where I paused on the sidewalk. It was that woman. I couldn't forget those eyes, the flat gray color, and the way she stared piercingly, like she did when I looked down at her from the attic. Did she recognize me, or was it a look she threw at everyone? It had to be…we had never met.

"You're back," Sally called with a laugh in her voice, but she looked a little different than earlier, tired or strained. "Forget something?"

"Just meeting someone in a few minutes." I looked over at the woman in the booth. Her eyes darted away this time, she didn't connect with me.

Sally shot her eyes at the woman, brandishing the same stare. An eye for an eye. Who was that woman? I had to find out. She had been at Gina's with the death card in hand, and Sally seemed to give her a death stare.

"Gina?" I called out as Jenna and I entered the foyer.

"Well, hello," she boomed back at me and laughed.

I hadn't looked up when we entered. Jenna was in the middle of telling me about how she met Graham. "Oops, sorry." I shut the door behind us. "Gina, this is Jenna. Jenna, Gina."

Gina wrapped her arms around Jenna. I was surprised, but Jenna hugged back. Two people who loved Nathalie—they already had a bond. I felt that familiar void stretching across my chest that I had never met Nathalie, mixed with that nagging sensation of presence and absence—black and white.

They pulled apart and stared at one another—like a search into a loved one's eyes to check in, to make sure the other is okay. And again, I was back on the street with the young woman, the emptiness expanded, sunk into my gut—I wondered how long it had been since anyone had checked in with her, had given her that look.

"Come in, come in." Gina pulled off our coats almost at the same time.

"Mmmm, it's so warm in here," Jenna said.

I followed her eyes, remembering that rush of taking it all in. It was easy to go there with her, that first dance around the room.

"Tea?" Gina asked. Always the first question.

"Would love one, thank you." Jenna's gaze stretched down the hallway.

Gina turned to Jenna and put a hand on her arm. "If you woke Ali at three in the morning she'd say yes to tea. I think she can hear the kettle whistle from the attic. I can't get away with it." I liked her funny faces when she pretended things were wicked.

We settled around the kitchen table. I watched Jenna as she looked around, piggybacking on her experience. Gina got right into it. She wanted to know all about Nathalie as a girl. Jenna lit up as she spoke about her childhood friend, but her smile faded to pain as she picked up one of the memories, and it hung over us like a hot July night. It was so warm in the kitchen—it tightened around us as we went back…down to the river. We joined Jenna and Nathalie…five years ago.

Chapter Eight
Jenna

The days after Nathalie's little sister Mia fell into the river were heavy, black, Gorilla Glue sticky. The air felt thick, too close to the ground—like a dome pushing our grief into us and everything it could get its hands on. Whenever I hear a helicopter, I go to the banks along that river, to where it happened. And my mood goes flat—I get that sucking pull to the ground. I spent those first days walking along the river with Nathalie as they went from search to recovery, but we didn't know that... I wasn't supposed to know that. I overheard my parents in their hushed bedroom voices talking about the recovery. My dad had said something about the cost of the helicopter—I didn't understand, but I felt it wedge into my stomach.

Every day, I watched Nathalie fade away under the helicopter that had become a drone, like a metronome.

The beat, I remember thinking of as a continuous machine gun…dakka, dakka, dakka, and then the staccato increase of the slapping blades as it accelerated, pulling out for a break. Nathalie didn't seem to take anything in. I started to feel hollow next to her as she broke from herself. Those days I took everything in, every sound, every detail. The sky seemed always full of one big, dense cloud, white-gray without definition, the atmosphere closing in, pushing down. The wind ripped at our faces, but nothing moved, a layer of moisture stuck to our cheeks.

Each day when we arrived, I looked for the familiar faces at the incident command set up high on the shore. On the third day, I couldn't pull away from a man and woman, laughing in their uniforms, laughing while Mia was out there somewhere in the river. The scene looked the same every day—at some point, there was a crew of divers either coming in from the river or heading out, pulling on their wetsuit or peeling it off, and there was always at least one zodiac buzzing along the river. Fewer and fewer camera crews. At night, I'd wake with a sheen of sweat sticking my pajamas to my chest, horrible images of Mia floating near the shore, Nathalie's narrowed gaze, drifting ahead over the packed tracks, stepping over her.

The last day we went to the river was the last time Nathalie, and I hung out. I wanted to hang on to her, but there was nothing to grab. I had the urge to shake her. I wanted her to spiral into one of her laughing fits. Listen to her talk about how she wanted to kiss Mr. Lahey or didn't want to kiss Rod Jenkins, even though neither of those options made any sense to me. But we silently combed the shore as we had done that week, me looking, hoping not to see tips of fingers surfacing above the water's edge, Nathalie's vacant eyes a foot ahead of us, and then she turned to me when we were as far as we usually got until we made our turn. I stared at her even though I didn't want to meet her dead eyes, but she didn't look at me, just over my shoulder.

"I pushed her." It didn't sound like her voice, but I wasn't surprised.

Dakka, dakka, dakka. I hadn't heard her, I don't think. I didn't want her to repeat it, though, but she did and waited—I could feel her looking at me then, but I stared way back at the incident command station. Dakka, dakka, dakka. After a moment, I tried to lift my arm to touch her shoulder, but I couldn't pull it away from my side.

"Nattie," I finally said. I had nothing else. The whop of the blades above didn't startle me. It was the first time that week I didn't watch the helicopter pull away. We were left with silence, the faint buzz of the lone zodiac.

Maybe if I would have had more to say. I know she didn't mean to push her, if she had, in fact, pushed her— I doubted it. I could picture them walking along the shore as Nathalie and I had done forever, sometimes with Mia. Running with the blur of gray beside us, icy moisture whipping our cheeks, our tracks the only ones by the river's edge.

All three of us jumped when we heard the bang from above. Gina and I exchanged a startled stare, not only from the interruption. That glimpse of Nathalie's life hit like a cross-check to the ribs, winding me. Plus, Gina had that look that there might be other possibilities than something falling for no reason—that there was a reason. None of us moved after that initial jerk back from the table. We all waited—looking at one another. I would find out—I was going to find out.

I shot up, Gina with me. I think our push against the table and jump to attention startled Jenna more than the bang from above. But she fell into line right behind us. We marched up the first flight, the second flight. That nagging prickle creeping along the back of my neck that had become so familiar on those stairs. We reached the second landing, and Jenna bent to pick something off the floor. It was an envelope. I had seen it before but chose to ignore it. It had made its way back into the hallway. Another bang.

"Ah, Gina, Awli!" Kiki shot out of her bedroom door, her eyes were wider than usual. She was surprised to see *us*? She was never home this time of day.

We all stared at her.

She looked at the three of us and then to the letter in Jenna's hand. "Nice to meet you, ah, um?"

"Kiki, this is Jenna…" Gina answered for Jenna, but the intro got stuck and fell off. Gina looked over Kiki's shoulder into her room, as though looking for something.

"Nice to meet you, Kiki," Jenna said.

"Nice meeting you, Jenna." She reached for the letter in Jenna's hand. "You come to dinner Christmas Eve. Here. Yes?"

Jenna stared. We all stared at Kiki.

"I invite." She looked at the letter. "Meant to be. You come. Yes?"

"Well..." It was all she managed. She looked to Gina and me for support.

I stared at the letter. It was the one I had seen in the hallway. I reached for it, on auto-pilot—wanting to know what the letter was.

"No. No. No." Kiki shook her head. "Jenna. It meant

to be. She must come Christmas. I know it."

I stared at her. I looked to Gina, willing her to make a move for the letter. I felt like a child…having to watch the younger one play with the toy. Maybe it would have been hard having a sister. Did the letter have something to do with Nathalie? Maybe it had been in her box of things Kiki held. Did Gina know about Kiki hoarding her things? I wanted to tell on her. I guess I would have been a bad sister. I kept my eyes on the letter. But Kiki had it gripped, she wasn't giving it up. I had missed my chance when it pushed into the hallway—right at my feet.

"You are more than welcome, of course." Gina touched Jenna's shoulder and smiled. "It would be lovely to have you here."

"Well, I…"

"You have, you must," Kiki said. "Natlie want."

"What?"

"What?"

"What?"

All three of us raised a 'what' with similar degrees of surprise.

"Christmas Eve her favorite. You need be there. Here." Kiki looked at Jenna. "Set up?"

I think she meant settled.

"That's very kind. But Christmas Eve's at Graham's parents' place…"

"Ok. You come after." Kiki smiled widely and reached for Jenna's hand. "Nice to meeting you." She wasn't letting go of her guest. I didn't blame her. Maybe I could tag onto that. I brought her here…or I could claim Graham.

Jenna hesitated but offered her hand, sealing the deal with the little devil.

Kiki stomped into her room, slammed the letter into

a drawer. "No peeky." She looked at me, then flew down the stairs. My mind stayed stuck on the drawer. I know, I know, but I can't let this one go.

We stood in the hallway and listened to her push around the coats in the front closet and pull on her boots. The door banged, and we jumped again. I started to laugh. Gina looked at me and joined in, and Jenna surprised us with kind of a honking laugh. Gina laughed even harder, slid down, and sat hunched over on the landing, her long legs, reaching down a couple of the steps. Jenna and I leaned our hands onto Gina's shoulder and continued our laughs in varying degrees, honks and gasps. At some point, I swear, through the breaks for breath of the three of us, I heard a fourth laugh. I didn't mind. It didn't make me jump or look over my shoulder. Maybe I wanted to hear it.

Later in the day, the blend of sweet and spicy aromas drew me to the kitchen. I found Gina there, every counter covered with cookies and cakes and loaves and squares. She must have a whopper of a freezer somewhere. "Hey, Gina." I wondered if this was her normal, or if she was in there more because of Christmas. It smelled like butter, cinnamon, and sugar. "Do you need anything at the store or anything? Just heading out for a walk."

She shook her head. I had caught her with a cookie in her mouth. She pointed to a pan. "Have one. Before they're gone."

I laughed as I bit into a warm cookie. "Mm-mmm, so oh good. My mom used to make these or something like these." I gave her a look. "I was wondering where you were storing all the cookies. I see how you work now."

"Very funny, wabbit." She lifted clusters of cookies up with an unusually large spatula. "Don't count them." She pretended to cover the plate they piled onto. "Enjoy your walk."

I crunched along into the dusk. Christmas lights blinked on as I moved up Union. It was my favorite time of day. I hurried through the heavy snow. I wanted to get to the graveyard before dark. I don't like to think of myself as a grave hunter, but I like cemeteries, and without sounding too morbid, I like them best at dusk and around the holidays. When I'm haunting them at Halloween, I am always out before the dark covers the gravestones. Not that I'm prone to fright—I don't believe in spirits roaming around trying to communicate, but I still don't like to be around the dead at dark. I wouldn't call it a hobby, I guess the term is taphophile, which fits—I like cemeteries and looking at the tombstones. Of course, I don't mention this on a first date. Reading the epitaphs, I often wonder if it was what the dead had said or if the sentiment is what the living wished the dead had said. I trawled for the funny ones. My favorite that I can easily recall: *Don't tell my wife where I am. It's quiet here, and I've got lots of cold ones with me.*

I opened the iron gate and relished the moan against the quiet falling snow. About a foot of white rested fresh and glistening on the tombstones in the dwindling light. The moon caught the tops of their theads, snow stuck to their faces, covering their words. I wouldn't go so far as to dust off graves, but I started my stroll—it wasn't all about the epitaphs. Poinsettias dotted the cemetery, vibrant green and red leaves against the white. Was Nathalie here? The thought pulled me out of the beauty.

With that in my head, I started to look at the graves differently. What would it say on *her* tombstone?

I paused in front of a grave. *A Life Well-lived, A Life Well-loved.* I calculated the years and smiled, ninety-seven. Was that easier if the life was long or did that make a difference? I suppose it would if one knew the pain of the loss of a life well-loved, but not well-lived. It was worse when there wasn't enough time to live it. I thought of my mom's sister. I don't remember her as an aunt as she died when I was three, she was only twenty-four. I remember her birthday, though, and I hated the non-celebration of it every year as a child—my mom often home before me, having left work early, her face drawn, her eyes red, her not as interested in what happened at school as I tried to penetrate the dark with my stupid stories I wasn't interested in either.

I spied an older man a few rows over brushing off a headstone. I wondered what the date was and hoped it was a well-lived one. He was singing *Have Yourself A Merry Little Christmas,* which led me in the direction it was a well-lived life, or perhaps enough time had passed to allow carols back into his life. I had the urge to join his choir but turned away and left him with his memories. The light was fading, so I turned around and looped back to the gate, humming his tune under my breath. On the edge of the graveyard, I saw another mourner. There was something familiar. The coat—the figure hunched over a grave, tugged on her camel-colored hood. Had she seen me? It was the woman who left Gina's, who had a reading. Whose grave was she stooped over? I had a feeling I knew.

I headed toward Union but stopped, my breath fogging around me, catching me in a cloud. I stepped around it, looking back into the graveyard. I didn't see the woman. Had she seen me? I scanned the cemetery, but it was empty, well, sort of. No one was walking around. Just that man and his muffled tune, heading out the other way. The creak of the gate wasn't as welcoming with the dark, falling over the headstones.

The gravestone had its face hid from me. I looked around and then stepped closer. I'd never touched one before. The snow was fresh and fell away with a soft brush.

I gasped a big cloud, creating a mist over the grave. Even though I knew, it was still a jolt to see it carved into the granite. Like proof popped into my head. Snow stuck to the dates. I couldn't touch it again.

NATHALIE HOWARD
Your Beautiful Memory Lingers

The epitaph chiseled through me. *Your beautiful memory lingers.* Yes, it does linger. It wasn't just lingering... There was more than her memory here…

My phone rang. My blood drained to my feet, zipped down like a falling elevator, a cable snapped. My hand shook as I unzipped my coat to get at it, to stop the ringing. It sounded so loud in the dark, with the dead. I looked at the number—it was Gwen from my cold case group.

"Ali, it's Gwen."

My eyes stayed stuck on the tombstone. "Hey," I whispered.

"Don't know if you're busy…some of us are meeting this evening. Now, actually. I tried to reach you earlier, didn't leave a message, sorry."

"Everything okay?"

"Yeah, yeah. I was just thinking of Lynn's case. I

wanted to get to it. So, thought I'd offer the option to anyone who's free…you know, since we'll be locked out for a week. I know nobody likes the time off." Her words ran quicker than usual.

"I'm thinking of something, too. I'll be there. See you in about twenty. I have to run home to get my laptop." I was thinking of Nathalie's case, not a cold case, but I would mention it to Gwen. The case. I know, I have a problem.

Half the group was there when I squeezed into our bunker. I noticed Michelle first, her curtain of black hair a shield around her and her laptop. What was her life like outside our foxhole? She seemed the most at home down here. I couldn't picture her elsewhere. I saw her once ordering a coffee on campus—she had the same look, the same drawn shade around as though she didn't want to be seen. Maybe she wanted to hide her piercing eyes, eyes that looked like black magnets, catching everything.

"You good?" Gwen asked as I set up beside her. Her eyes remained on her screen. I paused and watched her eyes move. The strain of looking for something that wasn't there or couldn't be found came to my mind.

"What's going on?"

Gwen chewed her bottom lip, then turned to me. "I got another letter… I wish people would email me, you know. It's harder to track a letter…"

I moved to the edge of my seat. "What did it say?"

Gwen handed the letter to me. "Says she's sort of a half-sister, whatever 'sort of' means…of Tom Dern, the guy they questioned the most but didn't have anything to hold…"

I scanned the few lines. It said she lived in some group home with him at the time it happened. Most of these leads were people either trying to frame someone or trying to get their CSI on. But all worth a look, of course. "What did McCool say?"

Gwen shrugged. "Just got it today. I don't know, just wanted to take a look first…"

"I'll go with you," I said and closed my laptop. Gwen looked like she needed someone to take over. "Gwen…" I put my hand on her forearm, gripped it to bring her to the present. "It could be important. You have to bring it in."

"You're right."

Walking to the station, Gwen started to talk about Christmas. Christmas! We had lots to talk about. We didn't need *that* distraction. I didn't care for that distraction. I wanted to steer back to the case…if not Lynn's, then Nathalie's. We crunched along, taking in the Christmas lights. I looked through the puff of white in front of her to the other side of the street. We took turns laying fog—walking deeper into it. "Do you remember the drowning in the Champlain last year around this time? Nathalie Howard." I watched my own puff of breath meld with hers, two dragons walking side-by-side.

"Yeah, sure. Why's that?"

"I live at the house she lived at…"

"Really?" Gwen grabbed my arm. I got the impression she stopped herself from saying 'cool' or something. I got it. "Did you find something?" she asked, her pace slowing. "I remember her drowning, for sure. It seemed to baffle people who knew her."

"Yeah. Well, I feel there's something more there that didn't get looked at, you know?"

"What do you mean?"

"No one thinks she jumped."

"She fell then?" Gwen shrugged, seeming to lose interest.

"Maybe." I paused. We walked for a moment in silence. "Did you ever see her around before it happened? Did you know who she was?" I asked.

"I didn't know her, but after her picture was in the paper, I recognized her right away. I often saw her on the street, talking to people... She volunteered at that detox center."

"Huh."

"What?"

"There's a young woman on the street I keep seeing…I don't know. I wonder if she knew Nathalie." One thing I knew, I would stop by that detox center.

"Where are you going with this?"

"Probably nowhere." I didn't like going nowhere, though…

"You're worse than me, I think." Gwen laughed, nudged my elbow as we arrived at the station.

McCool wasn't working. I stayed with Gwen while she went over the details and handed over the letter to the on-shift homicide detective. I felt a pang for Gwen's loss as we went separate ways into the falling snow and faded sky. I wished I had some evidence to hand over to the police so we could talk about Nathalie. Not as a ghost…as a case.

Chapter Nine

We stretched out in the den, watching wreaths of smoke curl and drift. The house smacked of Christmas more than ever, it being only three days away. Every room's ambiance seemed warmer, aglow with its candles and tiny lights sparkling from the trees and mantles. Cinnamon, nutmeg, and cider wafted from room to room. And the pipe—I think Gina may have had a little puff in the kitchen when no one was around. I would have loved to have caught her with it held between her teeth as she punched the dough. The scent of warm cakes and molasses oozed from every corner, and the constant fire, like a well-tended pet in the background, murmured and sighed.

"Looks like I'm going to lose you early, this evening," Gina said.

"Hmmm." I sat up. "No, just comfy, just perfect."

We both looked into the fluttering glow of the

candle wicks resting beside Gina.

I broke our silent doze. "Do you have your guest picked out?"

"I do."

I waited for a name. I was the only one now without a guest. She didn't seem like she was going to tell me without a push. "Well…is it a secret?"

"I invited Joe from the diner."

"Oh. I didn't know you knew him?"

"Really? I know everyone." She smiled. "He's done a lot of work for me. It seemed right. What about you, any ideas?"

"I don't know." I paused. "Well, there is a young woman… I think she lives on the street." I felt my throat catch as I looked at the snow bouncing off the window. Such a cozy picture—from the inside of a warm house. I rubbed my hands on my thick fleece leggings, with the vibrant snowflakes, while thinking of her thin black ones, nothing cute or warm about them.

"Do you think she would come?" Gina asked.

I shrugged and shook my head. "I doubt it."

"You could ask?"

"I don't know. She seems sort of…skittish. I don't want to push her away."

"Push her away? Makes it sound like you have a relationship?" Gina wiggled to the edge of her chair, her elbow nudging the pipe in its tray. She pushed it back without looking as she leaned toward me.

"No. I've seen her on the street a few times. She came into the diner, briefly, to get out of the cold. When I noticed her, she scurried out. I have this feeling maybe I can connect with her…but asking her to this house." I fanned my hands. "On Christmas Eve…maybe it's too much…" The words bunched in my chest as if hitting a wall.

I didn't hear Gina move over to me. She sat beside me on the floor and put her arm around my shoulders. "I think I know who you are talking about." Gina was a comfort, but I felt the strain within her. Like she was holding me and herself from falling.

I looked up at her through a blur. Her eyes glistened in the candlelight.

"She was friends with Nathalie."

"Oh?" I pulled away slightly. Awed that Nathalie was linked to all aspects of my life. Something had drawn me into her life, into the pieces left behind. I made a noise but couldn't speak.

"She feels guilty, I think. She was with her earlier that evening…" Gina pulled me closer, leaning her head on the side of mine. "I don't know, be careful." She shook her head, moving mine along in alliance. "I think she's troubled…" She squeezed me twice before pulling away to look at me. "I think she may still be into trouble... When I've seen her…she doesn't look like she's doing too well. Nathalie was trying to help her. But I don't know. I wonder about her. I feel bad saying it, but, I don't know… I get a bad vibe from Sarah…"

"Sarah?" Her name hung in the air, layering. I whispered it again, "Sarah."

"Yes. Sarah." She shook her head. "That's terrible of me. I don't know, I feel for her, I do. It's heartbreaking is what it is. I shouldn't have said anything. I suppose you could ask her." She tapped my arm, an encouraging tap. "I think you should ask her. Maybe that could help, poor sweetheart. I tried to approach her a few times after that night, but she was so withdrawn. Maybe you could reach her?"

My mind reeled. I pictured Sarah. I *was* drawn to

her. I had thought it was to help her, but maybe it was to help me with something…maybe she knew something. "I don't know," I said. But my mind kept moving. I had to meet her.

"I know. It's a tough situation." But Gina shrugged off any bad vibe, just like that. I was starting to see that about Gina. She had these strong reactions, but then she did something, she let them go. But when someone presented something to me, whether you wanted to call it a hunch or a "vibe," I didn't easily dismiss it. For one reason or another, I thought, I wanted Sarah to be my guest Christmas Eve. But, how do you ask a stranger? *A stranger is a friend you have not met yet*, popped into my head. It had been one of the fortunes I liked putting into those cookies I made. I borrowed it, like others, from a Chinese food order. But a stranger who was possibly homeless and maybe on drugs…

"And, really, it always works out. It always does. You'll see. Look at Kiki, she invited Jenna, that was meant to be." She touched my chin. "You have a beautiful heart, Ali. You remind me of Nathalie in a way."

A wave of heat crept up my sweater as I attached to the compliment or perhaps from my need to attach to Nathalie.

We both looked up to watch snow shimmer against the window.

"Now. Should we have a cider? Maybe with a dash of something wicked?" Gina winked at me.

I wondered how she was going to get up off the floor. I got up quickly so I could help her, but she surprised me by standing without the use of her twisted hands. I stared at her with awe. I didn't know if I could do it that easily.

"What are you gaping at?"

"Didn't know you were a gymnast."

"Not bad for an old gal, hey?" She walked out of the den with her shoulders back. "My grandfather used to say challenge yourself every day, mentally and physically, or you get lazy, or something gives up on you." She laughed. "I couldn't agree with him more as the years move along."

"That is good advice."

"We used to do that…it was sort of a little thing between us whenever I saw him. At some point, we'd cross our feet, back straight, sit down, and then stand up in a swoop, no hands. I don't want to let it go. Kind of funny, isn't it? He said that's how to tell if you've still got it."

When we arrived in the kitchen, I crossed my feet and wobbled down, and wobbled more on the way up and started laughing. "That's not easy!"

"Not bad, for a first go of it." Gina walked straight to the door and locked it. She looked out. "I think Kiki is doing this," she said, her voice muffled against the window.

I liked that reasoning the best. "You think?" But I wanted convincing.

"I do. Kiki is determined we all spend Christmas with Nathalie."

She moved away from the door, and I took her place. "Well," I said, more to myself, dismissing the whims of Kiki. I stared out at the lit tree along the back, the branches heavy with snow, the muted lights barely shining through.

Gina put her hands around a large clay pot to check its warmth, then grabbed two Christmas-themed mugs.

I watched the steam, anticipating the cider. She

handed me my mug, and I took a sip. I hovered over the warmth, inhaled the steam and the spice, took another sip. "I wish I could have met her." I looked down at the caramel-colored liquid. "Part of me wants Nathalie here for Christmas, too." Part of me wished I believed that was possible.

Gina looked at me and smiled, her eyes full of warmth and mystery. "She is. She will be." She reached for some brandy and lifted the bottle.

I shook my head.

"It's like Santa Clause. If you believe…" She poured the smallest amount of brandy into her mug, then smiled at me, her eyes full of magic.

I thought of Gramps. Forever hinting about clues of Santa's whereabouts and making me believe. He would have loved Gina. I moved to the sink to rinse my mug.

Gina leaned over my shoulder. "Holy smokes. How did you manage that? It's hot, still."

"Charred esophagus. Inherited. That's what gets passed down in my family. We're a long line of hot tea drinkers." I smiled at Gina. "Well, that's it for me. I think I'll head up."

"You go ahead. I have a cup that will occupy a good twenty minutes." She raised her brows at me.

I paused. Then went over and gave her a hug.

I propped myself up in bed with my notebook, keeping the Christmas tree lights and my bedside lamp on. I hadn't had an opportunity to look over my notes or to add anything since I had moved into Gina's. I pulled my quilt up and paged passed the cold cases. My last entry, unrelated to murder, was the day before I arrived at

Union Street. I scanned all the "Eric's" on the page but didn't linger. I loved a fresh white page, and I didn't want to spend any more time in a basement apartment. I took in the room. I was starting to want to be in Christmas, not avoid it…and here I was. I pictured Gina, snug in the den, sipping her cider, waiting for Kiki and Harry to get home, our sleepy sentry with her pipe.

I blemished the page with the date. I didn't hold back. I started with the background noise—Kiki believed in Nathalie's ghost. Gina maybe believed. I didn't believe. But I had witnessed Gina react to my Christmas tree lights. My Christmas tree lights always greeted me, and I never remembered turning them on. Maybe Gina turned them on. Was it possible Gina wanted me to believe? The light in Nathalie's room going off…not sure, but it could happen. Gina, Mr. Brooks, and Jenna all admitted there was something odd about Nathalie's death—they didn't believe she jumped. Gina had said Sarah was with Nathalie earlier that evening. I underlined Sarah a few times. I had to connect with her. Weird connection—Nathalie's little sister had drowned. According to Jenna, Nathalie had said she pushed her. Of course, she didn't mean it, if she had even pushed her.

I had been playfully pushed along a river shore. Kids do that. One of those summers when we rented that cottage, My Aunt Karen and Uncle Mike had spent a week. I was thrilled to have my cousin Lee to play with. Most of the time we ran along the river's edge, and most days he pushed me, daringly close to the edge. And I loved every minute of it. I loved that someone wanted to push me and laugh as we stumbled on the gravel, racing for an ice cream cone at the corner store.

I tapped my pen against my book, thinking of the details of what happened from a year ago. When I had searched the net, I pulled up anything I could find. There was a lot of the same. Medical examiners said there was no sign of foul play. There had been drugs nearby, but the toxicology report confirmed no evidence of drugs in her system. I stared at what I just wrote, shocked I had written those words: *Accidental vs. homicidal drowning.* It had never been mentioned, not publicly, anyway. I paused…had I pressed harder on the word homicidal? The ink looked darker. Or was I looking for something…always chasing a case. This case wasn't even cold. It was closed. Professionals had done the work.

Maybe the reaction of Gina and everyone else was simply normal, as with most unwitnessed deaths on the water, the tragedy leaving them grasping for closure. Without a suicide note or signs of a struggle, all cases are usually ruled an accident. Homicidal drowning is rare, or a rare charge—you need a witness, evidence of a struggle, or a note. But there were hints of suicide.

There *was* that letter. I had to get my hands on it. What was it doing in Kiki's room? The police would have seen it last year. They dismissed it then. Just a red herring. I know from my cold case group people write letters. For the fun of it, for the attention, to lead the case or push it off the path. Sometimes to try to implicate someone. They left it in Kiki's room. So, it wasn't anything.

But I felt there was something I needed to do with that letter. What was up with Kiki? Had she read the letter? Did she understand the letter? Maybe it was just a fun game for her to build her own anticipation, or maybe overstimulation from energy drinks had dulled her senses—she was looking for things. And maybe I was looking for things… I have a history.

Next morning, I woke an hour before the alarm. I had slept well, but excitement roused me. The first thought on my mind was Joe. How old was he? He could possibly be…maybe seven years older than me, but maybe not. Aunt Diana was ten years younger than Uncle Frank. They were happy. I shook my head. Already marrying the cook. I gathered my things and crept down to the bathroom. When I arrived on the landing, I noticed a crack of light from under Harry's door. I stopped for a second, froze—for some reason I didn't want to meet him then. It had been so long. I thought it would be fun to keep the mystery going and meet him Christmas Eve. I hurried along into the bathroom. I kept the light off but lit a large candle. The glow of the Christmas tree night light and the flame bounced around the room as I showered.

The mystery ended—Harry was coming out of his room when I opened the bathroom door. I stifled a yelp. He was younger than I imagined, maybe mid-twenties, and wow, he was tall. He had a short Superman bathrobe—too short. Maybe he'd hung on to it from fourth grade. It showed off his hairy legs. Hairy Harry. I smiled. Hari-kari. I stopped smiling. That was a zinger. But I smiled again as I focused back on Superman.

"Shit, sorry, dude."

Dude? He started to move toward me. I let go of the doorknob and met him in the hallway. His eyes were startled, too, but he looked like he was trying like the devil not to laugh. I helped him out and let go of a few giggly gurgles, still recovering from being startled by him and his 'Harry' legs. I extended my hand. "Hey, Harry. Ali. Nice to meet you."

"Nice to meet you. I think you're lying, though, I nearly gave you a heart attack. Shit." He pushed his hair up, and it kind of stuck up in a messy tuft. It looked good that way. "So, how you settling in here?" His eyes shot up to the attic. "Any ghosts up there?"

I stared at him and furrowed my brow.

"Kidding." He gave me a look. I think if he knew me another minute, it would have been an eye-roll. "But please tell me there isn't."

"Funny."

"Gotta pee, see you again, Al." He brushed past me and turned with a salute as he closed the door.

Al? Mags was the only one who ever called me that. Harry kind of reminded me of Joe. They had similar mannerisms, familiar right away with people. I liked that, so the opposite of me—I couldn't even utter a word to the girl I was tracking on the street. Harry just met me, and he was calling me Al.

'You can call me Al.' I thought and smiled.

I crunched along the familiar snowy streets. Almost every house had Christmas lights kept on day and night. Two days until Christmas Eve. I felt as much anticipation as I had felt as a little girl. Like walking in a recurring dream with my blanket of snow, in a concentrated quiet with only my footsteps, my plumes of wintery breath, and the Christmas lights as guides. I started to near my favorite house with the woman in the window, there every morning, every afternoon. Although I couldn't see the details of her expression or if she wore a house robe, I hoped it was a dress of black satin with beads in blood or jewel tones to fit in with the Gothic architecture of the mid-19th-century design. I kept my hat pulled low, almost covering my eyes so I could carry my stare up to her window that was tucked into the sharp pitched gable in the middle of the roofline. I wanted to draw her out of her gingerbread house to sit on the lacy verandah in the snow-covered chairs. What was she thinking as she looked down from her window? Was she keeping any secrets? I pictured someone behind her in the shadows, calling her to move away from the window, or perhaps in another one of the rooms, trying to escape her quiet…her secrets.

I savored the tour up Main Street, joy spreading across my chest as I caught the glow in the distance. The diner looked like a Christmas card—warmth emanating from its frosted windows; the streetlamps, lining the route like iron-clad escorts with polished heads, guarding the path from dusk until dawn. Just before I arrived, it started to snow again. Big, fluffy flakes took over the scene. I paused in the quiet, alone on Main, but embraced by the calm. I stared up at the streetlamp in front of the diner, watching the flakes swirling around and spiraling down away from me.

"Hey, what are you doing, crazy-thing?" It was Joe.

I looked behind me at the diner. He was just outside the door, hugging his arms around his torso, shifting his feet.

"It's beautiful, isn't it?" My whisper carried across the stillness.

He moved over to me and looked up at the streetlamp. "I guess." But I saw in his eyes that he was seeing what I saw.

"Hey, get your jacket!" I said.

"Huh?"

"Let's do a snow angel."

"I've never done one." He looked up the street, then back to me as he shoved his hands into the front pockets of his jeans.

"Get your jacket. You have to do one!"

He hesitated a second, then tramped back into the diner. I hoped he was coming back without that hesitation… I hoped he was coming back.

"Ok, show me how it's done." He had his coat on and his mitts, a good thing.

"Put your hood up. Here. Over here. Under this lamppost, it's all fresh snow here."

I dropped my bag and leaned back slowly, making my way onto my back without disturbing the surface too much. Joe stared at me.

"Come on. There's room beside me."

"You're an odd duck, Ali." He smiled and made his way over.

We swooshed our arms a few times, then we lay there, arms in wing-position, the snow spiraling down on our cheeks and lashes. It was so quiet—like a vacuum. I felt Joe next to me, his arm outstretched, barely touching mine. He picked up my mitted hand. We stayed quiet. My heart didn't.

"It's beautiful," he finally whispered.

"Yeah."

After a few moments of bliss, he asked, "So how do we get out of this?"

"Very carefully." I laughed. "Try not to squish your angel."

"Sounds like a book title you'd find in that old house of yours."

I looked over at him and smiled—that's something I would have thought. It wasn't a bad one, kind of a weird title, but those were the best. I made my way up, thinking of Gina, and trying to match her dexterity. I stumbled forward and laughed. Joe got up pretty easily. We turned and reviewed our prints.

"Cool," Joe said. He moved closer and looked down at me. "Just like you." He stared at me, and I felt every part, every fiber that could move or feel, twitch, and tremble. And then he kissed me. Well.

I had to hold back. All of me wanted all of him. When he pulled away, he looked at me again. I had to look away. A hot shiver ran through me. The after-shock continued—I could feel myself trembling.

"You're cold," Joe said and put his arm around me. "Buy you a coffee?"

He gently nudged me ahead of him as he opened the door to the diner.

I wanted to stay in the vestibule, under the warmth, under Joe's arm. If I stepped in too far, maybe all that happened outside might fall away. The magic of a first snow angel of the season, a first snow angel for Joe could be fleeting, just a set of prints. I worried it would be weird getting back to business in the diner. But no. Joe kissed the top of my head and reached alongside me to push the door open ahead of me. When we were inside, he put his hands on my hips and lifted me up for a moment, and put me back down to the right, pretending to move me out of his way.

"I don't know about you, but I'm freezing." He looked at me as he passed by. "You have a long coat. I'm soaked. Gonna change."

"Right." I smiled and got to look at his butt guilt-free.

"You stay here." He pointed at me.

"Get over it." I laughed. My mind zipped over the week as the quiet hung around me. *How did we get here?* But the rush of happiness surged through me. Kind of a pattern for me as Caroline always said. I seemed to form relationships too quickly...once I connected with someone. I usually only had two years for them before we moved again. I didn't need to do that anymore. I didn't have to leave town. But Joe was different. I felt him feel it too in that kiss. I took off my coat and put it on the bar as I glanced at the clock. Still lots of time.

As usual, the diner offered that wonderful warmth. Joe must have been there earlier than usual, again. I smelled the coffee and moved behind the bar. The pot was three-quarters full. I poured us our mugs, adding cream to mine. I leaned back against the counter and held the coffee under my nose with anticipation, taking in the diner before it was roused by the crowd. With the overhead lights so dim, the Christmas tree's warm glow looked like our welcoming custodian. The mugs, facedown and nestled in twos or fours, gleamed from every table, while cutlery shone with multi-colored reflections. Sporadic shots of light flashed around the diner; and always, the constant backdrop of snow on the other side of the windows. I took my first sip.

And then I saw her.

I spilled some of my coffee as I put down my mug. I hurried over to the window and craned my head, pressing up against the glass as she passed by on her gazelle-legs. I don't know what I was thinking I would do, but I hustled out onto the street. The cold hit me like a frozen sheet after being incubated by the diner…only moments from that rush of lying in the snow beside Joe. Choosing to lay there for the fun of it. My stomach felt tight as I thought of how cold she must be, where had she not wanted to coil up for the night?

"Hey," I called out feebly. Hoping or not hoping she'd hear me…I was a coward. "Hey!" I gave it everything. I was shocked by my voice. It sounded unfamiliar against the cold, quiet morning. It made me feel lonely. I felt lonely every time I saw her. Sarah. "Sarah." But the strength in my voice fell away, as I whispered her name into the snowbanks.

I think there was a slight pause to her pace, but she kept going. And then, what looked like an old flip phone fell out of her coat pocket, she reached down to pick it up, opened and closed it, fiddled with it, opened and closed it again, then turned in my direction. I held my breath as she pocketed the phone and kept moving. Who still had one of those? Maybe she had found it, or maybe it was a remnant of the life that had slipped away from her. What was it she couldn't hold on to or didn't want to hold on to? I stared at her for a long while. When she had moved enough away from me, she half-turned, but only for a moment. Where was she going? I stood there, feeling like I had woken from sleepwalking, everything looked too still, as though I was thrown onto a movie set. I couldn't move, I couldn't call out, as though caught in sleep paralysis. The only thing I could feel were my toes starting to get cold—I wanted them to go numb in solidarity. Feel something she felt.

I scanned the empty street, only one car parked on the other side, a little snowed-in, must have been there all night. No other shop windows were lit yet; the diner the only light under the lampposts. On the other side of the street, I saw an outline move in the distance…moving away from me, heading in the same direction as Sarah. The frame looked familiar—the coat looked familiar, that camel-colored coat.

"Hey!"

I jumped. I heard steps on the snow behind me and turned to Joe.

"What are you doing now?" He put his hands on my shoulders. He pulled me around to face him. I wondered if he had moved a lot, too. "You okay? What are you doing out here?" He looked beyond me, down the street.

"I wanted to ask her for dinner."

"Who? Let's go inside first. I haven't warmed up yet from your last trick." He put his arm around me.

We took our usual posts, leaning on the counter looking out. We didn't say anything for a while. His shoulder against mine was all I wanted. And his hip. That was new. Our sides connected, and I felt a blush spread over my cheeks, across my collar bone.

"There's a young woman I keep running into. Or keep trying to run into, maybe. I want to invite her to Gina's for Christmas Eve."

Joe looked down at me, waiting for me to continue. He nuzzled even closer when he looked at me. He was so cozy.

"I don't know, though. I'm sure she would never come. And I'm sure she thinks I'm stalking her now."

"Who is she?"

"I think she lives…on the street." I dug my thumbnail into my hand. "Something's drawing me to her. It's so cold out. She could be me."

"What do you mean?" He took my hand, interrupting my dig into my palm.

"Just that. She looks like someone…like me, I don't know. She looks lost, but like she's edging away from something. I guess like anyone would in that situation. I don't know what the answer is."

"To homelessness?"

"No." I squinted up at him. "Well, yeah, but I meant, what's the answer to approaching her, or do I leave well enough alone? I don't know."

"Guess you could try?"

I nodded.

"Don't be so hard on yourself." Joe wrapped his arm around my waist and kissed my forehead.

"Thanks." I loved the forehead kiss.

"For what?"

"For being here. You're like a cozy blanket." I fought the urge to turn to him and kiss him gently on his eye-lids, my mom's angel kisses—too intimate, too cutesy.

"Hmmm." He looked down at me and narrowed his eyes.

"What?"

"I don't know if I want to be your cozy."

"You can be more than cozy." I couldn't believe I said that…and in a diner—at least the lights were dimmed. But I held on to it, turned my face up to him and he kissed me. Really kissed me. My head spun. I was grateful for the counter behind us.

"Okay, cozy works…I can handle that," he said. "But I better get to the line or something un-cozy's gonna happen." He winked at me and dumped a few inches of coffee into the sink. He gave me a last quick kiss and headed through the kitchen door.

Whoa. There was something different about Joe. Maybe because he was older. I hoped he wasn't that much older. He was so easy going. So confident…but not arrogant. Such a good kisser. I stood a moment longer and lingered on those kisses. But then Eric popped into my mind like an unwelcome commercial— that unfair zinger across the screen for the latest horror movie. I hadn't thought about him in a while. Such opposites, he and Joe.

I was jolted by the sound of a siren. The pitch a piercing yelp, and then I felt it saw right through me. I knelt in one of the booths and peered up the street to follow the flash of red-white, red-white, red-white. The siren zipped off, but the strobe continued to flash in the distance. My eyes stuck in the rhythm, for a while. I couldn't move, couldn't let go of the story—Sarah? My knees molded into the vinyl. I kept sinking…I couldn't let her go.

The jingle of the door opening ripped me out of that thought. My gaze shot up at the clock before the guest. We hadn't relocked the door.

Mr. Brooks.

He looked crazed—his hat was pulled sideways as though he had been pulling it on and off. His eyes darted around the diner.

"Mr. Brooks!" I rushed over to him.

He tried to smile, but his mouth only reached a straight line.

"Are you okay?" I looked him up and down.

He removed his hat. "A young woman was hit by a car…" His face was white underneath red patches that stood out on his cheeks, his jaw trembled. Was he in shock?

I looked over his shoulder into the dark, then back to him. I had seen her only minutes before. Had it been Sarah that got hit…. "Is she okay?" My stomach felt as though it was pulling back to my spine, holding, waiting.

He nodded. There was a weird slouch to his face, as though he'd had a stroke. Was *he* okay?

"Here. Have a seat." I led him to his usual booth, my arm brushing ahead from side-to-side as though I was pushing people out of the way. "Let me get you a tea." I hurried away from him as my mind reeled.

I watched him take off his coat. He looked older. Everyone always looks older when stressed. Wrinkles deepen, eyes hood, faces turn waxen.

"Here." This time I took the seat across from him.

"I think she meant it…" He looked outside and put his hands close to the teapot for warmth. His eyes moved back and forth. The quick movement such a contrast to the quiet that had descended after the whoop of the sirens.

"She meant what?" I asked. Suddenly, I felt irritated. Must have been my nerves, the tension that stretched them taut and trembling. I wanted to push it— move it along, out of here. I dug my thumbs into the outside of my knees under the table.

"I don't know. I didn't really see…it looked like she may have stepped in front of that car." He paused and looked at me. "On purpose. But it kind of looked like she was propelled…like she was pushed or fell…I don't know. I wasn't close enough."

"Sarah?" I whispered.

He looked startled. "You know her?"

"No. Yes. I don't know her, but I know who she is. It was her?"

He gave me a half nod as he seemed to struggle to swallow. His Adam's apple barely lifted.

"I just saw her this morning…" I trailed off, staring out as though I might see her.

"You saw her? When?" He looked out the diner window, over his shoulder in the direction I had seen her flee.

"I called out to her."

"You called out to her?" Why did he look so concerned that I knew her, that I saw her?

"I wanted to invite her to Gina's. For Christmas Eve."

He put one of his hands on the teapot. I wanted to reach out and touch the metal, to test it—it had to be scalding hot, too hot to pause that long.

"Who is she?" I pulled my eyes away from his red hand that now rested cupped beside the other, so white. I thought of my first-year Roman civilization course. I remember reading red and white have a long history of symbolism, indicating present or imminent death. I dug harder into my knees. He had said she would be okay.

He looked at me funny and shrugged. "I don't really know."

"You don't know what?"

"Her. Sarah."

"But you knew…know her name?"

He tried to stifle a sigh, took a moment before he spoke again. "I only know her name through Nathalie. Nathalie was sort of helping her out, I think." He opened the lid of the pot, took the tea bag out without squeezing it against the side. "And you?" he asked. "How do you know her name?"

"Gina said Sarah was friends with Nathalie. That she was…" The siren came to life again.

Mr. Brooks closed his eyes briefly.

"But you saw her…she'll be okay?"

"She'll be okay."

We both looked outside at the snow. I could see the snow angels underneath the streetlamp. Imprints of a moment of whimsy and happiness Sarah didn't know. The angels looked connected by hand and foot. I thought of the paper chain of snowflakes I used to make and hang in the window. I thought of Nathalie…and Sarah…picturing another link…me linked-in… Sarah the link in the middle. Was she my link to Nathalie? The snow continued to soften the edges…dusting the prints.

"I'm sorry to bring this news to you. Right before work. She will be fine." It seemed a struggle to raise his droopy eyelids, to bring an expression to his face.

I watched him try to look convincing, I looked hard to hold onto something…and then pulled my hands together as though gathering them up off the table. "So." I pushed against the table and slid out of the booth. I reached for a smile. I did have to work.

"So?" He looked startled.

"So, what's for breakfast, today?"

I served Mr. Brooks poached eggs and toast as the diner started to fill. And fill and fill. I ran through the morning with hardly a thought in my head. I barely had a moment to exchange more than the details of an order with the customers with whom I'd become so familiar— like Adam, like Boston. But it was comforting to have them there. And Joe. It was hard to see him under the heat lamps as he passed an order through and not be able to touch him. It was like looking through the window at a pet store and longing for that puppy.

Joe and I didn't even have a chance to connect after breakfast before the lunch rush. He was busy with prep in the kitchen. I was busy with cleaning and resetting tables and my own prep with refilling the creamers on the tables, topping off ketchup bottles, lining up coffee filters. I welcomed the diversion. It was strange to want a distraction from intense good and overwhelming sadness at the other extreme. I thought of my mom. Of that brief period when she took to yoga. Her talking about yin and yang all the time. I smiled when I thought of her standing in tree pose in the middle of the kitchen with her eyes closed when my dad and she had started to argue. Too bad the yoga didn't take. When her tree fell, my dad heard it. I wondered where all that anger came from, until I realized it wasn't my dad making her angry, I think she was angry she wanted to leave.

After three, Joe came through from the kitchen. There was still one table, but they were good—served and happy. Everyone *did* look happy who came into the diner. Such a nice time of the year…for most people. My happy face dropped when I thought of Sarah and others who thought this was a crappy time of year.

"Nice to see you, too." Joe looked at me funny.

"Sorry. Coffee?" I moved to pour our mugs.

"What's up?" He took his mug, and it seemed like he was about to lean in to kiss me but thought better of it as he looked at the table by the window.

I smiled. I imagined his kiss. "That was quite the rush. Quite the day."

"Yeah." He raised his brow. "But? You look upset?"

I hesitated and looked over at the booth. I leaned back against the counter, mirroring him, meeting his shoulder with mine.

"Mr. Brooks was here earlier..."

"Yes, of course." Joe smiled.

"There was an accident. That girl I mentioned to you this morning. She was hit by a car."

Joe turned to me and put his mug down. He looked shocked. "Really? Is she okay? Do you know?"

"I think so. Mr. Brooks said she'd be okay."

"But not really, right?"

"Right." I put my hand on his arm. He covered it with his own and squeezed.

"Why don't you go cash out and get ready to head home? I'll keep an eye on that last table. Sally should be here soon enough."

But I don't want to leave you. But I nodded. "Thank you. Can we do that?"

"I think I can handle it." He touched my cheek. "And Sally will be here any minute, you might as well.

What's the point hanging around?"

You. I looked at him and said as much with my expression. He looked over at the couple engaged over their coffee, then leaned in and kissed my neck. *Damn.* He lingered for a moment, his warm nose and lips soft on my skin. The surge of endorphins made me weak and charged all at once.

"Wow," I finally said.

"What?"

"I think I like you." I smiled up at him.

"Really?" He pulled away from me, pretending to be surprised.

"You know it."

"You know it, too."

I looked at him funny. "What? I know what?"

"You know, I think I like you, too. How did you do that, you witch?" He narrowed his eyes, but the outer corners lifted into his laugh lines. I loved that he was always ready to laugh. "Damn, I think you could make me crazy. Now, you better leave, you little witch."

It was harder than ever to walk away from the diner. I hated leaving Joe behind. Weird falling for him after only knowing him such a short time. He said I could make him crazy. He hadn't pulled back like a lot of guys did after a first kiss, as though making sure you kept wondering…not Joe. I got that rush that turned me over. I liked his I-don't-care-what's-supposed-to-happen-here attitude, but mostly I liked that he did care—he had such a warmth and kindness about him. His parents must have been such opposites to get someone like him. He never mentioned his family. Were they even in town? Probably not if he was going to be at Gina's Christmas Eve. I thought of everyone I had met who seemed alone without their families. Me included. Even Mr. Brooks. It was like a town of misfits. But such wonderful misfits. Maybe that was part of the charm of the place—all the misfits wandering around made everyone so accessible.

When we lived on a base in Saudi, those two years had been the only other time I felt instant connections. The day after I arrived, that evening, a dusty orange sunset hung close to the dunes. It looked like Armageddon, but soon became normal, the normal backdrop of the desert. A group of six pre-teens in jeans, boys with red-and-white headbands (Springsteen was Boss, he was still the Boss, well, he still is), girls with innocent blue eyeshadow and glossy lips came and brought me to a dance at the Rec Center. I felt a misfit as I sat in my frilly blouse, and Patty nudged her boyfriend to ask me to slow dance. I didn't get my own first boyfriend until the second year—a guy with Van shoes who said dude too much, but I fit in and enjoyed kissing at parties, everyone kissing in the corners. Those blissful, innocent kisses soon got pulled apart by another move— my heart ripping apart at fifteen, or so I thought.

I looked up and realized I hadn't planned my route or noticed the shop windows blurring by as I strode into the white. I started to take in Main Street. It was like being bathed in Christmas—each window garbed in festive lights, tiny villages, moving trains…and my favorite—fake snow. It rimmed and crept up the panes, veiling the warm glow from inside some of the shops. So old-fashioned. I paused in front of Kaffee Brik. I longed again for the experience of that hot chocolate.

"I knew you would be back here. It's the hot chocolate, yes?" The same counter woman greeted me.

"I'm hooked." I laughed. "It's the best."

She smiled at me and then started the process. I glanced at the display case, but was drawn back to the silver pots, the ladle of rich chocolate.

"Something else?" Her eyes gleamed as she paused on the presentation of baked goods as though seeing them for the first time.

"No, this is perfect—I just want all of this." I tapped the side of the mug as I held it close with anticipation. "For now."

I grabbed one of the last two-seater booths by the window and checked in with the other guests, bonding with chocolate and the Christmas spirit. I had to admit the Brik gave the diner a run for comfort—it was a place you wanted to settle in for a long while. But the diner had Joe. I peeked at the woman behind the counter, feeling a little self-conscious about reducing the café to the Brik. I suppressed a giggle by diving into the whipping cream. I hesitated before spooning through more, knowing as soon as I broke through the barrier, I'd drink it too quickly, but as I daydreamed, I tunneled and sipped. When I looked up, a young woman was pushing through the washroom door. My mind flashed to Sarah, walking out with wet hair the other day. My eyes sank down to the remaining swirl of chocolate. I slid the mug off the table and moved to the counter.

"Another one?"

I stared at the cup in my hand. "Oh, no…" I moved to the dirty dish bin, then returned to the counter.

"You decided on some treats?" She looked like my dad used to, when he would come into my room a few days after Christmas with a present he found that must have fallen out of Santa's pack.

"Yes. And may I have another hot chocolate to go?"

"Should we be worried?" She tried to look serious, but her eyes sparkled.

"I'm sorry?"

"I think I've addicted you, yes?"

We both laughed. I quickly chose an assortment and watched her tie the box with a trio of gold, red, and green ribbons.

I picked up my pace. I knew where the hospital was—you know where everything is in a small place. It was a few blocks away. What would I say to her? They probably wouldn't even let me... I'd be able to leave the box, anyway… I hoped.

I paused by the front doors. They opened, but I froze. I didn't know her last name. I didn't know her. The doors closed partway, reopened. There's no way I could visit without knowing her last name. I stood in a few rounds of the motion sensor, open, close, open, close.

"Excuse me." A tall woman started to pass me but then stopped. "Are you okay, miss? It's cold out there. You coming in?" She had a bulky sweater wrapped around her; it looked as though it had been thrown on from a wrong hook on the wall—borrowed by mistake. The crisp white blouse looked more like hers underneath the shaggy sleeves.

I took a step forward, and she swept her arm ahead of me. I could tell by her expression and the look she shot over my shoulder, she thought there was something wrong with me. She probably hoped I had a chaperone. I spoke up. "I'm okay."

"Someone's going to be happy to see you." She smiled at me as she looked at the box in my hands.

"Well…"

She had been about to pull away from me, but then stopped. "Something wrong?"

"It's just…I don't know her last name," I blurted out.

"What's that?" She looked over her shoulder at

reception and put her arm out to lead me away from the front entrance. "Whose last name?"

I wanted to move back to the doors that kept opening and closing from the motion sensor, where I felt I had a choice, I wasn't committed. They'd never let me in this way. I should have had a better plan. I could have found out her last name. I winced against the antiseptic soap that crept in along with the smell of disinfectant, stale coffee, stale people. "A young woman was brought here this morning. She was hit by a car. Her name is Sarah. I don't know her last name." With each sentence, I paused. I knew how it sounded. It sounded stalker-like.

"But you know her?"

I looked over at reception. How much do you have to know someone for a visit? What could I say here? "Sort of. I want to give her this. I just want her to have something."

The woman frowned. She didn't seem concerned with me too much, more like she was trying to piece it together. I got it. My thoughts were hard to piece together *inside* my head at that moment.

"I'm Doctor Brennan, by the way. Were you there this morning? Did you see it happen?"

"I'm Ali. No. I just..." *I'm just obsessed with people. Nathalie and Sarah.*

She looked disappointed. "But you *sort* of know her?"

"I know this all sounds crazy. To be honest, it sounds crazy to me. I have seen her on the street." I cringed. I felt like I was outing her. "I hate seeing her out there."

She nodded. "I see." There was an exchange with reception again. Maybe a nod, an 'I got your back' look, even though the young woman seemed bored and looked as though she wouldn't move too fast.

I looked over my shoulder at the door. I should leave. "I'm sorry. Anyway, thanks…but I think this was a bad idea." I started to turn away. I'd have to figure out another way…

But I turned back. I was here. "I know it seems weird. It's just something. I don't know…" I hesitated. I told her about Nathalie—what I had learned last evening from Gina—that Sarah had been with her the night she had jumped in the lake by the Red Rocks—at some point before, anyway. I thought if I gave her something… I'd seem credible… I knew about Nathalie more than Sarah, but Nathalie was dead…

She pulled me over to an area away from reception. She kept her hand firm on my arm as we stood in front of an office, but we didn't go in. I looked at her hand on my arm and glanced in the door. There was no one in the bare cube of an office.

"Sorry." She let go of me. "I didn't know she knew this Nathalie. I mean Nathalie…"

"I think they were close. I guess Nathalie was a good support to Sarah." I paused. "Sarah was doing well, Gina told me." I paused again. "That's my landlord." I felt funny calling Gina that, she was way more than that. She smoked her pipe with me. "Nathalie had helped her find a job, even, but she fell apart again after Nathalie passed away." That's all I knew. I was there to learn more. I had to get in there. But all I could add was, "I wish I could help." I meant that, too.

She pursed her lips. "You know, I think she could use a little kindness. And I think she would appreciate a few of those." She tapped her finger on the gold Kaffee Brik decal. "I love that place."

I looked down at the box.

She paused. "Come with me. I am heading to her floor. I suppose…why don't we see if she would be okay with a visitor?"

How was that going to work? Sarah didn't know me…how would she 'okay' the visit?

"I was here when she was admitted. I left to get something in my car." She reached her hand into a large pocket as though making sure whatever she needed was in there.

Did she pull that sweater out of a lost and found bin on the way out?

"Do you live around here?" she asked as we walked across the shiny linoleum.

"I live on Union Street." I had the urge to give her details. Talk about Gina and her place. My place. Just saying Union Street seemed too dull. I lived in Christmas with a Boho Mrs. Claus. I smiled.

As we rode the elevator, there was no shortage of things she had to say. Mostly questions. I think she was sizing me up. Making sure it was okay that I visit a stranger.

"She's going to be okay, then?" I asked before the elevator opened.

"She's fine. Mostly, I want to keep her warm."

The doors opened onto the reception area. She said hello to a few people and grabbed a clipboard and scribbled. Her quick strokes led me to believe she was signing her name. "She's with me," she said. We headed down a hall. The linoleum gleamed.

She stopped halfway down the hall. "Just hold up a second, okay? I'll check in with her."

My throat pulled tight into a dry knot. I looked behind me. It was so quiet. My only other experience visiting a hospital had been much different. That last week with Gran, the gurgling and hissing from machines and patients. Vacant or scared eyes passing by on gurneys or wheeling down the hall without their teeth. There had been no shortage of people during our visits. But there didn't seem to be anyone in Sarah's ward. It still smelled like the usual suspects were there. I craned my head to get a glimpse into a room. All I saw was a bed, no sheets. It didn't seem like anyone else was on the floor. A fierce pang of loneliness ripped through me.

"You can come in," Dr. Brennan said as she gave me an encouraging smile and beckoned me to the door.

I felt warm suddenly.

Doctor Brennan moved closer to me and touched my arm. "Do you want to come in?"

I looked down, then back at her. "I feel funny now. I don't know what to say."

"That's okay. I can help."

I wanted to meet Sarah. I looked ahead.

Sarah was sitting cross-legged on her bed. I looked at her for signs of injury, but she didn't show any, not that I could see. It made me happy that she looked warm, but there was a torn-out hollowness, a lack of expression, that looked too pained, too permanent. She had one of those deep lines between her brows. Her eyes darted at the door, then to her lap. Her hands shook. She pulled at the sleeves of her hospital gown. I saw a few cuts, where the sleeves didn't quite cover, but they looked like scars.

"Sarah, this is Ali."

Her eyes shifted back and forth before she lifted them to me, the recognition flickered, and then she dropped her gaze back to her lap.

"I keep seeing you around. So, thought it was a sign we should meet," I said, sounding like I was reading cue cards in front of an audience, with uninterested attendees. But worse, I was a solicitor. I was selling cookies. My voice sounded too loud for the small room, too cheerful, too fake. Heat rose up through my coat.

Dr. Brennan smiled at me. "Ali's brought you some treats, Sarah."

I shifted the box up and away from me only a few inches. I had the urge to throw it onto the bed and take off. This was too uncomfortable.

"What do you say? Let's have a look." Dr. Brennan took the box from me and set it down on the high table to the right of Sarah's bed. There was nothing on the shiny veneer, except one of those plastic cups with water and a bendy straw. I wished I had brought flowers instead. She didn't look like she ate.

I took in Sarah out of the corner of my eye as we both watched Dr. Brennan untie the ribbons and open the box. "Wow. They look good." Dr. Brennan placed the box in front of Sarah on the bed. Sarah stared at its contents and then lifted the box and reached it out to me. My eyes shifted to Dr. Brennan, back to Sarah, back to the box.

"Thank you." I felt I better take one. My hand hovered over the cookies, searching for the smallest one. I chose a round shortbread edged with dark chocolate.

Sarah reached the box out to Dr. Brennan. The sleeve of her gown pulled up, and I winced away from more scars that ran up her twig of an arm. Fire scars flashed through my mind. I remembered an article in National Geographic I had read at a doctor's office a few years ago. Something about an injured tree develops fire scars, boundaries around the injury to protect it, new growth to close over the injured place. What was Sarah's injury that lay deep beneath her skin?

Dr. Brennan didn't pause. She chose a thick star

with dark chocolate edges.

Sarah put the box down on the bed and stared into it. Her long index finger and thumb reached in and twitched back and forth over the assortment—she finally chose one in the shape of a Christmas tree.

I was grateful for Dr. Brennan and her mmm's and longer mmm mmm's. I just wanted to be able to swallow the dry shortbread, be done with snack time.

Sarah extended the box in my direction again when we were done, and I shook my head. "Thank you." I stared at the full cup of water, wanting my own sippy cup to dislodge the clump that had formed in my throat.

Sarah took another one as I tried not to keep my hands from pulling at my scarf. I wished I had kept my hat on to pull down. She picked another Christmas tree which surprised me. Was it the familiarity? That struck me—*that* cookie, could be her constant. A moment-to-moment she needed to adhere to.

Sarah looked fine. Was there a broken rib under the gown or banged up knees? How could you get hit by a car and look so normal only hours later? I gave a sidelong glance to Dr. Brennan, waiting for her to say something, direct the conversation, or cue me to leave. This wasn't heading anywhere. I wasn't going to be inviting Sarah over for Christmas Eve. They'd both think I was crazy. The directory at the reception area suddenly flashed before me. It had said Psychiatry or something with that word or a derivative of that word. Oh. I thought of what Mr. Brooks had said about Sarah meaning to step in front of the car. But he also said or led me to believe she could have been pushed. *He pushed her.* I nearly gasped. He had seemed funny at the diner. No, it was shock. The emptiness of the ward wrapped around me— I sank into the linoleum.

"Well, it was so nice of you, Ali, to come to the hospital with those wonderful cookies."

"Of course." I managed to speak, that was my exit cue. What could I say? I hadn't gotten anywhere. I couldn't start asking Sarah about Nathalie and that night. Even though she looked fine, she'd just been hit by a car.

"Thank you," Sarah said. Her head bobbed at me. She stared at her hands, twisted them in and out of steeples. She looked back at me…did she want to say something?

I took a step closer to her. "You're welcome." I nodded, like a hospital visitor bobble-head, wanting her to say something. Tell me something. Tell me something! I reeled for something to offer, for a way to keep us connected. I realized I still had the hot chocolate for her in my hand. "Oh, here." I placed it down and then stared at the empty bed beside her. "Well, if you ever want a coffee, come by the diner…I work…"

"I know where you work," Sarah blurted out, but she sounded shy at the same time.

"Oh." I was surprised by the strength in her voice, but also by her admission—I thought of the pay phone and then that old cell phone she had dropped earlier. "Just there through the holidays, but, come by if you're able." I felt stupid after I said it—it was only two days until Christmas. I wondered how long she would have to stay here. The thought of her in here for Christmas pushed around my stomach. I hesitated. In my head, I asked her to come to Gina's. No. We'd only exchanged a few words…in a psychiatric ward.

Our eyes met. I tried to see underneath the hooded fear that held her hostage. She had been with Nathalie earlier on that evening. At what point had they parted ways? An unwanted but not unexpected thought popped into my mind…was Sarah with her until the end…

"Okay, then. Hope you feel better?" I said, placing a hesitant question mark after feel and better.

"Thanks." She looked out the door behind me. Did she feel our connection was gone, was she following it out the door?

"I'll walk you out," Dr. Brennan said, interrupting me from hanging on—trying to stay connected.

When the elevator doors closed, I felt a hollow ache of isolation as I left Sarah in that empty ward. What a place to put someone who's already in a bad place. I shuddered, thinking of the long night, the deserted halls glowing in the dim lights. There must be other patients. I don't know if that made me feel better or worse.

I gulped in big clouds of my breath, cumulus ones that took away my view, but I kept my eyes wide open, not squinting against the snow. Flakes hit the back of my throat, melting into cool drops as I moved away from the isolation ward, that's what it felt like, anyway. I hated to walk away from her, but it was a relief to be out of there. It was kind of weird that Dr. Brennan let me see her, probably a choice based on no boundaries, no family to care. Who didn't want whom? I didn't know which was worse, her wanting to get out of a family or a family wanting to close the door on her. I picked up my pace. Maybe I'd ask Mr. Brooks to be my guest—probably should ask Gina first based on how she stared off when I spoke of him, maybe they needed a little meddler.

When I got back on Main, I slowed my pace. There was the familiar hum of snow ploughs and the scrape of shovels. It was hard for everyone to keep up. But the massive snow berms blocking curbs and driveways didn't stop too many—all the little shops were busy. A warm glow from the windows lit my path as I paused to look at the displays. I neared the bookstore—I'd pop in to say hello on the way home. But I kept moving. I caught a glimpse of Harry talking with Mr. Brooks. They didn't look happy. Were they arguing? If I hadn't met him this morning, I wouldn't have known who he was. Weird to see someone mad at Mr. Brooks or the other way around? I pictured Harry's smile, him calling me Al. I instinctively bent my knees to lower myself, as I hurried by. A few shops down, I stopped and turned. If I went in, I could get a vibe of what was going on. The store was open—I wouldn't be doing anything wrong, normal to pass by. I twisted a few times in both directions, but that wouldn't get me anywhere, anyway. It would make me seem like a snoop, and if there was something to snoop about, it would place my nose smack into it for Mr. Brooks to see…for Harry to see.

Back on Union, I pulled down my hat to mask my stare that jetted up to the woman in the window. Did she watch me while I watched her—it was hard to tell if she was looking at anything. I could just see the direction of her head. It snapped to the right, and I looked to where she had turned and saw someone coming out of Gina's place. I slowed and shot my gaze back up to the window, but she was gone. It looked eerie, the window without her in it. I got a chill, imagining her still there, but away from my view, her watching me…watching the woman leaving Gina's house. We were the neighborhood watch—I seemed to have signed up for that, spying on everyone, my neighborhood or not.

It was the same death card woman I had seen the other day. When she neared the sidewalk, she turned and looked up to the attic as she had done the other day. I stopped, pulled my arms around myself, feeling like she could see me, even though I was away from the attic. Nathalie jumped into my mind. Not often far from my thoughts, but this was unsolicited. I knew then my answer was in the attic. I was meant to rent that space.

The door under the stairs was open when I walked into the house. Although it was my opportunity to go peek, call down to Gina…I wanted to go upstairs. Gina had said Nathalie spent time up there…she had to have left something behind.

I paused outside Kiki's room. The letter.

I'd been waiting for a perfect moment. There it was. I moved into her room and flipped the light switch. I opened the drawer she had slammed the letter into, hoping she had more trust in me than she should—that she hadn't moved it. Yes! I peeked inside the envelope, making sure there was a letter. I resisted the urge to pull it out and read it right there. Then a plan I'd been toying with came together. I just had to get the letter back before Kiki got home.

The shadows reached out and met me at the door. I stared across at my window, rimmed with snow and fogged with condensation and then the tree, the lights on, as I had come to expect. I creaked across the floor.

I turned on the desk lamp and noticed a small key on its base. I shook my head. The key from Nathalie's apron. But my mind was on the letter. I studied the handwriting on the envelope, then slid my hand under the slip and eased the letter out. The date hit me—just days before Nathalie drowned. It *was* a suicide note. But it couldn't be Nathalie who wrote it. It felt heavy in my hand. Someone I knew had written it or someone I had yet to meet.

I pulled out my journal and scribbled notes and scanned the letter a few more times, making sure I had everything I needed before returning it. *Return to sender.* I gasped. Kiki. Why was she holding on to it? I paused at the top of my stairs, listening for Gina, or any movement on the floor below me. I was a good listener. Years of eavesdropping on a potential 'case.' I returned the letter to Kiki's drawer and headed back up to the key in the attic.

I picked up the key and considered the desk. I hadn't tried this key in the locked drawer yet. It had been in Nathalie's apron, after all, and it would make sense it belonged to something in the diner. I hadn't tried it here…I'd been more mystified with the N on the strap.

The key fit in the lock and turned, click. My heart thumped as I tugged on the drawer. It stuck a bit, snug against the wood. I tightened my grip and pulled harder, and it slid open. My heart drumming in my ears, I looked inside, a frisson of guilt running up my spine because I'd opened a locked drawer that wasn't mine.

A small box lay in the middle, a brass latch shining around a tiny keyhole.

My mind went straight to the wardrobe. The other key, it had been smaller. No. I couldn't. I'd scoffed at Kiki for looking at Nathalie's things that weren't even locked away from spies. But a locked box—I couldn't just flip open the lid, it wasn't meant to be flipped open. I ran my hand along the wood. I felt the seam and tested its cover. I wasn't surprised I made the effort, I still felt that strong pull that I was meant to look.

It was locked. The drawer jammed to one side as I started to close it, but I finally got it shut.

It dawned on me—maybe it wasn't even Nathalie's. It could be Gina's, or even a former resident—someone from a long time ago, like the finds I used to unearth at the cottage those summers. But then, the key to the desk was in Nathalie's apron. Maybe Nathalie had found the box, but couldn't bring herself to open it, had more restraint than me. But she hung on to the key…or forgot about the key. Well, whatever scenario, I was going to leave it there and leave it locked.

My Christmas tree lights went off.

"Tomorrow's the eve of Christmas Eve," Gina said as she eased into her chair in the den. Her eyes shone in the flickering light.

I think there were more candles. I scanned the room. "Yes. I can't believe it's here. Almost here."

"Ready for it?"

"I still don't have a guest." I looked at her as though looking for suggestions.

"Someone might turn up for you at the last minute." She looked like she was telling me Santa might show up.

I wished. If there were ever a place he'd want to visit, 334 Union Street would be it. I looked around again and out the window at the monstrous snowbanks. The wind chimes jangled more than usual with the gusts of wind. I stared at Gina as the smoke circled her head like a wreath, but the thought didn't make me laugh as it normally would.

"What's up?" Gina asked.

I thought of Sarah. She hadn't been a minute from my mind since I saw her at the hospital. I told Gina about the accident and my visit.

"The sweetheart," Gina said.

"I know. I just wish…" My voice cut off.

"Maybe she'll come see you. If she said she knows where you work, then she's probably interested. I don't think she would have said anything."

"You think?"

"I think I know." She smiled, that deep, knowing smile of hers.

"Did you hear that?" I looked at Gina but didn't move—other than my initial jump from being startled. I knew she had heard it too, as her eyes had lifted over the top of my head.

"Kiki's rubbing off on you." Gina pushed herself out of her chair. "Probably the wind blew over a garbage can or something." Gina looked out the front window. "It is windy out there tonight."

The noise hadn't come from the front.

I followed Gina into the kitchen. We both looked up the stairs on our way. There was another noise. Gina paused for a second and then marched ahead into the kitchen. It sounded like the gate latch. I hurried to the back door and squeezed in beside Gina to see out.

"Huh," I said, just above a whisper.

"What is it?" She kept staring out. Both of us gently pushing against each other for a view of the yard.

"The snow angel."

"Oh." Gina pulled away and looked down at me.

"That's odd. I did a snow angel this morning with Joe."

"Here?" Gina looked down at me with raised and knitted brows.

I laughed despite my racing thoughts. It struck me as funny, Joe and I doing a snow angel here. "No, no. Not here. At the diner."

"Oh," she said.

We both stared at the outline, lit by the moon.

"Kiki?" I asked.

"I suppose." She didn't sound convinced. "Doesn't it look a little big for Kiki?"

I hesitated. "It's the aura. It makes them bigger."

Gina looked at me with surprise, and then we lost it. Our laughter filled the kitchen. Gina bent over and leaned on the kitchen table. "Love it," she said between her rolling laughs.

"You bring it out in me."

"Good. Good on you," she said. "I'm glad you're here."

"Me, too."

"So?" she asked.

"So?"

"A snow angel with Joe?" Gina looked like she was about to rub her hands together but then held them in a sort of braid.

I felt a warm rush flood through me. "It's just a snow angel."

"It's never just a snow angel."

"You're a romantic."

"A-ha. A romance?" Then she did rub her hands together.

I mocked her hand rubbing, by joining her, then gently pulled her hands to stop them. "That was a trap."

"He's a good one."

I nodded.

"I knew he should be here Christmas Eve." She snapped her fingers together as she did a little jig around the kitchen.

"You're a nut." I laughed at her as she finished her little snaps and bumped her hip against mine. "You said he had done a lot of work for you? Fixing tiles?" I couldn't resist.

"Tiles? God, no. He was my accountant." Gina put air quotes around accountant. "Well, he still is. I'm one of the lucky ones he didn't let go of." I was glad she didn't seem to notice my sarcasm about the tile flapping against the attic roof, scaring previous tenants.

"Accountant?" My voice was too loud. Why had she put air quotes around accountant?

"He never mentioned it to you?"

I shook my head. "So, he has another job…" I hadn't got that vibe from Joe.

"No, not really. He's just good with numbers. I think he set out to be an accountant and then…"

I stared at Gina. "Did something happen?" I felt bad talking about Joe, asking about him. But why hadn't he told me? Well…I guess we didn't have that much time together before we kissed. Part of me wished I could take back the kiss. It was too soon for a kiss, that type of kiss.

"No. Well, I think he liked working more than going to school. Plus, he loves the diner. When Rick took over, he joined him. He's planning on buying it off him soon, I think."

I leaned both my hands on the table and scoffed. "Why wouldn't he tell me?" It wasn't that big of a deal, I know, but I think it was more I was mad at myself for not getting to know him first. I had fallen for his smile, his easygoingness, him laughing, and his getting to know *me* too quickly.

Gina poured a cider and lifted a mug. I shook my head. She leaned back on the counter and crossed her arms, giving my question some thought. "Maybe he wanted you to truly kiss the cook, you know?"

"If so, I'm a bit..." I tapped my fingers on the table. "I don't know…"

Gina stared at my drumming hands, and I stopped.

"I wouldn't be upset." She absently lifted a tin cover and bit into a cookie. "He's a good one." She stretched the tin out to me. "He doesn't like a lot of attention. He likes working at the diner." Gina smiled.

Me, too. And I loved eating molasses cookies in Gina's kitchen.

I made a few notes in my journal, then turned off my light. It felt good to enjoy the comfort of the bed, the weight of the duvet. I hung on to the luxury of being snug in bed but still awake for as long as I could, fighting sleep to relish the feeling of being tucked in my nest, Gina still awake in the den. And then my phone lit and vibrated. I stared at it a moment, turned on my light.

"Ali." The familiar voice sunk into my hand, into my heart.

I sat up and pushed my duvet down and then back up, tight to my chest. "Eric."

"Sorry, were you sleeping?"

"Almost. It's late?"

"Yeah. Sorry. I just… I miss you."

What! My heart started to roll, and I coughed as it caught in my throat. *No.*

"How are you?" he continued as my silence hung, as my heart raced.

"Well, I'm fine. You?"

"Can we meet?"

"Now?"

He laughed. His laughter gave me a rush I didn't want. I had kissed Joe.

"I would. But no, tomorrow? I could come by the diner?" I could picture his smile, kind of like Joe's…

The diner? No. "How do you know I work at the diner?"

"Small town, as you say."

I threw my duvet to the end of the bed. "I don't know, Eric, I…" I tried to take the hesitation out of my voice. I had come this far. I fought the memory of his kisses, his familiarity, his intensity as it rushed over me as though he was right beside me. Did he have a sixth sense? I had kissed Joe, just that morning. Did I kiss Joe too quickly?

"Sorry, Ali. I've just been thinking of you. A lot."

I looked around my room, taking everything in as though slowly waking, slowly grounding. *No. No. No.* "I don't think so, Eric. I'm sorry, I can't…" I sighed into the phone. "No." The sound of my 'no' surprised me— it sounded like I had snapped at a dog to stop chewing on a shoe.

"Okay, okay. Sorry to call… I didn't mean to..." he paused, "…well, anyway, Merry Christmas."

Bah.

I picked up my novel. I waited to nod off…it took at least an hour until I finally couldn't keep my eyes open.

Chapter Ten

I woke too early, from a dream—a nightmare. Someone was tapping on the window. I couldn't make her out in the dream, but she had a camel-colored cloak…like the woman under the stairs. But I knew it wasn't her. I leaned against the glass, my hands splayed open, trying to connect, get her to look, turn just enough for me to see her face. My index finger curled and I drummed a few beats, but she kept bowed, slightly turned…the *tap, tap, tap* an unremitting plea. But I sensed who hid in the hood…I could feel her like the familiar pulse throughout the house.

I woke tangled in a damp, cold sheet, a thump in my ears that joined the persistent vibration, the faint tapping on the glass. I stared out into the dark. I turned onto my side, and the light of the moon shone onto my book splayed down on my nightstand. I was in the middle of chapter three when I couldn't keep my eyes on the pages as they bounced over the words then blurred. But it was right at the part when Catherine had been at the window. Funny I should reread *Wuthering Heights*...be led to the room that Heathcliff allowed no one to stay in. Gina had invited me, but I was the first in years. My mom was right. I did look for scenes in my own closet, in attics, in every tap at a window…even though I hated a horror movie.

I flipped over and pulled the quilt over my head. I tried to quiet my breathing… I waited for it to slow and lead me back to sleep. It wasn't going to happen. I reached for my phone, and the screen lit up—3:58. *Oh, God.* The sick hangover of Eric's call pulsed in my head. I untangled my foot from the twisted sheet and threw the bedding aside. I thought of everyone I knew in different time zones…but it was still too early. I was too wound up to read. I closed the book and turned it face-down. I wouldn't finish it; I'd exchange it for something lighter, there was a tattered copy of *Emma* in the wardrobe, nothing scary about that. I wrapped my housecoat a little too tight and crept down the stairs. I paused on the landing in the glow of the nightlight, listening for movement in Kiki's room, hoping I'd hear her thump out of bed. I avoided the emptiness from the other room. I resisted looking into the dark. I crept down the next flight of stairs and paused on that landing, waiting, listening for Gina or Harry. I kept creeping to the kitchen.

"Oh." I gasped.

"Hey, Al." Harry was sitting at the kitchen table with a half-eaten monstrous sandwich. "Couldn't sleep either, hey?"

I shook my head and pulled the belt of my housecoat, but it couldn't get any tighter.

"Grab a seat. There's tea…" He looked at his

sandwich. "Want this half?" He nudged the plate. "I kind of overbuilt it."

I shook my head and smiled. "Yeah, looks like it." I laughed as I poured a tea.

"What's funny at four in the morning?' Harry turned in his chair, but he had a look, ready to laugh.

I slid into the seat across from him. I was glad he was sitting in Gina's chair. "I never had a brother…" I shook my head. "But this is one of the images I think of when I think of you guys…getting up in the middle of the night and eating a humungous Scooby-Doo sandwich."

"It's what we do..." He touched the plate. "I suppose I should finish this now…"

I kept my tea cupped in my hands and sipped as he ate and spoke through his bites. He had a lot to say about everything. I think he'd been awake for a long time, or perhaps he never fell asleep.

"Who are you bringing to dinner tomorrow night?" Harry rubbed his hands over the plate and pushed it to the side.

"I haven't found anyone yet." I lifted my shoulders.

He drained his mug. "You work at the diner. Should be easy?"

I shook my head. "There's this woman…Sarah." I paused, put my mug down. "I think she might live on the street…she knew…" I felt heat rise through my housecoat. I didn't want to get into this with Harry.

"Sarah?" Maybe there was a little twitch at the corner of his mouth.

"You know her?" I asked.

"Sort of. Nathalie knew her." He looked like he was holding back. "My girlfriend, my sort of girlfriend…Olivia…" He made a face. I didn't know what the face meant. "She said something about Sarah being with Nathalie that night. Olivia doesn't trust her. I don't know." He shrugged. "Sarah seems harmless to me. If Nathalie was friends with her…" He looked into his mug.

I nodded, wanting to agree with him.

"What time is it now, anyway?" He turned and looked over his shoulder at the stove. It was close to five. "You know, I'm going to see if I can sleep for…oh God, an hour and a half…" He rinsed his mug and plate. "Guess you'll get ready and be off soon. Thanks for the company, Al." He gave my shoulder a light squeeze when he passed. "You're in charge."

I sat for a moment, listening to the cracks and creaks up the stairs and then to the noises I hadn't noticed when he sat across from me. My back became rigid against the chair…I heard a *tap, tap, tap*. No. I bowed my head toward the door, my gaze froze and stuck on the brass handle. No. It was the radiator, the steam getting trapped… I heard the familiar whistle and hiss.

I rushed getting ready, wanting to be at the diner to have some time with Joe. Weird he never mentioned anything about the diner…about taking it over. I left my drapes shut. I didn't have the nerve to open them against the dark morning, to see my reflection bounce back and startle me. I didn't trust I wouldn't allow my face to morph into hers—then screech, waking up the rest of the house. I wondered if Harry made it to sleep as I passed his room.

I could see Joe shoveling the front path to the diner in the distance. I picked up my pace to the rhythm of the faint scrape against the sidewalk. The town tempo. The snow was slow, steady and straight, like a moving screen. You walked into it, and it walked into you.

Everything took on the snow—houses topped with mounds of white, tracks constantly snowed over on the streets, and the trees, with their laden boughs, some with muted lights barely poking through. Cars on side streets looked like they had been abandoned for weeks. But every so often, I was surprised to see headlights push through and then someone initiating an avalanche, starting from a sweep to the hood.

"Hey," I called out.

Joe's head jerked up. "Hey, Angel." He laughed as he leaned on the shovel. I was glad he didn't have a cigarette dangling out of his mouth.

"Humphrey Bogart barely pulls that off. Angel?"

He looked offended. "Huh? No. I just shortened snow angel."

"Just teasing." I stopped in front of him but wanted to keep going into his arms.

He leaned down, paused close to my lips, and looked into my eyes. My body had already started to tremble. He let go of the shovel and wrapped his arms around me. *You can call me Angel.*

"You're cold." He pulled away. "I'll be in…in a few minutes." He looked down at the snow. "Maybe ten. I keep getting more and more work dumped on me."

"There another shovel?"

"Nah, go ahead, it won't take me long." He leaned over and kissed me. "But thanks."

I walked through the diner, absorbing the dim glow, the flashes of light that bounced off the cutlery, the smell of the coffee…hmmm, Joe hadn't smelled or tasted like cigarettes. I hurried out of my coat and boots, shaking snow all over the floor, avoiding the puddles as I put on my sneakers. I didn't like being back there, especially with Joe outside. I pictured Sally folding her coat and placing it under the counter, avoiding the back room, Joe saying it felt weird after I had had that sensation…or whatever it was when I had nodded off…the sound of rushing water. I caught the picture Joe had brought in of the river out of the corner of my eye as I brushed passed it. The water looked like it was moving. But I was moving, I had to stop searching for things that weren't there, hearing things…

I poured us our coffee and leaned on the counter, waiting for Joe's shoulder, arm, hip to connect with mine. I had decided not to mention I knew about his other life. It wasn't a big deal. I felt weird holding out, but I was sure he'd tell me soon enough. I didn't tell him about Eric. About him calling me. But I told him about the snow angel at Gina's.

"You're kidding?" He kind of moved away from me.

"Weird, huh?"

"No."

"No?"

"It was me. Saying goodnight."

"Really?"

"I thought you would have known that. Didn't think you would jump straight to the supernatural." He shook his head and put his arm around my waist. "It was that good, huh?"

"You know, you shouldn't go around terrorizing the neighborhood. Leaving your print of a snow angel."

"Okay, now that sounds creepy. It was just goodnight. It was just for you. I didn't go lawn hopping." He rubbed my back. "You're an odd duck, Ali. But I like you, anyway."

"What if we saw you—in the middle of your act?"

"I would have done a blue angel."

"Weirdo." But I laughed. He *was* funny. I only knew what a blue angel was because of Caroline's brothers. One time when I had visited her, we bounded down into the basement, and her brother Pat appeared to have fire streaming out his backside. I had yelped, and Caroline had thumped down onto the bottom step and howled. They all had howled while I begged Pat to do it again. I was shocked. I wasn't used to boys farting in a basement, but who could look away from someone turning their butt into a human cannon. Crazy. If you've never seen one first-hand, search it on Google, there are lots of people with no shame on YouTube. Well, you knew that.

We sipped, Mahalia Jackson's *O Holy Night* in the background. I told Joe about Sarah and my visit at the hospital. Maybe because I always talked about Sarah or Nathalie…I never gave him a chance to tell me anything.

"Is she going to have to be there for Christmas? Does she have family?" Joe asked.

"I don't know. I wanted to ask the doctor so much about her, but it was none of my business. It was good enough for her to let me see her."

"Right."

We stared out at the snow. The record snow that kept falling. As we stood, it started to come down heavier.

"It's a banner year for snow angels," Joe said, lightening the mood.

"You obsessed or something?" I leaned my face up, and he kissed me—a long head-spinning kiss. The counter was my savior. I didn't know how I would ever manage a free-standing kiss with Joe. He'd have to have a good hold on me as he had outside. Again, no hint of a cigarette. We pulled apart, and I looked up at him.

"What's that look for?"

"You're an even better kisser without Marlborough-mouth."

"Yeah." He laughed. "I quit."

"Just like that?"

"How else?"

"I don't know, don't you need to stick something to you, chew something…just cold turkey?"

"That's right, Angel." He laughed and tickled my ribs.

I yelped and pulled away from him. I continued to giggle, and he caught my arm. "Don't, please don't tickle me." I tried to twist out of his grip.

"I won't." He pulled me in for another kiss. "But now, I know…that's some valuable information…"

Joe went back to the kitchen and left me with Dean Martin and *Baby It's Cold Outside*. I piled creamers into bowls and straightened cutlery. I floated around the diner thinking, I get it, I could work here. This could be my job. My mom would have a heart attack. I shook my head. "*I really can't stay…*" I sang along with the song. But maybe I could keep a shift on the weekend… "*…maybe just a half a drink more…*"

Adam was first in, like the first day I came to the diner. "Hey, ho, Ali!" he called as he stomped his feet. "Still snowing out there." He pointed behind him and laughed.

"I hope it doesn't stop until New Year's." I poured him coffee.

He looked at me funny, then leaned forward as he folded his parka on a bar stool. "Me too, but don't tell anyone."

"Really? Must slow your route quite a bit?"

"I don't mind. Plus, people are nicer…feel sorry for me, I guess." He laughed. "But they can never know…"

He pointed a finger at me.

I put my hand up, then zipped my lip. "The usual?"

"Look at you, already knowing my usual…hmmm, I'm that boring, huh? Maybe in the New Year, I'll try something new, maybe when the snow stops…"

The door jingled. "Hey, Boston," I called. I couldn't believe I called him Boston, blah. I had only known him less than a week.

But he smiled. "Hey. You know, no one's called me that in a while. How are ya today?"

He took a seat, leaving a few spots between him and Adam. "Adam." He nodded.

"Boston." Adam nodded.

Boston gave him a look but smiled. He put his paper down. They started talking hockey. I was beginning to recognize the Bruins players' names. The bell jingled again and again.

Mr. Brooks came in somewhere between the jingles before eight. I told him about going to see Sarah, that she seemed to be okay, physically, anyway, but I didn't get into that.

"Good," he said, but his face still had that stiffness, his expression didn't reach his eyes. He folded his coat and ruffled his hair as he finished his usual scan, then looked back up at me. "And what did she have to say?" He opened the lid of his teapot, closed it.

"Not too much." I adjusted my apron, retied the straps a little tighter. "I didn't stay long."

"Well, glad she's okay." His smile lifted, it hit his eyes. "Okay, so I have to be good today…" He looked toward the kitchen.

"Why's that?"

"Because I'm going to be bad tomorrow. All day." He laughed. "It's Christmas Eve tomorrow. Sugar starts early." He squeezed the tea bag against the side of the pot but left it to steep. "Just a muffin and half a grapefruit."

I raised my eyebrows. "You sure?"

"Ah, I don't need your sympathy."

I felt better walking away from him and his sparkly face and words. Springsteen was belting out *Santa Claus is Coming to Town.* He was still the Boss. I zipped around with coffee, ketchup, and syrup. And did it again and again. The morning shot by, and so did the afternoon. I only had one shoulder-to-shoulder with Joe before lunch.

"How are you doing…cold turkey?" I asked Joe on my way out.

He laughed. "Not bad, sticky monkey."

"Sticky?"

"I don't know." He shrugged. "So, you're okay with monkey…but not angel?" He moved around the pass-through and pulled up my zipper on my coat.

"Eek, eek."

"I like monkeys," he said and kissed me.

I floated along with the snow up Main. I paused outside Kaffee Brik, taking in the cuckoo clock, the shiny bags on the tables—there wasn't an empty seat, but I wasn't planning on going in. I kept going until I reached the flower shop. I stared into the contrast through the steamed windows, snow up to my ankles, anticipating the sweet smell, the freshness of the cut flowers.

I pushed into the green, pink heads peeking out at the front of the shop, the heady scent of the roses mostly holding on to their blooms. I inhaled the spicy, peppery carnations, moved into the meld, the coming together of the freshness, the sweetness, and woodiness.

"Afternoon," a woman called to me, coming out of the cooler.

"Hello." I inhaled a big breath. "You must always smell like flowers. I worked in a restaurant once that served fajitas. No one was happy when I walked in the door after a shift."

She laughed. "I guess. I think I take it for granted. But to be honest, sometimes I have to say, it's like finally getting your own air when you get away from these flowers." She waved her hands around the shop, her bangles jingling up and down her wrists. "Try hanging out with them for ten hours." She put her hand to the side of her mouth, letting me in on a secret. "And between you and me… I hate carnations." But she laughed. "What can I do for you today? A special occasion before Christmas or would you like something Christmassy?" She looked over her shoulder. "Maybe some carnations?"

I laughed, but at the same time, my eye caught a beautiful planter of poinsettias and English ivy that was very Christmassy. It would last longer than fresh-cut flowers. I pointed at it. "I like this one here." I walked toward it and scanned for a price. Holy smokes. I thought of Gina, who always said 'Holy smokes.'

"That's one of my favorites." She picked it up.

Of course, it is, I thought. She lifted it up for admiration and turned to the cash register. She was good. But I liked her and liked the arrangement. "Yes, thank you."

As she rang it in, I looked at all the cards she had displayed on the counter. Her business card, ads for nearby shops…the bookstore. I scanned back to her card, then the one beside it. I bent toward it. "Is that you?" The name was the same on both cards, but the image was quite different, with one showing this woman with a conservative blouse buttoned to the top, her hair in a bun, the other a somewhat younger woman with cropped hair and a relaxed smile.

She picked it up, flipped it toward her and leaned on the counter as though considering it for the first time. Her bangles fell to her elbows. I couldn't imagine working with those things, all the moving around she had to do, each bracelet moving with her every move. "Yeah, that's me. I kind of like that picture." She brought it up closer and squinted at it. "It looks nothing like me." She rubbed her thumb over the image as though trying to see what lay beneath. I was starting to kind of wonder. "Think it looks like me?" she asked.

Suddenly, I could only smell the carnations. The humid surround started to feel thick and sticky…the aromas too sweet. She had said she liked the picture of herself…but it didn't look anything like her, neither of the images did. "Sure, well, I thought it was you…" I stared at the planter, willing her to wrap it up.

She shrugged, pushed the card toward me and started to cover the planter in stiff green paper, with a pattern of darker green Christmas trees. "You interested?"

I stared at the card. I hadn't noticed the words in gold cursive…the word. *Medium.* I wanted to say I thought I might have one of those at home but thought I might laugh. Plus, I didn't want to laugh at all. I wondered if Gina *was* a medium or just a card player. I shuddered thinking of that death card. "Thank you…" I finally said. I straightened away from the counter.

She paused in her wrapping, lifting a hand placatingly. "Hey, no worries. I just thought…"

I looked at her, happy she hadn't said 'sensed'… I

wasn't comfortable when people sensed things or said they sensed things.

"Never mind." She shook her head, pushed the planter forward and fiddled with the paper.

I fought the urge to say: What? What is it?

"Anyway, take my card…if you ever want to…" She slid the planter toward me and took my Visa, "…whatever you're comfortable with."

I looked at the card and pocketed it. "Thanks…Rose?"

"I know." She laughed. "My name had a bit of an influence…pulled me into the biz…"

The cold hit my face like a glass of ice water, but the rest of me celebrated its release from the heat of the flower shop. I inhaled a big breath of winter. Snowflakes washed the back of my throat as I hurried toward the hospital, away from fake spring. I couldn't have borne another suffocating minute with the roses…with Rose. It was close to the time I had stopped by the day before. I hoped Dr. Brennan would be there.

When I arrived at the entrance, I paused, the doors opening and then closing. On the second sweep, I stepped inside. I nodded at the woman behind the information booth. She gave me a bored nod, her head bent, cradling her cell between her chin and shoulder.

I took the stairs to the fourth floor, not wanting to get into another enclosed space like an elevator. I nearly dropped the planter when the door handle didn't move when I pulled the handle. I balanced the planter, hugging it between my side and in the crook of my elbow, but the door was locked. I hesitated, then turned and tried the third floor. The heavy door clicked, and I moved down the hall to the elevators. When the elevator doors opened, and I caught Level 4 Psychiatry, my stomach tightened.

The locked door. I hesitated, thinking maybe I would leave the planter with reception.

I turned left and started to move into the emptiness of the ward.

"Excuse me. Miss, excuse me." The voice got louder.

I turned to reception.

She waved me over. "You have to sign in." She tapped a clipboard.

"Oh." I put the planter on the counter. "Sorry. I didn't know…"

"That's okay," she said. She had a singing voice. "You here to see Sarah?"

Is she the only one here, really? "Yes."

"She just left for a meeting. She won't be in her room for another hour."

A meeting? "Oh."

"Do you want to wait? Or you could leave that in her room, if you like."

"I'll leave them."

The phone rang. She waved down the hall. "You can leave them on her table."

I passed the stripped beds, now wishing for the confines of the flower shop and its sickening sweetness. The table beside Sarah's bed had the box from Kaffee Brik, that cup of water, with its bendy straw, still looking untouched and…flowers. Oh.

I felt a wave of happiness. Maybe she did have family, or a close friend, at least. I stepped in, feeling strange in her room. I just wanted to place the planter and leave her space. But when I squeezed it in beside the vase, I noticed one of those flower message cards bent in half, facedown. I had forgotten to pick up one of those little tags. I looked over my shoulder. No one was in sight. I turned over the card. *Merry Christmas, Love Nathalie.*

I heard a click…but it was me, my tongue pulling from the roof of my mouth. My hand trembled as I picked up the card and turned it back over. I looked over my shoulder… I had to get back to reception, but I wanted to stay—find out who brought the flowers. I prayed there was another Nathalie in her life…but…what were the chances… The alternative was either someone trying to be nice…weird…or…someone diabolically mean had been in her room. I shuddered. I stepped back, turned away from the floral arrangement, heavy with white stargazer sympathetic lilies. I summoned everything in me not to run. The receptionist was on the phone, still…or again, and gave an enthusiastic wave, a cheery smile. Thank God she was on the phone. I couldn't idle for any form of chat.

I rushed into the bookstore, scanning for shoppers or browsers, but unfortunately, it seemed empty, as usual. I heard a step and then another, Mr. Brooks coming down from a ladder. He poked his head around one of the bookcases. What was he doing with those shelves all the time? No one was taking anything off them.

"Well, hello." He moved to greet me as he placed the book that was in his hand on the counter. "This is a nice surprise. Hot chocolate?"

I shook my head. I didn't have the heart to tell him about the hot chocolate at Kaffee Brik. I'd have to bring him one next time, though. "You busy?"

He looked around. "Not overly." He laughed.

I grinned and walked with him. We took a seat in

those comfy chairs.

"What's up, kiddo?"

"You were close to Nathalie. Did she have anyone, I don't know…who may have been mad at her?"

Mr. Brooks' face dropped. He had been ready for a hot chocolate.

"I'm sorry. I was just at the hospital." I shook my head. "Someone brought Sarah flowers. And the card…" I winced. "The message on the card was, Merry Christmas, Love Nathalie." I stared at Mr. Brooks. I noticed a little twitch under his eye as his face drained to a gray-white.

"Was she upset?" he finally asked.

"Sarah? No. Well, I don't know. I didn't see her. She wasn't in her room. The card was wrinkled, bent in half." My cheeks felt hot. Mr. Brooks would think I was nosy. Well, I was, I am, when I think it's okay to be. "Not the usual reaction to a card you'd want to keep."

I was starting to see *he* had an odd reaction to stress. The way he responded at the diner to the accident, and then right then in his store—it was as though he was pulling away, trying to hide from it…or was he hiding something? I was glad I was here. I felt there was something here. Maybe his reaction to pull away was normal, mine to push into everything wasn't. I had been en route to Gina's, but something drew me into the bookstore. I scanned the bookcases, all those bound words feeling heavy around me. Was he holding on to any words or bound to something…someone? Had Harry been mad at him or he mad at Harry? I stuck to silence, waiting for Mr. Brooks.

"There was someone," he finally said. "Someone Nathalie was helping out." He looked at me as though he didn't want to continue. But I stared at him, nodding too much, I know it. I always lack decorum when I want to know something. He continued, "I got this vibe I didn't like." He made a face, maybe because he was embarrassed he had said vibe. I wanted to tell him I was used to it, I lived with Gina. "Nathalie stopped in with her a few times. I don't know..." He shook his head. "I think she was off, you know, or on, I guess...on something. I believe Nathalie was helping her with that, but I didn't like that glaze in her eyes, and there was a tension I picked up on."

"Is she still around?" My heart fluttered at my neck as I imagined finding this woman.

"Olivia?" He gave me a closed look. "That's the thing. Harry seems to have become involved with her. I really don't think it's a good idea..."

Harry's girlfriend. "Do you think Olivia's...I don't know..." I wanted to say dangerous but realized that sounded much too dramatic. My mind zoomed back to the kitchen on Union that morning. Harry had said that Olivia had thought Sarah was untrustworthy. Maybe the note with the flowers was an 'I know' note from someone who had seen something. Witnessed something Sarah did. I shuddered. That was too fantastic. I shook my head. If someone knew anything, they would have told the police. I know I would. *I will.*

Mr. Brooks frowned. "I think she's not good for him. I don't know if she's taking anything still, but..." He paused again. "Harry stopped in here with her the other day. It was odd. I waved them in. Harry's never around town during the day. Always at work, never takes a break. So, at first, I was happy. But then when I saw her... I got that feeling I got when Nathalie had brought her in here." He rubbed his arms, as though getting the vibe again. "She didn't stay. It was as though she got caught in a trap. She looked at me. I'll never forget that look, then kissed Harry and took off. I told Harry how I felt, but no one likes to be told something like that." He tapped his thumbs together then looked at me and shrugged. "Anyway, maybe I'm just a crazy old guy… I think I need a hobby. Around all these books all day…" He half-smiled.

My mom and some of my friends had said that to me many times when I had mooned over a case or over a neighbor I thought looked 'off,' as Mr. Brooks had said. But I supported Mr. Brooks, maybe he did need a hobby, but it wasn't because of this. This was something, or there was something about all this—about Nathalie. "I'd like to meet her…" I said more to myself but got it out there in case Mr. Brooks had an idea of going east or west.

"Olivia?"

"Olivia." I repeated her name. "Yes." I twisted my lips. "Maybe see if I get the same vibe."

I saw Mr. Brooks' eyes return to the present, that big smile of his reaching up to them. "You…" He shook his head but laughed.

"I'm serious." I held up my hand even though I giggled.

"Well, you're in luck, she'll be Harry's guest Christmas Eve. You can let me know what you think. You'll have to come back for another meeting here…" He patted the armrest. "And we can compare notes."

When I pushed the door closed behind me, I heard a faint thumping, as though someone was jumping upstairs. Kiki. I called out as I rested my hand on the newel post, waiting to see if Gina responded from the kitchen.

"Hello," I called again as I started up the stairs. There was music and a persistent thump with a bit of rhythm.

Gina poked her head out of her room. I could hear her breath now. She waved an arm and went back in. It was her thumps. "Come on in," she called. "Join me…" she said, panting. "I'm Zumba-ing."

I stood in the doorway, shaking. I had long ago mastered the laugh without sound, but it only worked in large auditoriums or when no one was looking right at me. Gina continued her jerky movements as I admired the king-sized canopy bed, with its dark hardwood and the elaborate carved accents. Her bedspread was a rich floral in gold and red. I wanted to take everything in. I think the dresser and night tables were topped with marble. But I couldn't avoid the main attraction—Gina. She had a blue fitted tunic and orange spandex leggings. And that braided headband!

"You can't do that. You can only laugh if you join me." She waved me in again.

"I'm too uncoordinated." I laughed with impunity as Gina laughed with me.

"Look at me. Do you think I have any grace? No grace at the dinner table, no grace on the dance floor, Hail Mary."

"Where did you get that headband?" I bent over as she jutted out a leg and an arm in different directions. I don't think she knew a sequence. "You're doing it on purpose."

"What? What?" She made an exaggerated hip bump and swooped forward, now trying to make me laugh harder.

I thought of my mom. She used to get into one of her workout outfits when I was little and spin around the house. I remember she had these tricolor hippie-type pants. I think they were tie-dye, even. Oftentimes she would pull them up to her ribs to make me laugh. It was before she wanted to leave, when our laughs echoed together throughout the house…before she felt guilty. Those days when she wasn't restless, when she was home after dinner or for dinner every night. When my dad didn't make me fish sticks.

I shook my head, got into the moment with Gina, who was always there, right in the moment. I stumbled along with the moves she made up as she made her funny faces. I felt a sense of familiarity after so many years of wanting to avoid the moment after my mom retired her hippie pants.

"OW!" Gina whooped as I stomped on her foot. She gave me a push but started to laugh. "Okay, okay." She put her hands up in surrender. "You're right. You've got some African elephant in you."

"Sorry." I giggled and shaped my arm into an attempt at an elephant trunk, extending it to give her a peck on the cheek. "Aroooooouhhh."

She laughed. "Okay, get out of here you nut, I'm going to shower…and tape my foot."

I headed up to my room. I was startled by the dark when I opened the door to the attic. I stared at the drapes and shuddered, thinking of my dream, the tapping on the window. I strode over and pushed the heavy material to the sides. There wasn't much day left in the sky, but the storm of white from the constant snow brought some light and comfort into the room. I looked down onto the street, into the dusk layering the snow and muted lights, like an opaque curtain descending on a theater set. I felt a pang of sadness that at some point the snow would end, the season would pass. It would be weird to not be Christmastime in this house. Funny that only days ago I couldn't imagine Gina and Christmas in the same room, now I couldn't imagine her without Christmas in the house. And what would happen with Nathalie and her memory…would that pass, too, after the holidays?

The pipes started to rattle and then the *tick, tick, tick* pulsed in the walls. My mind zipped down to the door under the stairs. No one was home…Gina was in the shower. My heart thumped along with the ticking. No. Maybe I had been so mortified at Kiki, elbows deep in Nathalie's things, because I was just like her. I looked at the desk…the drawer. For the love of Christmas…

We settled into the den a little earlier than usual. I was happy to have that extra time with Gina. As much as I was excited about having our guests Christmas Eve, I would miss our den-time, just her and me and her pipe. I had just put more logs on the fire. The pop of sap filled the den along with the Christmas music. I felt a sense of urgency, as though this was it…if not now, forever hold my peace. Gina startled me by tapping the foot I was wagging back-and-forth.

"What's with the ants?"

I looked up at her. "Ants?"

"You've got ants in your pants. Excited about tomorrow?" She finished packing the bowl, raised a brow, and lit the pipe. The smell pulled the room together, wrapped us in.

I nodded but got to the point…the first point. "Do you know Rose—I forget her last name—from the flower shop on Main?"

"I do. She's a character, Rose." Gina shook her head. "And a good medium if you ever…no, not really your thing, though, I think…" She looked at me through a cloud. "You met her today?"

I thought it funny, a character calling out another character. And a medium? "Do you do that, too? Are you…a medium?"

She scrunched her nose. "No, not really. I do readings, cards, gimmicky stuff." She laughed through a cough.

I looked at her and paused. "I heard you one day…" I wagged my foot, and she kicked it gently. "Sorry." I grabbed my toes and pulled my legs up, hugging my knees into my chest. "I never said anything to you…a few days ago I eavesdropped on you. I heard you and a woman under the stairs. Is that what you were doing? A reading?"

She waved her hand at me. "That's okay, little Snoopy." She winked at me. "Yes, that's what I was doing."

I straightened out my legs again. "Do you have a crystal ball down there?" I giggled. "Sorry."

"Oh…I see how it is with you." She laughed and tapped her pipe. "Do you want a tour? You might be disappointed, though. I think you've got a big imagination." She leaned forward and tapped me on the nose. "I think it's sticking out, actually…"

I twisted my lip and shrugged my shoulders.

"Come on, then." She stood and looked like she was going to pull me up.

I put my finger up and wobbled up, with a lot less wobble than I had in the kitchen the other day. "Ha." I laughed.

"Ha, what? Don't tell me you're competing with an old horse?"

I followed her down the hall. I had the same

sensation I had had as she led me up to the attic not that long ago. She paused, her hand on the brass doorknob. It seemed to be her thing, that perfect pause—she loved drama.

"Honestly, it's nothing much." She turned to me. "You're going to be disappointed."

"Oh, come off it." I gave her a little nudge.

She gulped a giggle down, opened the door, then turned to me and waggled her eyebrows. She flipped on a light; it lit a few of the stairs below us. I nudged her again and kept my hand touching her elbow as we went down into the 'reading room.' As we reached the bottom of the stairs, I couldn't see anything. It was black and then blacker as I strained into a flat darkness. Gina pulled away, and I lost my tether. But I heard a pull, then click as the bulb shed barely enough light to showcase a table with a gauzy cloth cover as I imagined, candles with dips and peaks from the dripping wax, a book bound in black leather…and a deck of cards…*the* deck of cards?

"There you have it." She splayed her hands out. "All that you imagined?" She pulled the cloth straight on our side of the table, picked up the cards, and started to shuffle.

I stared at her hands, like grasshopper legs shuffling the cards, with the constant bend at her knuckles. I don't know how she managed. Then one snapped out of the deck and landed on the floor. Our heads snapped down at it. *Please, no.*

A man in a long red robe cand a yellow crown stared out from the card, a sword in one hand, a set of balances in the other. I squinted. The lettering at the bottom read JUSTICE. I sighed. I didn't see the word DEATH written anywhere. That would have been too much. I would have called Gina out on having a fixed deck.

She bent and picked it up with her grasshopper fingers. "Justice," she said. She looked at me with a flicker of something in her eye. I didn't recognize it…it could have been surprise, or it could have been her interest in teasing or embellishing.

"And?" My voice fell into the darkness.

"Have a seat." She tapped the table.

I looked around and drew my sweater tighter. I squeezed into the chair without pulling it out, not wanting to settle in, not wanting to make it my space.

"It's natural to strive for the world to be one way…to have wrongs righted…to want a happy ending." She was staring at the card, holding it up. I wondered if she was reading off the card, but I hadn't seen any other words. She placed it down. "But sometimes the pursuit of justice…" She tapped the card. "Can become an obsession."

I pulled my sweater tighter and kept my arms wrapped around me. I felt like it was a warning. I tried to push the chair back, but it didn't move. I was happy it wasn't the death card, but I wasn't too comfortable with it, either.

"The card represents change…"

I thought the death card represented change, I wanted to say. Maybe she said that to everyone.

"A lot of the cards represent change," she said as though she picked up my thought. I didn't mind when she did that upstairs. But under the minimal light, in the cold, underneath the stairs… I just wanted her to stop talking. "This one, Justice," she continued, "represents the change that occurs when the facts sink in as deeply as the verdict."

I never liked cards. I never liked games. I pushed against the table and squeezed out to stand. "Gina…I, ah…"

"I'm sorry, Ali. Pauvre petite bête." She stood and stuffed the card back into the deck. "I know you don't like this, it's just fun, really…" She moved over to my side of the table and wrapped her arm around my shoulder. "Let's go up."

I couldn't get comfortable as we took our posts back in the den. I looked at Gina's pipe, wanting her to light up again—recreate the scene before the card game. Had she pulled that card on purpose? But then I thought of how those cards can all be read to see something…to see what we want to see…

Since it was hard to get back into the Christmas spirit, I brought up the flowers. "When I went to the hospital to drop off a planter for Sarah, someone else had been there." I pulled my knees into my chest, but slid them back out, started to wave my feet back and forth, then stopped. "There was a card with flowers…the card was signed, 'Nathalie.'"

"Nathalie?"

"Yeah. Merry Christmas, Love Nathalie."

Gina pulled her head back, a half-chicken, my dad used to call that move. She frowned. "Well. Maybe…maybe there's another Nathalie?" That's how a normal person thinks.

"That's what I hoped…but…" I had initially had that same thought…just maybe. But I'm more of a skeptic.

"No. You're right. And Nathalie never mentioned another Nathalie in her circle, either." Gina shuddered. "Who would do that? It's not cute. I don't think someone would think it's cute."

I shook my head. "No."

"I wonder how Sarah took it."

"I am going to drop by the hospital again. I'll go after work. Or after *The Night Before Christmas.*" I was looking forward to Mr. Brooks' reading at the bookstore.

"After tomorrow?" Gina's lips twitched into a smile. Her expression that familiar—I couldn't help myself. I loved that about her.

"Very funny, wabbit, as you say."

I brushed my teeth, the Christmas tree night light shimmering a soft green with little glints of red and white. I had become used to getting ready for bed with its dim glow, along with the moon on the white tiles. There was an added spicy scent that hadn't been there that morning. I bent toward the soap dish. It was filled with little red and gold soap balls. I wanted to take a bite out of one but resisted the urge and headed up to make some notes.

I got snuggled in, propped with pillows, the heavy duvet pulled up, then took a moment and looked around—there were so many favorite times of the day. I couldn't order which one topped my list if I tried. This, that moment seemed to win each time. I opened my book to my last entry, and my gaze dropped into the dark ink of *homicidal drowning*. Maybe I did need a hobby.

I heard a book fall. I stared ahead at the wardrobe. Those books didn't want to stay in a neat row. *In front of the box*, popped into my mind, of course, it did. I stepped onto the shag beside my bed and went to make sure they were all down. I'd leave them on their backs. I didn't want another one falling in the middle of the night.

I stared at the box, then over my shoulder toward the desk. Maybe there was something in that box in the drawer. Maybe I was supposed to look. I plucked the small key by the lamp and brought the box from the desk over to my bed. I wasn't even sure if it would fit, I had just assumed.

It did.

I paused after it easily clicked in the lock. I looked up at the ceiling—is that where you look for a spirit…a ghost? Or I guess they're in the room with you if they're trying to tell you something. I felt a giggle lift in my chest. Maybe Nathalie was nudging me to this. I lifted the lid. There was a picture, worn, bent on the edges. I recognized Nathalie from the papers, from the images on the internet. She had her arm around a smaller version of herself—it would be her little sister. They both looked like they had just finished laughing. They were both dead. Both drowned. I stared at their image for a long while. It was hard to pull away. There was something so alive, so present. I remember a front page of a newspaper on a Saturday morning when I was young—it had given me a similar feel—it was of a family who had died in a car accident. All images I'd seen, that last glimpse of the departed, had the same look—like they were happy, that they knew. They had an 'I'm okay' look. Maybe they did that for the living…maybe there was a premonition…I have to make this picture a good one.

Underneath that photo was another—a picture of a couple, probably Nathalie's parents. It must have been taken after Nathalie's little sister had died. They didn't have the look of the dead taken away too soon. Although they smiled from the image, they had the look of the heartbroken. They had two daughters, both dead. They knew they were going to be left behind.

There was one more photo. It was stuck to the back of the parents. I peeled it away—it was Nathalie, with her front tooth missing, a big grin, looking again like she had just finished laughing or was still laughing and I recognized the little girl slung under her arm. It was Jenna. Jenna had a tooth missing, too, her head was tilted back a little, she was still laughing. They had posed, proud of their matching missing teeth.

I smiled and looked underneath the photos. I guess I *wasn't* meant to look inside the box. I shrugged. There was a barrette, just one, with pink and yellow butterflies clipped on as though just resting for a moment. There was what looked like a small battery of some sort, and a pencil, with vibrant flowers on it—it had never even been sharpened, it must have been a favorite, too pretty to use. I skimmed back over the photos, looking for something…was there a clue in one of those images? I didn't think so. Maybe I was just meant to be here. To just be. Stop searching. Continue to form a base with my new friends, with Gina, Mr. Brooks…Joe. I didn't need a base—like the ones where I was brought together with others in a new city or a foreign land, creating a bond to survive. I didn't need to latch onto anything.

Chapter Eleven

Joe was leaning back against the counter when I arrived. I couldn't wait to get in and settled beside him to his left—shoulder-to-shoulder.

"Morning," he said as he walked toward me.

"Morning. Wow, does it ever smell good in here. It smells like Christmas!" I *didn't* need to latch onto anything. I smiled. When left well enough alone a moment latched onto me…along with Christmas. It rushed over me. Over and over. The bass-baritone of Johnny Cash's voice played in my head: *And then I felt the Christmas spirit.*

"Perfect," he said and kissed me gently on the cheek.

"Gingerbread pancakes?" I asked.

"Gingerbread cookies. I always make some Christmas Eve to give everyone when they get their bill." He kissed me again.

I looked up at him and smiled. "That's a nice thing to do." I kissed him.

"That was a nice thing, too." He kissed me back.

"You smell like Santa," I said.

"You would know, wouldn't you, you little tramp."

We laughed, and I pulled myself away to put my coat in the back and change out of my boots. I peeked into the kitchen on my way out. There were pans and pans of gingerbread cookies shaped into stars, snowflakes, and snowmen.

"Did you hire some elves?"

"I wish. They were busy. Tough time of year. I got up a little early."

He poured me a coffee and handed it to me. I added cream, and we leaned back. *Christmas Bells* by Patti Page was playing softly. I looked up at Joe and smiled.

"What's up, kiddo?" He nudged my elbow.

"This is my favorite."

"Me, too," he said and kissed the top of my head.

"This song is *your* favorite?"

"No. *This* is my favorite." He kissed me beside my eye. "This right here. It's the highlight of my day."

How could he do that? How could he be so right? He delivered lines like gentlemen from the era of Patti Page, yet he was so...he had an edge I loved that went with it. He was such a guy-guy. My type. But more. My stomach felt warm and scrambled. I felt dizzy, like the effect of that first drink when you're a bit too young for it.

"Me, too," I said. My voice sounded hoarse. That hoarse sound I seemed to get when infatuated. It felt more than that. But that was crazy.

"On that note, I better get back at it. It's going to be another day like yesterday. But at least we close early.

Looking forward to tonight."

"Me, too." I started to separate coffee filters.

"What are you going to do about a guest?"

"I don't know. I still have time?" I said but didn't mean it.

"I could ditch Gina?" He raised his eyebrows.

"I'll figure something out." I paused and turned to him. "I finally met Harry." I thought of his casualness, his lightness like Joe, but then his oppositional stance at the bookstore, facing Mr. Brooks.

"Hmmm."

"What?"

"He's better looking than me. I'm going to have to step it up. Maybe I should shave. I'm hiding this face."

"No, don't do that!"

"No? You like the beard, huh? Remind you of Santa, does it? You little minx."

"Okay. Go on, you nut job." I smiled, thinking of Mags. She had wanted to submit the name for a red lipstick to Revlon—*Sleeping with Santa.*

As I got ready for the rush, it hit me that my days were numbered at the diner. I was scheduled another week until New Year's Eve. Even though I was enjoying every minute, I made a note to enjoy every second. My gaze swept every corner, every table, every light bouncing around. I moved to the window and looked out at the snowy street. I peered under the lamppost for a hint of our angels of the morning before, but they'd already been more than dusted over with fresh snow. I stared into the memory and enjoyed the impression in my mind, in my heart. It was more than enough… I was completely transported. A thud abruptly ripped away the vision. A snowball smacked straight into the glass in line with my face, which was nearly pressed against the window. I yelped and jumped back. Then I heard, "Ho, ho, ho," and laughter from outside.

"Mr. Brooks," I screamed at him as I opened the door. "You trying to give me a heart attack on Christmas Eve? It's not Halloween." I smiled at him despite my racing heart.

"Sorry, Ali." He shook his head and put his hand on his stomach as he continued to laugh. "Sorry I'm laughing. Don't know what I was thinking. Ho, ho, ho."

"What's with the ho, ho, ho's?" I gave him a narrowed look but couldn't land it. I giggled with him. "That's not a very Santa-like thing to do, is it?"

"You were miles away. You okay?" He bit the corner of his lower lip, more like a little chew I had noticed him doing the last few times we spoke. A nervous tic or something.

"Yes. I was in a good place."

"Sorry, then." But he seemed relieved.

"No, no. It had to be done. Maybe not in that way, but…" I smiled.

"Wow, sure smells good in here. Like Christmas. Joe makes the diner an even better place to be today."

"Yeah, I love it." I paused and took a deep inhale before getting Mr. Brooks' tea. I wanted to absorb everything with every sense—I wanted to take a bite. *A Bite of Christmas. Winter bites my fingers…* I stopped. I wasn't going anywhere with songwriting. But was I ready for a bite? I had started to nibble on Christmas.

"Yes, there's a lot of love here, that's for sure," Mr. Brooks said as he eased into his booth.

I looked over at him. He didn't look at me. Did he know? Was it obvious, or had he seen Joe and I together in a kiss? Maybe he was simply feeling that Christmas spirit. I tried for a poker face and brought over his tea.

"You're more than jolly, today," I said. I flashed to the image of Harry at the bookstore. He didn't seem to be nursing a hangover from that.

"If you can't be merry today, then when? And I know from experience I get a cookie after breakfast." He laughed.

"You can have a plate of cookies, if you want."

"Are you hinting that I'm Santa?" He tapped his non-existent belly.

"There *is* something about you that reminds me of the big guy. But it's not your belly, that's for sure." I smiled, thinking of my dad. I felt a pang in the gut, but let it go. I wanted to be in the diner. To be right here. "So, what will you have for your Christmas Eve breakfast?"

"Sugar all the way, today. I will have those candy cane pancakes."

"Candy cane pancakes?"

"Joe didn't make them?"

"Oh, I don't know."

"He always does." Mr. Brooks looked over at the kitchen as though he was trying to see through the wall.

"I'll check it out."

"If not, I will have whatever pancakes he made today."

"You got it." I hoped Joe had made them. What would they be like? Shaped like candy canes or maybe crushed candy canes in the batter? You'd need a sweet tooth for those.

Neither.

When I walked into the kitchen, Joe was plating a beautiful stack of pancakes with red and white swirls. They were beautiful.

"You made them!" I rushed over and peered through

the pass-through to get a better look.

"Huh?"

"I didn't know about the candy cane pancakes."

"No?" Joe smiled as he topped the stack with crushed candy canes. "They *are* famous."

"I can see why."

"I can't imagine, to be honest. That's a lot of sugar." He laughed and put them under the heat lamps.

I stared at them.

"He did want them, right?"

"He sure did."

"You look like *you* want some? I have connections, you know."

I shook my head. "Thanks. But, I have to agree. Too sweet for me, but so perfectly Christmassy. Thanks." I slid the plate down and kept looking at them.

"You sure?"

I looked up into Joe's eyes. I wasn't sure of anything. I swallowed as I didn't think I could speak. "Uh-huh." I blushed and turned away.

"Hey," Joe called.

I turned. He was moving around the pass-through. "Have a good day." He leaned down and kissed me slowly.

I looked up at him. I couldn't even say 'have a good day.'

"It will be my last chance until tonight to see you."

I looked at him funny.

"Really see you, that is. It's going to get busy. Just wanted one more kiss." He gave me another. "Okay, that's it."

I gave him a quick kiss. "It is hard to have just one of those kisses."

"A kiss is a kiss, no?"

"No."

"Agreed." He went back to the grill. "Okay, you better leave me here, or I will forget what I am doing. What am I doing?"

Mr. Brooks' face lit up when he saw me, saw the pancakes. "You know I'm never disappointed when I'm here," he said. His hands moved up to reach for the plate, but he put them back down and watched as I set it on the table.

"They *are* pretty," I said.

"And they're wretched." He rubbed his hands. "Wonderfully wretched."

I smiled. I thought of my uncle and of Gina, who had said wretched in that same way about her pipe smoking.

"Do you really like them, or just the look of them?"

"Hmmm. I like the look of them, the thought of them, the smell of them. And it's Christmas." He leaned closer to me and put his hand beside his mouth, feigning a whisper. "And I kind of *do* like them."

"Good. It's very Santa-like that you like them."

"Ho, ho, ho."

"Okay, okay." I waved at him and left him with his pancakes.

"We still on for *The Night Before Christmas* at the bookstore at three today?"

"For sure. Looking forward to it."

The door jingled. In came Boston. And then Adam. And then it jingled all the way until after 1:00 p.m. I'd never known busy until then. As busy as it was, I enjoyed the wonderful Christmas moments of a diner on Christmas Eve. The energy of those taking a break from the last-minute shopping, mingled with those who like being caught up in that energy, leaving a few last-minute items on purpose to bring them down to Main Street. I thought fondly of my dad. He was one of those. He used to leave the house around 3:00 p.m. every Christmas Eve with a sparkle in his eye. Would he do that this year? But for whom? I hated to think of him without that sparkle. At least he wouldn't be alone. I made sure he had said yes to the invitation to the Stewarts' for Christmas Eve and Day. The Stewarts had been in our lives since I could remember. In and out always because of our moves—but they stuck. They were our extended family by choice.

At 1:30 p.m., I went and flipped the sign on the front door to closed. The diner was still half full, but all were served and happy. I looked around. Everyone did seem happy. It *was* the happiest place to be.

"What are you smiling about?" Joe said as he poured a coffee. He passed the mug to me and then poured another for himself.

"This place." I stirred cream into my coffee and then leaned back against the counter. "It's a happy place."

Joe looked around and then back at me, his shoulder against mine. "It is." He nudged my elbow a few times.

"I still don't have a guest."

"Just say the word. I'll dump Gina."

"That's not very Christmassy." I laughed. "Gina told me not to worry. I had enough time. It's just I had a one-track mind."

"I hear you." Joe put his arm around me for a moment but didn't linger. We still had guests.

I pulled away from him to clear some plates from tables. I topped up a few coffees, but most people wanted to get moving, get in their final stops before settling in with family and friends. I couldn't wait to snuggle in at Gina's. That morning when I left, the kitchen was full of baked goods. Tins piled on tins, pies on cast-iron tiers, loaves covered with tea cloths on the counter and table. She wasn't up before I left, but she must have stayed up until the wee hours, the nighthawk that she was. It smelled like cinnamon, pastry, and baked bread. And a hint of her pipe, I think. Maybe she'd snuck an extra puff between pastries. I'd have to tell that pun to Gina, to watch her face crumple in a cringe.

"You go ahead," Joe called to me as I cleared one of the last tables.

"You sure?" I looked around. I didn't have much left to do, and it was twenty minutes to three. I had promised Mr. Brooks I'd be there.

"For sure."

I walked over to Joe, and he pulled me into the kitchen. "Just leave me with a kiss."

It *was* a kiss. I don't remember my path to the bookstore. Just a blur of Christmas lights.

Every candle was lit at Mr. Brooks' shop. I looked around in awe at the magical landscape. My gaze gathered the radiance, lifting to the bookcases that seemed to hold space. A soft dance of wicks flickered from various heights.

"Ali," Mr. Brooks called over the little heads that hovered around the table with the cookies—the torturous centerpiece they wanted to touch.

"Hello! It's so beautiful."

Mr. Brooks looked around satisfied, and extended one of his arms to welcome me further in. The door jingled behind me.

"Welcome, folks. Come on in." Mr. Brooks' eyes sparkled as he walked toward the door to greet a young mother and her two girls.

Just after 3:00 p.m., the circle was close to full. I went to the front door and peeked out to make sure there were no stragglers. I gave a thumbs-up to Mr. Brooks, and he settled into a chair. The young ones squirmed as they eyed the cookies Mr. Brooks had brought from the diner. I made an executive decision and handed them out on the snowflake napkins. Mr. Brooks winked at me, and everyone seemed happier and quieter. I watched Mr. Brooks in his element, and the children, who were mesmerized by him, the bookstore, the story, and the anticipation of the evening ahead, waiting for Santa. I shuttered my eyes. I listened, remembering my own childhood when Gramps or my dad had read *The Night Before Christmas* by the fire. I was sitting from an ideal vantage point, glimpsing every angle, with the bonus of the snowy street outside, the light starting to dim under the heavy snow of the afternoon. The lampposts glowed in the fading daylight, illuminating the seemingly endless falling snow. Christmas-perfect. I wished I could have taken out my phone for a picture. I would never have captured all that moment, anyway. So, I enjoyed it and knew I'd always have it framed in my mind. The picturesque scene of a Christmas card I could be satisfied sending to just myself.

Then someone walked into the card. I could just see their silhouette slow to linger in front of the bookstore. I sat up straighter in my chair. Was it her? Sarah? No. A Christmas Eve mirage, precipitated by wishful thinking and the propensity to believe in the magic of Christmas. It was my turn to squirm. Luckily, the next thing I heard was: "And to all a good night."

The parents clapped, and the kids started to move. Mr. Brooks looked at me funny. I clapped and went to him. "That was wonderful, thank you." But I had my eye on the window.

"What's up with you?" He followed my gaze. "Who's that out there?" He squinted his Santa-eyes.

"I think it's Sarah." I started toward the door.

I could feel my heart hammer in my throat. I wondered if Sarah was okay. Was she supposed to be out of the hospital? What was she doing here? What would I say to her? Despite the thump in my ears, I didn't hesitate, I opened the door.

"Sarah?" I questioned. It was easier to throw a name at someone when you put a question mark at the end. A copout, but it worked.

She stared at me and shifted. I thought of a little greyhound, fussy with the cold snow under foot.

"Are you okay?" I asked but hung with the door as a shield—part coward, part not wanting to spook her.

"I followed you," she said.

"You followed me?" I let the door go behind me and hugged my arms around me.

"From the diner."

"Oh?" The thump was full out in my ears. My face burned, but my hands were ice right away.

"You remind me of her." Her eyes darted into the bookstore, and she shifted to the left, as though moving out of sight.

"I remind you of her?" My mind started to spin. "Who?" *Was* she okay?

"Nathalie."

My cheeks were wet from the snow, but they were still warm. I felt kind of sick. For some reason, it made me uneasy. It was weird to hear Sarah say her name.

"I can see your heart," she said.

I'd never heard anyone say that. "Oh?" I think I

could hear me say it but didn't know if Sarah could hear me.

"I just wanted to thank you," she continued.

I didn't know what to say.

She turned and looked down the street.

We both stared down Main. It was so quiet. It was as though we were in a vacuum.

I heard her move.

I didn't want to lose her. "Wait." My voice sounded loud against the snow. It hung on the trees, on the banks around us. "Are you okay?"

She nodded.

"Would you like to come with me…for Christmas Eve at Gina's?" I blurted out. I wanted her to be there. But my reason was twofold—I wanted to see how Harry's girlfriend reacted to her after what Harry had said. "We are having a get-together there…a few people…" I started to turn my shoulder to point and tell her Mr. Brooks would be there. But I heard her boots, restless on the snow.

She paused again and smiled, sadly. She shook her head. "I'm okay," she said. She said it as though she wanted to comfort me. She fully turned and started to make her way through the snow. "Merry Christmas," she said. She didn't turn back.

I wiggled my toes. I knew she was going, and I couldn't stop her. "Merry Christmas," I called.

"Merry Christmas," someone called with cheer from behind me.

I jumped. "Merry Christmas," I shot back, a knee-jerk reaction. My heart felt exposed, I imagined *I* could see it—a red blur bouncing away from me into the white. I couldn't imagine Sarah had anything to do with Nathalie…

Parents and children piled out of the bookstore, lots of 'Merry Christmases.'

I held the door and smiled down at the gingerbread-kissed faces. Their anticipation, joy, bringing me back. "I hear Santa's going to be in town a little earlier this evening. Supposedly Blitzen's in top form this year. He recently won the Irondeer in Norway." Wide eyes looked up at me. "It's the race of all races for reindeer."

"Nice touch," Mr. Brooks said as he flipped the closed sign on the door. But he looked to the right up Main before turning to me.

"My grandfather always had some update or news on Santa and his reindeer. I craved the moment he offered some of that on Christmas Eve."

"I liked the Irondeer, very cute."

"Yeah." I laughed. "It just came to me."

"Have time for a hot chocolate?"

"Definitely. I want a moment to bask in this." I looked around at the beautiful bookstore. "These are my favorite Christmas moments. In the quiet. In the magic." All the Christmas that had encompassed me since I moved into Gina's, me subtly deflecting, now settled. I let it stick, bond as the snow hugged the trees, nudged up against the windows, like white batts of cotton.

"Me, too," Mr. Brooks said as he started preparing our mugs. But his back looked stiff. I didn't feel his 'me too.' "Just have a seat, Ali. I want you to have that moment."

Despite that little tug of something from Mr. Brooks, I let it go. I eased into the sofa and blurred my vision, taking in the candlelight, the snow falling outside the storefront window. It was the moment. There's always one on Christmas Eve. I felt a blanket of peace swaddle me. I felt love. Love for Gina, love for Joe, Mr.

Brooks, and love for Sarah, even—an indistinct love I wanted to form, to latch onto, to hold her in.

Mr. Brooks eased down beside me and set my mug on the table. We sat in the moment. It was right in the quiet. It felt like you could hear the snow spiraling down, the hum of the lamppost out front.

"Thank you." I finally broke the silence. I picked up my mug and lifted it to him.

"Thank you." He tipped his mug against mine. After a few sips, he set down his mug and leaned back. "So, it was Sarah earlier?"

"Yeah. I wanted her to come to Gina's. I really wanted her to be there."

"I know." He tapped my knee.

"I wish she was at least inside."

"I know. Me, too."

There was a thud.

My head jerked toward Mr. Brooks. We didn't move for a second.

He stood, but he didn't seem alarmed. And when I tentatively snugged in behind him, he didn't stop me.

"Sounds like something fell," he said as he flipped on a light by his desk.

As casual as Mr. Brooks was, I felt too warm, and my heart broke through the silence of the bookstore.

He leaned down to pick up a book.

I caught the title before he pulled it away from me and placed it behind the desk. *Reviving Ophelia.* My mind raced to Hamlet. It zipped right there, like a shock from a light switch. The drowning of Ophelia…of Nathalie. References to Ophelia bumped through my mind—love, suicide, mental instability. I smelled the smoke of a snuffed candle.

"Did somebody order that?" I asked. I wanted to

head home, walk back into Christmas. But something ran through me. He caught me looking over the counter where he had placed the book.

"No," he said quickly, then paused. "I haven't seen this since she left it here. And then I couldn't find it. Huh." He looked stunned, but at the same time, he looked like he wanted to stand in front of it, hide it from me?

"Who?"

"Nathalie."

"It was her book?"

He looked at me, confused. "I think so." He looked around again. "It was a few days before…" He frowned. "She dropped by for a little visit. She didn't seem herself." His eyes glistened.

"I'm sorry." I put my hand on his shoulder. I wanted to say something to comfort him but didn't have anything. But I wanted the book. I wanted a look at it…if it had been Nathalie's, I wanted a look.

"It was on the counter here." He tapped his hand on the wood. "I noticed it after she left and then I didn't see her. And then I couldn't find it. I forgot all about it."

"Yeah… I forgot about a key," I said.

His eyes lifted. "What's that?" He still seemed muddled in remembrance and disbelief at finding the book after all this time. But then his stance shifted, his shoulder pulled back. "A key?"

I told him about the box in the desk. I watched his face pull tight. He seemed to care, and that's what I cared about. I cared about reactions. I put it away, but it was stored.

"What are you doing this evening?" I wrenched the conversation in a different direction.

He frowned. "I usually have a quiet night, linger

here, a long walk, take in all the Christmas lights, then home, watch *It's a Wonderful Life*."

I had no guest. "Would you like to come to Gina's tonight?"

"Still, no guest?" He smiled.

"No. I'd love you to come. I just thought… I thought you might have other plans…" What pounded in my head was Gina might not want him there. But no, Gina would be fine with anyone who didn't have somewhere to go. Maybe she'd be happy.

He crossed his arms and put one of his hands under his chin. Perhaps he was looking forward to his evening alone. "Well, okay, then." He rubbed his arm—the one I had noticed the scar on. "I think it's time." Then he tapped both of my shoulders. "I'd love to come. I know the company will be good…and the food…that might even be better." He laughed and then sobered. "It's funny I hadn't seen this. Where did it come from? It had to fall off here?" He tapped his hand on his desk. "But it wasn't here."

I hadn't forgotten that. It was a hard one to dismiss. I shrugged. I didn't want to weigh in on the possibility of the supernatural. "I guess you were meant to find it." I conceded. But why would he be meant to find that? I imagined Dickens would have liked this little scenario.

I had never seen Mr. Brooks so taken aback. But he had told me about his late wife turning on lights beside his bed. Tapping him on the shoulder, even, I think he had said. But a simple misplaced book? That was easier to dismiss. I didn't like the drowning reference, though. I wanted to leave to get back to Christmas. But I wanted the book.

"Maybe she knew." His voice was so empty but so heavy.

The books seemed to catch his words and hold onto them, squeezing them into their spines. I straightened mine.

That could only mean one thing, and I didn't like the thought of that. It wasn't an accident.

"Maybe she had meant it, maybe she did jump?" He pulled at my thoughts. I felt like he was testing me.

"Mr. Brooks…" I wanted to stop him. I wanted to see his Santa-eyes, hear his ho, ho, ho.

"I'm sorry, Ali. It's Christmas Eve. Sorry." He tapped his desk. "Go ahead. I have a few things to do here."

"Is there anything I can help you out with? I can wait and walk over with you, if you like?"

"No, but thanks. You go on ahead. It's still a little early."

He handed me my coat.

I paused. "Do you mind if I take that book. Borrow it off you?"

"Well…why would you want the book?" He put his hand to his throat. That meant he was uncomfortable. That's an easy read. But why? He was close to Nathalie. Maybe I asked too many questions.

"I don't know. It's odd Nathalie would have that book. I wouldn't mind taking a closer look at it." I wanted to show it to Jenna as well. I was meeting her at Kaffee Brik. She knew Nathalie when she felt guilty about her sister drowning. How deep was that?

"Okay." He handed it over to me. Like evidence, I thought. I hoped. "When I see you at Gina's I will have the Christmas spirit with me. Promise." He smiled.

I put the book in my backpack then stepped toward him and hugged him. I got a 'ho ho' out of him.

I pushed out against the snow and looked down

Main. It was like stepping into Narnia. Always a winter wonderland, but Christmas *had* come. I paused, looking in the direction Sarah had taken. I squinted into the white, hoping to see her. I turned the other way. It was Christmas Eve. And there was still time.

I made my way through the heavy snow to the Church Street market I had been avoiding. I started to lean into Christmas. The heavy snow, more than a constant—it held the town in its embrace. Oftentimes, it felt like night was halfway there by 3:30 p.m. I walked in its hold and was pulled into the scene and time stood still when I turned onto Church and saw all the lights, stringing across the street, on the rooflines and windows of the shops, on the magnificent tree.

I didn't need to lean, it completely took me in as I strolled along. A few stragglers laden with bags, called Merry Christmas as they hopefully left their last store. A last guest for some of the owners as I watched closed signs flip over, lights dim. A final look out into the snow before a blind pulled down, anticipation for a day off, at least one day at home for everyone. Maybe this was why my dad did this every year, got out in the last minute of it all…maybe it was his moment.

I thought of everyone in their homes, tucked in for Christmas. I thought of Gina and her embrace, her house that took you in. And then I thought of Sarah and my heart expanded, I imagined it traveling the streets, nudging up alongside her—I sent it out there with all I could muster. With all my loved ones, old and new, gathered with me in my mind's eye, in my heart, I turned and toured with them slowly the other way, taking in the storefronts on the other side of the street.

Back on Main, a few of the shops were still open. At Kaffee Brik, Jenna smiled and waved at me through the window.

"Hey!" I scanned the café, waved at my hot chocolate maker under the cuckoo clock.

We sat in our little mini-booth with our hot chocolates and chatted about her past few days, the size of Graham's parents' place and her need for places like this, about the night ahead, but there was something beneath her smiles and laughs. I could feel her leading me somewhere, but I didn't mind, I had mounds of whipped cream and insatiable interest in Nathalie.

Chapter Twelve
Jenna

Before Nathalie disappeared, she went away for a while. I overheard my mom on the phone talking to the neighborhood gossip, Mrs. Roberts. I didn't like when my mom was on the phone with her—there was always a sigh before she answered when she saw 'incoming Roberts' scroll across the screen, then she jittered a lot through the conversation, twisting one leg over the other, scribbling random words or arrows in deep ink, and then made a lot of noise with the pots and pans when she hung up. One time, I picked up the pad and saw she had almost torn through the page with the word "HELP." I didn't understand why my mom put up with the gossip, but as I got older, I understood, it was hard to tell people to mind their own business, and sometimes hard not to get into the business, too. I was watching TV in the living room, and she was in the kitchen, quiet still, but bobbing her leg rapidly, crossed over her other one. The volume had been down when I turned on the TV, so I kept it low when I heard my mom say 'Mrs. Howard' and 'Nathalie.' I pulled out snippets and then asked my mom about it after she cracked a few pots against the stove and closed a few cupboards too hard.

"What's up Jenna-bug?" my mom asked, her usual smile starting to push away the fatigue, but there was another layer of real fatigue beneath, not just from other people's words.

I leaned on the counter. I picked up the pad and looked at her arrows and what looked like a monkey with a banana she had doodled. My mom couldn't draw, but Mrs. Roberts seemed to bring out some form or need of artistic release. Mom pulled the pad away from me, rolled her eyes, and whipped it into the drawer. "Nathalie's going away for six weeks." She put her hand on my shoulder and turned me toward the kitchen nook. I found it hard to look at my mom as she talked about addiction and drugs with Nathalie's name tight in her throat. Heat started to build under my sweater, sweat dripped down my sides. I felt as though I'd been cornered at a table in an adult conversation—I didn't want to picture the treatment center and Nathalie alone in her skinny tights or would they put her in a hospital gown?

She was only back for maybe a few weeks before her picture started to appear everywhere. I saw her once leaving the community center. I overheard my dad saying something about a meeting held there for people like Nathalie. I hated that he said people like Nathalie, she was my best friend. She was still thin, but it looked like there was more of her or something, maybe thicker hair. She wasn't wearing a short skirt or smoking a cigarette. I didn't speak to her, I think she saw me, but she didn't even pause. My mom said that Mrs. Howard said she was better and on the right track, but it'd take some time. I had hoped we could get back to giggling into the morning, eating salt and vinegar chips from the bag until our lips swelled. But then she was gone.

We both stared into our cups for a moment and looked up at the same time. "Sorry," I said, flat like the cream spreading to the edges in my mug. "From what I've heard from Gina, it seems she was happy?" I scrunched my nose and lifted my shoulders. "But it's weird…"

"It is."

I looked at her and paused. "Do you think she jumped?"

"Not for a second."

I wasn't expecting her to be so sure. So, then what? She fell? I waited on her for a moment to see if she would continue. "I've been doing a little digging," I said and scanned the coffee shop.

The bird shot out of the cuckoo clock and my shoulders jerked back. We waited out another three cuckoo-cuckoos.

"I found out she was a sponsor for addicts." I looked into my mug, pushed it aside. "Or addict…I don't know how it works." I shrugged. "I went down to the center and spoke to some people about her. From what everyone says, Gina, Mr. Brooks…it seems she was happy enough."

Jenna shook her head. "Yeah. Doesn't make sense. She had to have fallen in… I don't know why they think she jumped."

I thought of Mia. Nathalie telling her she had pushed

her into the river…the book *Reviving Ophelia* that had fallen at Mr. Brooks' bookstore… I thought of her continued unrest… I shook my head.

"What is it?" Jenna asked. She reached her hand out and put her hand over mine. I thought of the game on the Price Is Right—that shell game. I had a letter under one hand…a book under another. I wasn't going to win, was I? I needed some more evidence. You need hard evidence to open a closed case.

"Go ahead. What are you thinking? It's obvious your mind's spinning." She sat back, as though bracing herself in the booth.

"I need a little favor tonight."

I pictured the death card, the justice card, and then I imagined my own deck. I flipped up a picture of Sarah, *snap*, the woman under the stairs who went to Gina's for the reading, *snap*, and then a blank face, the wild card… Harry's girlfriend—the name without a face… Olivia, *snap*.

Chapter Thirteen

I arrived at Gina's and paused on the stone steps, reflecting back to a week earlier when I had hesitated on those steps. I wanted to shake off the new uncertainty I felt about a lot of things. I wanted to land as a guest—experience that first burst of the magic of the house, of Gina. I giggled through a puffy cloud, thinking of her pipe. Would she have a puff with all her other guests? I felt a whirl of happiness pulse up through me to the crown of my head as I pushed against the front door.

"Hello, Gina," I called.

"Happy Christmas Eve, Ali," Gina called back. I could feel her energy move down the hallway to greet me.

I looked at her apron. "Still cooking? Where are you putting it? The kitchen was magnificent this morning."

She laughed. "I can't stop myself this time of year." She turned her back to me and touched the back of her neck. "Is there an off switch? I always remember one more thing, from my mother, my grandmother, or an aunt. So many recipes compiled in one family. Thank goodness it's Christmas Eve. I'd have to rent a storage locker."

"What can I do?" I followed her down the hallway and noted she had a beautiful red velvet dress underneath her apron. Good. I could wear my white turtleneck dress. It was my favorite holiday outfit. Another cashmere from my dad. I wouldn't feel overdressed. I smiled, thinking of my dad. He was such a jeans and sweater dude, but he had great taste. Always buying me the latest fashion. I would take a few minutes to call him before the guests arrived.

"Not much left to do, Sweetie. Why don't you get ready for the evening and then maybe light the candles and check on the fire?"

My heart swelled at her calling me sweetie. It had come out so naturally. I felt Gina's love, and mine soared.

"Thank you, Gina." I stood close to her, like a puppy waiting for affection.

She wrapped her arms around me. "For what?"

"For this. For that. For everything. For you."

"Ditto, my dear. It's such a pleasure. I feel like you've been here for years. You are a snuggly fit."

I did feel a snuggly fit here.

"Okay, I will be a few moments. I am going to try calling my dad."

"And your mom?"

I paused and felt an ache in my chest. I still had that pang of abandonment rise up and sting my heart when I thought of her. She had wanted the divorce. She had met another man. She had left town. But it was Christmas. "And my mom."

"Good stuff." She winked at me.

As I walked up the stairs, I started to hear faint tinny music. It sounded like it was coming from Nathalie's room. But the room to the left was dark. My eyes locked on the entrance. My heart's heavy beats veiled the music. I wanted to dismiss, ignore, move on, but I couldn't. It was always that way. Along with everyone else, I scoffed at movies when someone searched out the nightmare they were alone in the house with. But I wasn't alone in the house. I pictured Gina in the kitchen below. I flipped on the light in a quick sweep, like ripping off a Band-Aid.

The source of the music was a little pink jewelry box. I had had a similar one as a child. The lid was open, and a tiny dancer twirled with jerky motions to the music. I stared into the open box, and my hand trembled over the lid, wanting to stop the reedy sound. I looked around the room, feeling conspicuous, intrusive. I tapped the lid down, and it made a louder noise than I imagined. I jumped and quickly made my exit, hitting the light, and not looking back. I thought of Mags. She would take it as a sign, a message, or something. Mags was into that crap. One summer she had been really into it. I remembered her saying spirits hung around when they had something they couldn't let go of or something to say. I shuddered and moved into the bathroom to wash up.

I heard a voice outside the bathroom door. *Please no.* I didn't want that. I didn't summon that…anything…anyone. I thought Mags said you have to attract these things. Supposedly they don't sneak up on you, you have to wave them in... It wasn't fair play. But then I heard a familiar voice. I swept the door open for confirmation. Kiki…and Harry. He *was* cute. It was only my third time meeting him. I flashed to the image of him at the bookstore.

"Oh. Hi," I said with relief.

Harry moved toward me. "Hey, Al." He pretended to push ahead of Kiki but stepped back and swept his arm into the bathroom.

Kiki brushed past me. "Hi, Al." She grinned, and her dark eyes bounced to Harry before she closed the door.

Harry put a hand on the door and pretended to bang on it. "I guess it's a blessing we're all never here at the same time."

"Right." I didn't agree, though. I always thought it would be fun to have siblings, even if we had to compete for the bathroom. Caroline used to whine about her bathroom wait-times, but I always envied her.

I was happy to find my Christmas tree lights on earlier than usual. Whether it was Gina, Kiki, or a ghost, I didn't care…as long as it was just a light. A laugh bubbled. I went to the window and looked down onto Union. The peaceful landscape calmed my giddiness. The snowflakes sparkled under the lamppost. I ran my fingers along the drapes, now like a favored blanket. I turned and breathed a happy sigh into the cozy mantle of my space. I toured the familiar setting, took a seat on the bench, and called my dad.

"Hey, Gator!" He sounded out of breath.

"Dad." I felt winded suddenly when I heard his voice.

"I'm glad you caught me. I am just on my way out."

"Good and good."

He chuckled. "How are you doing, kiddo? Lots of

snow there, I hear.”

“I’m good, Dad. I miss you. Yeah, it hasn’t stopped snowing for a month it seems.”

“I know, you’re on the map every night. It’s big news.” He laughed again. I pictured him in the kitchen with his coat on, the yellow glow of the light underneath the hood fan turned on for the evening.

“So, what are you taking over to the Stewarts?” I asked.

“I have to bring something?”

“Ha, ha. Did you make your meatballs?”

“I did. I have to make an impression, so…” I heard what sounded like a plate move on the counter, probably him adjusting the tray, admiring his trophy meatballs.

“Oh, lucky them. Wish we could be together.”

“They’re that good, huh?”

“Get over yourself.” I laughed.

“So, what are you up to at the old draughty mausoleum this evening?”

“Dad. It’s the opposite. God, you’d be down to your skivvies. You’d love this place.”

“I know. Settle down.” He joked.

“We are having a Christmas Eve get-together here. Lots of guests. Well, not that many, but you should see all the food Gina made. I wish you were here, Dad.”

“Me, too, Honey. Next year for sure we’ll be together. We won’t do this again.”

“Well, I can hear the hurry in your voice. And I should get ready. Just wanted to say Merry Christmas.”

“Merry Christmas, Gator. Love you.”

“Love you too, Dad. Enjoy your evening. Snap, snap.”

He laughed. “Miss your gator-snap kisses.”

I savored the moment before calling my mom. I

heard the scrape of a shovel and leaned against the window to spot Harry clearing the path to the front door. He must have decided to tackle that before his shower. It was hard to keep it clear these days, these weeks, and in the moment—it was as though a snowmaker followed his route. My gazed moved across the street to four people lifting boots up high out of snow to get up a walkway. The front door opened, and light and smiles shone from the hosting family, including a little one jumping on her tippy toes in her Christmas dress. I thought of the stiff white cotton dress with printed candy canes I had when I was about four, the memory implanted from photos of that Christmas. My mom had secured candy canes in the high twists on our heads. My dad would have taken that picture, I could tell by the way my mom was smiling at the camera, at him. Who could imagine that one day that beam would recede and she would make smiley-faced pictures with someone else? But it was Christmas Eve, and I wasn't four, so it was time I let it go.

"Allison." My mom's voice caught.

"Mom." I was held in the same emotion.

"Oh, Sweetie. How are you? God, I miss you, especially today."

"Me, too. How are you? How's Colorado?"

"I'm fine. It's fine. I wouldn't do this again, though. I don't want us to be apart for Christmas ever again."

I wanted to say Dad had said the same thing, but I didn't want to open anything up that I didn't want her to defend. I just wanted my mom, my happy, loving mom. I wished she were here. "I agree. But it must be beautiful this time of year."

"It is. And you, I hear you're completely snowed-in. You must love it."

"Yeah. It reminds me of when I used to imagine walking around in Gran's snow globes."

My mom laughed. I could feel the emotion through the line. I could see her emerald eyes glisten at the thought of her mom, our Christmases all together. "She would love it too. So, what are you up to this Christmas Eve?"

"We're having a little get-together here." I could feel the lift in my voice as I spoke the words.

"Wonderful."

"And what about you?" I didn't say, 'you and Brad.'

"The same. Just staying at the place. We're having about a dozen guests or so."

"Nice."

"You're doing okay, Ali? The new place working out?"

I felt that tug on my throat, wanting her more in my life again. I had been so distant. But I was more than okay. "I'm doing really well, Mom. Just miss you. Can't wait to see you when you get back."

"Me, too, Honey, me, too."

"Well, I better get a move on, I don't have many jobs here, but I said I'd light the candles and stoke the fire. Just wanted to hear your voice. Merry Christmas, Mom."

"Merry Christmas, my angel."

I sat and savored that connection. All the awkwardness I had in mind had fallen away at the sound of her voice. I felt good, more than content with everything…and now a party. I didn't have any more time to linger. I moved quickly and changed, pausing by the mirror to straighten the seams and smoothed it down over my hips. It was a nice dress and so comfortable. I looked back at my room on the way out and smiled, and then returned to the tree and nabbed a candy cane for my hair—borrowing the memory, securing a bond in my heart with my mom across the miles.

I ran my hand down the wood banister, linking hands with the house, feeling the warmth reach up further as I paused on each landing. The soft beats of the Christmas music amplified as I made my way to the living room to attend the fire. Pops and crackles mingled with Frank Sinatra as I placed another log and poked the healthy flames. I added another for insurance, as the hearth had ample space to accommodate, and gave the logs another nudge to set the assembly. I crossed the foyer to the den to retrieve a taper to light the rest of the candles. I could smell Gina's pipe and wondered if she had come in earlier to have a little puff, but I only stayed a moment as I felt like an intruder in the space without Gina. I lit the three wicks in front of the window by her chair, and then did rounds in the living and dining room, lighting the ones that would last the evening, which were many of them—Gina had replenished most so they could linger the evening with the guests. The guests. I felt a surge of joy, thinking of Joe.

"Oh, where's my camera?" Gina beamed as she put down a ladle, adjusted the flame on the stove, and then moved toward me. "You look like a Christmas card." She held my arms.

"Thank you. I feel like I'm in one, so I wanted to fit in."

"Oh, you fit in."

"What can I do? All the candles are lit. The fire should be good for a while." I scanned the kitchen, intimidated by the ordered chaos.

Gina looked around and took inventory. "Hmmm, why don't you give us a little pour?" She grinned as she returned to the stove.

"I can do that." I didn't mind the lackey jobs, it allowed me to be in the moment with Gina. She was a pro in the kitchen, naturally in the moment with five things on the go. "What are we having?"

"Let's be festive and open that sparkling wine. Just a taste."

"Sounds perfect." I wasn't a huge fan, but I loved the idea. I loved champagne flutes. I opened the cupboard with all the glasses and reached up to retrieve the crystal stems. "These are magnificent. They look like antiques—Royal antiques."

"Almost." Gina laughed. "They were some great-great-great aunt's. Maybe give them a little rinse, they haven't been used in a while, maybe since the second great aunt." She laughed again. She had one of my favorite laughs.

I popped the cork, Gina jumped and then set down everything and stood close by my side with her glass raised. "A toast. To you, to Nathalie, to all our guests. I feel such gratitude to have you here, Ali."

My voice caught, for the third time that evening. "Gina. To you, with more gratitude than you will ever know." We tapped the crystal rims, and our eyes held, lingering a moment longer. I didn't want to break it but remembered my guest. "Gina?" My tone was hesitant, but I didn't wait. "I invited Mr. Brooks." Blah. There. I lifted my shoulders and looked up at her.

"You did, did you?" She tried to narrow her eyes at me, but it didn't take. "God, don't look so worried. What's going to happen—I'm going to rave like a lunatic or swoon like a monkey? What's your bet?"

Swoon like a monkey? "You're a nut." I laughed. I thought of Joe calling me sticky monkey. What was with the monkeys? But I liked being a monkey with Gina. *Hey, hey, we're the monkeys.*

When I set my glass back on the table, I noticed what looked like a poem. It was in Gina's handwriting.

"Did you write this, Gina?"

"Oh, it's nothing." She shrugged and went back to the stove, increasing the heat on one burner and lifting lids.

"May I?"

She looked back and scrunched her nose.

"Sorry," I said and looked away from the notepad. "I'm such a snoop." I thought of the box in the attic. Should I mention it? Not tonight.

"No, no, it's fine, Ali. I'm still working on it. It's a New Year's poem."

"I didn't know you wrote poetry."

"Well, some wouldn't call it that." She chuckled. "Go ahead. Let me know what you think. Still needs some work."

I hesitated only moment, more than curious about yet another aspect of Gina. I picked up the pad.

New Year's Eve ~~Minutes~~ Moments
Step into black garb—
Glittery ~~gowns~~ tights, shiny cuffs.
I sparkle tonight; you sparkle tonight
Champagne in flutes of crystal
Golden bubbles, pinky fizz
Step into the stretch—
Starry night, twinkly snow lights.
I sparkle tonight; you sparkle tonight
Dust shimmers on outdoor rinks—

Hockey sticks and figure eights.
Step into the fête—
Noisemakers, feathery masks.
I sparkle tonight; you sparkle
tonight
A crowd of ~~anticipation~~
expectations
Balloons nudge the net, mesh
swells
Step into the dance—
The floor bounces; we glide, leap;
I sparkle tonight; you sparkle
tonight
Brass shimmers, brags, horns
trumpet
Drums boom, hips bump, the room
sways
Step into midnight—
Hands held, second to second.
I sparkle tonight; you sparkle
tonight
Streamers soar, balloons descend
Another year and this kiss
Step into the moment.

"Gina." I held the pad. "I love it. I can feel it—it feels exactly like a New Year's moment. It's really pretty good. It's kind of like a song."

"Well." Gina scrunched her nose again and took another sip of the bubbles. "Just having a little fun."

"Do you have any more?"

She waved her hand. "Ah, a few, in a box somewhere."

"I'd love to read them sometime."

She looked at me with what seemed to be surprise. "Thank you."

The doorbell rang. It felt strange to hear it. I hadn't heard it since the day I arrived. It sounded exactly as one would imagine for such a grand house. I looked at my reflection in the window and smoothed my dress. Gina raised her sparkly eyes at me and grinned. "Well, go on."

"And you." I reached my arm to take her hand.

"Wait, wait." She pulled the loop of the apron over her head, and I saw her look to the window.

I raised my eyes back to her and slung my arm into hers. "You look beautiful, Gina."

She squeezed our linked arms together into her side. She could have been Mags. She could have been Caroline. Keeping us connected, she did her usual wide sweep of the front door to welcome the first guest.

"Ho, ho, ho," Mr. Brooks bellowed. "Merry Christmas." He was weighed down by bags and boxes.

We unlinked our arms to help him. "Lawrence. You know you weren't supposed to bring anything. People can't just give back. But come on in. What have you got here? So many things." She peeked into one of the bags.

"Merry Christmas, Mr. Brooks." Lawrence. Lawrence Brooks. I liked it, but he'd always be Mr. Brooks to me.

"Hey, Brooks," Joe called as he jogged up the walk. He had a few colored bags. "Gina. Ali."

"Joe." Gina embraced him. "So nice to see you."

"You too," he said as we relieved him of his parcels so he could get out of his coat. He shook it outside before handing it to me.

"You walked," I said. I wanted to hug the coat, even though it was cold. I wanted a part of him to hold, I couldn't wait for a moment alone.

"Always. I love walking in the snow. Making snow angels." He winked. "Especially in this neighborhood. Love all the lights." He put his hand on my shoulder and kissed my cheek.

I stared at him for a moment, then paused, looking out at Union Street before I closed the door, hoping the cool air would calm my fiery cheeks. I guess it didn't have to be a secret, we weren't in grade six.

"Wow, you look beautiful," he said as we moved in, following Gina and Mr. Brooks into the living room to set the gifts under the tree.

"Thank you. And you look handsome. I'm glad you kept the beard." He smelled good. Soapy and clean, not greasy and eggy—not that I minded his diner smell. He had a navy collared shirt with a subtle white embossed pattern. I had never seen him in anything but a white smock and a white skull cap. He looked more than handsome.

He rubbed my back and kept his hand there. "I love this dress. It's so soft, too."

"Thanks. Yeah, I kind of feel like I'm wearing pajamas—it's so comfortable."

He laughed. "Fits in with the comfort here." He scanned the room, the fire, the tree. "Looks great in here, Gina."

"It's perfect," Mr. Brooks said. "As always, Gina."

"Okay, okay." Gina waved her hands. "Enough niceties. I can't take it." But she laughed and extended an arm down the hallway. "Now come in. We just opened some sparkling wine. There's beer or something else, maybe?"

Joe moved under the tree and picked up one of his bags, one that was in brown paper. "Actually, I brought some beer. Mr. Brooks, would you like one?"

"Wouldn't say no to that, thanks."

It was snug in the kitchen with the four of us and all that food. I reached for two beer glasses as Joe and Mr. Brooks eyed the plates of cookies, tiers of pies, and the pots nudged together on the stove. Joe lifted one of the glasses I set on the kitchen table. "Nice glass." He held it up before snapping the tab on the can.

We felt a vibration, like a distant roll, the twitch of an earthquake, and then *thump, thump, thump*—there came the little devil. Kiki slid into the kitchen on her striped-sock feet as though she had missed something. She scanned the faces, then shot her arm out at Mr. Brooks, grabbing his hand. "Kiki," she said. It was like an announcement.

"Well, hello, my dear." Mr. Brooks chuckled and pumped her hand, connecting with the same enthusiasm. His sleeves were pushed up, and I glimpsed that scar. "Nice to meet you, Kiki. I am Lawrence Brooks."

"Nice meeting you, Brooks." She pointed at his arm and touched it. "OW! It hurt?"

"That's old." He looked at Gina. "But now a part of my life history." He winked at Gina.

I looked at Gina to gauge her reaction. What was with them? And that scar?

"Oksee Dokesee, good, Brooks." Kiki pulled us out of the moment.

We all laughed. For me, it was because she had shortened his name with such familiarity. I rubbed her back, but she didn't need comforting as she joined our laughs. I didn't miss the rise and sparkle in her dark eyes as she extended her hand to Joe. She was a little bit of a flirt, but it was like a kid flirting with your older brother. I had seen it with Caroline's older brother, especially that first summer he came home from university. Me included, but only in my mind.

"Nice to meet you, Kiki. I'm Joe."

"Nice meeting you, Joe. You Awli friend, yes?"

"Yes."

"She a good friend to have." This time Kiki laughed first. Her personality was showing more and more with her increased ease with the language.

"Okay you, what would you like? Something to drink?" I asked her, my hand on her arm.

She looked around at all the glasses, and then to Gina. "You have cider, still, Gina?"

"I do." Gina tapped the clay pot to check the temperature.

"Hello, guys." Harry joined us.

Mr. Brooks lit up and held Harry's shoulder as they shook hands. "Good to see you, Harry." Mr. Brooks reminded me of Gina in a way. To the point, get it out, but let it go. And Harry seemed to have let go of anything Mr. Brooks had said to him the other day about his girlfriend. I couldn't wait to meet her, though. I wasn't so good at letting go when I thought I should maybe hold onto something…

Joe handed Harry a beer.

"Thanks, Dude." He snapped the tab of the can and didn't take a glass.

"Okay, as cozy as this is, let's move it into the living room," Gina said as she handed Kiki the cider. Turning back to the stove, she made a few adjustments and then lifted her arms up as if to lead a herd out.

Although there was space enough for a dozen, the six of us sprawled out nicely in the living room. I looked at Harry. He was missing his guest. Olivia. I hoped she was still coming. I wanted to see if I picked up on that same vibe that shuddered through Mr. Brooks. I continued around the circle to Kiki. All she had to do was hand over the letter. I was counting on that. That's why she invited Jenna.

Since I had moved in, the energy of something building, something bubbling, had pulsed through the house. I thought of Mags. She would have relished it. She'd have arranged a séance or something. I felt a chill and looked at the fire—this was the perfect setting for witching someone, or whatever you want to call it, summoning, maybe? Kiki caught me, and I smiled wanly at her—she grinned. I put some more strength in my smile and focused on the conversation.

But I couldn't focus. I heard the laughter, and although it was a comfort, I couldn't help but tally up all the loose ends of the past week and a half. I scanned the shiny bags and stacked presents underneath the tree. I wanted to enjoy the warmth, the touch of Joe's hand, the feeling of magic on Christmas Eve, but Nathalie was there, she was more present than ever since I had arrived. The spirit of Christmas was receiving a nudge from a different spirit—a veritable ghost from Christmas past. Joe squeezed my knee, and I jumped.

"You okay?" he asked.

"I'm okay," I said, and he looked at me, raising his brow. I smiled and tapped his hand before getting up to stoke the fire that didn't need attention.

I absently poked the logs. They hissed back at me. I followed the movement of the flames, the shifting of the wood, ashes letting go like exhales from the breath of the fire. I stayed fixed until my face could no longer take the heat. The room felt cool as I turned to everyone, but my cheeks felt tight from the blaze, the residual heat lingering. What if my plan didn't work? I had to find out who wrote that suicide note because Nathalie didn't. The doorbell rang, and Harry jumped up. Gina stood, and then the rest of us moved to the foyer to meet Harry's guest.

I recognized her coat. And her gray eyes that look like stones. Gina hugged her after Harry pulled away. "Come in. Come in." Gina kept a crooked clip on her shoulder as she introduced the woman from under the stairs. Olivia.

Her hand was cold and limp. Her long fingers skimmed my wrist as her eyes held a little long for a first intro. Did she recognize me? But when she pulled her hood down and stepped under the light, her features softened. I looked at Gina for signs of anything. She smiled at me. She sensed auras, she wouldn't let a bad one into her house. I didn't truly believe in it, but I believed in Gina.

"Why don't we go ahead into the dining room, gang?" Gina opened and closed her hands like castanets, *crick, crack*, and led the parade down the hall.

Harry, Kiki, and I followed Gina into the kitchen, while Mr. Brooks, Joe, and Olivia headed to the table after Gina told them to go on in. We all grabbed a dish, while Gina managed the pots on the stove and transferred them to beautiful serving plates and bowls to bring out. The aromas wafted into my soul, that feeling of homecoming that often came over me in her kitchen, despite the uniqueness of most dishes. When I came back in, she handed me a pie, and I cocked my head.

"Have you never had a tourtière? I'm not putting out the dessert, my dear." She laughed. "It's a meat pie. Oh, you'll love it, I'm sure of it. It's one of my favorites."

I bent my face toward it to take in its wonderful aroma. "It smells like heaven. You have a lot of favorites, you know." I gave Gina a teasing look. "I can see why. I'm starting to have a lot of favorites, too."

"Glad to hear it. Oh, and you look cute beside Joe, he looks cute beside you," she whispered.

My cheeks still felt hot from the fire, so I didn't have to worry about redness showing—the blush easily stretched beneath.

"Okay, settle down," I said straight-faced, but then we both started to laugh, a laugh that I know for me was a release of a lot of things.

Gina had set the table for the seven of us, removing the other place settings to allow lots of elbow room, but its surface didn't have space for one dish to nudge past another dish—they were all snug together as close as they could be. Even though I was growing accustomed to Gina's presentation of food, it always amazed me, and it was beyond any of the other dinners I had enjoyed to date. The aromas were starting to become familiar—molasses and salty boiled potatoes filled the dining room. As Joe cut into one of the meat pies, I took in the cinnamon and cloves that wafted up from the steam. I reached for one of my favorites, the poutine râpée—a boiled dumpling made from grated and mashed potato with that tasty center of seasoned pork. At both ends of the table were baskets of crêpes râpée, which Gina had only served once since I had arrived. They were these wonderful buttery, crunchy pancake-looking treats, but there were made with potatoes, of course—if you could fit a potato into a recipe, it was there, and flour, onions, and salt, then cooked until golden and crisp. I wasn't the only one whose eyes did a continuous sweep of all the dishes, waiting patiently for a pass to keep filling our plates.

We all loaded every inch of our china. The conversation resumed at a more relaxed pace. I took a moment to look around. What a beautiful table in every way. I sighed a little too loudly. Mr. Brooks looked across at me and nodded as though agreeing with my thoughts and then lifted his glass.

"To Gina, for hosting such a beautiful meal, to opening your home, as you always do to lucky ones like us." He paused as we all held up our glasses, a wave of emotion seemed to run through all of us. "And to all who can't be here but are here with us in spirit."

Ching, ching, ching.

Olivia looked at me. I felt a prickle down my neck, and then when I looked at Mr. Brooks, he raised his brow as if questioning me. I shot my eyes down. I didn't want anyone to pick up on our exchange. Plus, he looked too rigid. Had he wanted me to see that book in his bookstore?

I shifted in my chair. I heard a click from the kitchen—it sounded like the latch of the door. I shot Kiki a look, but she hadn't flinched, nor had anyone else. My spine stiffened against the back of the chair. Maybe I was trying to hear things, now—attempting to create a scene. Each time there had been an occurrence, I had dismissed it as something tangible, some coincidence, including the unlocked door and footprints in the snow—I had thought Kiki with purposely planting tracks, building suspense for some reason or another, to entice me or I don't know. But now, it was me, hearing things, watching for something… Kiki had succeeded…or was I laying tracks of my own? I resisted the urge to go to the kitchen to check the lock on the door. But I didn't resist giving Gina a sidelong glance, wondering if she was 'sensing' anything.

I felt a hand on my arm and looked down at it, and then up into Gina's eyes. "Ali?"

I heard Joe's voice and Harry's, and the Christmas music from the living room, all nudging me to stay present. I looked back at Gina.

"Why don't we put the kettle on?" she asked.

She waved her hand over our plates—leave them—when I moved to pick them up.

She held my arms gently when we arrived in the kitchen. I stared at the latch on the back door.

"Ali?" Gina waved her hand in front of me, keeping one hand gripped to my arm. "You seem funny…I don't know…really out of it. What's wrong? Why are you staring at the door?"

"It's locked?" I asked. "I heard something." I touched her hand to free myself and moved to the door, cupping my hands to look into the yard.

"There's nothing there, my dear." She stood behind me and rubbed my arms. "You're spooked is all."

I rested my hand on the doorknob and turned it, it was locked. But the metal met me with warmth. Was that normal?

"Okay, dear. Too many movies, too much of Kiki creating the perfect ambiance. 'The suspense is terrible, I hope it will last.'" She laughed and rubbed my arms again.

I turned to her and studied her face.

"It's an Oscar Wilde quote." She hugged me and then shook me, as though shaking me out of a trance.

I pulled away and looked at her again. I put my hands on her arms, gently nudged her to the far end of the kitchen. "Gina," I whispered. "I'm getting a bad feeling about something."

She looked over my shoulder and twisted her mouth. "I can see that. What's going on in there?" She tapped my head.

I whispered muddled details, feelings that had started to come up about Mr. Brooks, the book. Sarah. "It's all coming together for me—if Nathalie didn't jump, was she pushed? Does someone here have something to do with it…the book felt like a plant to me." Was it Mr. Brooks who planted that? I flashed to him, coming in the diner after Sarah got hit by a car.

"What book? A plant?" Gina jerked back.

I told her about the book. "Maybe someone wants it to look like Nathalie felt guilty, Ophelia? Come on, that's too…maybe it wasn't really hers, her book…" I mouthed the last few words, hardly a whisper. I sounded insane, I knew it.

Gina rubbed her chin, placating me with a thoughtful pause. "I think I've seen that book somewhere, too." She shrugged. "I don't know where though…not with her, I don't think. Doesn't sound like a book she would have, to be honest. She didn't like to examine things. I'd only ever seen her read fiction. She liked fantasy and romance, even." She looked down as though searching for the book, stuffed into a bag, peeking out under other books. "Ophelia…That's Hamlet, right?"

"That's right."

"You know who loves Shakespeare? Harry. I think he has every one of his books in his room. I guess there was a time he had time to read." She laughed and hugged me. "Anyway, that's fantastic, absolutely wild, my dear." She pulled away and kept hold of my shoulders with a firm grip—it felt like she was trying to stop the nonsense. "I think you are looking for something…" She rubbed my shoulders and smiled, nodded, waiting for a nod back from me. "Come on, now. *Pauvre petite bête.*"

I finally nodded, and she cupped my chin. "Now,

let's get this mess out of the way." She started to lift some pots, move dishes around. We filled stubborn pans with hot soapy liquid, leaving them in the laundry tub to soak and put the kettle on.

"Be back in a minute…" I pointed upstairs. I needed a break, more than I had to go to the washroom. I needed to get away from the steam in the kitchen.

I was halfway up the first flight of stairs when I heard a hiss, the hiss of my name. I turned. It was Olivia. She started up the stairs, and I turned full toward her. "What's up?" I asked.

"I just wanted to talk to you for a second."

"Oh?"

"I hear you work on cold cases?"

I frowned at her. Harry. Gina must have mentioned it to Harry. It wasn't a secret. I looked into her flat gray eyes. I wondered if she was taking anything, but although her eyes looked too still or something, they were clear. "That's right." I couldn't imagine where she was going with that.

"Well, I saw you talking to Sarah earlier…outside the bookstore."

I looked down into the foyer. I wanted to get off the middle of the stairs. I felt trapped. I wanted to be the one asking her the questions. "You were there?"

"I was passing by. I was across the street when I saw you."

"And?" I wished she'd get to the point.

She paused. "Are you working on her case?"

"Her case?"

"Nathalie's."

Did she think I was a real cop or something? The case was closed. There was no case, according to the department. I started to shake my head. But then I thought I could lead her to believe I was 'working' on it by not denying it. "Why's that?"

"I think Sarah and Nathalie had a fight that night. I saw them together."

"You saw them by the lake?"

"Not there. But not far from there."

"What are you implying?" I went for it.

She looked startled. "Well…nothing. I just saw you talking to her…and I heard you worked on cases…so, I wanted to tell you what I knew is all."

"And what you know is that they had a fight?" I thought of Detective McCool—that's what he would have said.

"Well, yes." It was her turn to look down into the foyer.

"Because if you know something or knew something, you should have gone to the police." I lowered my voice on the last half of the sentence. She pulled the stone on her necklace. It looked like she might break it. "*Should* you be going to the police?"

"Well…I don't know." She let go of the stone around her neck and lowered her stone eyes. "I guess not."

I continued to stare at her. I thought of Gina saying she got a bad vibe from Sarah. Mr. Brooks, Gina, now Olivia had mentioned Sarah being the last one to have been with Nathalie. But the police would have spoken to her. There was obviously nothing there. Nothing to talk about, nothing to look at. "Well…" I said as I made a motion to take a step, trying to lead her to return to the other guests.

"I just miss her. Nathalie was so good to us."

"I'm sorry." I lifted my hand, but it didn't make it to Olivia's arm where I thought it should go, to squeeze, to pat, at least. But my mind was with Sarah. If only I could get close to her, to find out what happened that night… I'd like to know until what point she was with Nathalie. I finally touched Olivia's arm. "Are you okay to go back down?"

She nodded.

I pointed up to the bathroom. "Be down in a minute."

I took my time, waiting until Olivia had turned around the newel post to head back into the laughter from the dining room. I heard the chairs pull away as everyone moved to transfer back to the living room to wait. That's how it felt to me—like a waiting game. I wished I could go to the station and talk things over with Detective McCool. I overheard him mention to Harris he was working Christmas Eve, the 11:00 p.m. to 7:00 a.m. shift. I knew I didn't have anything, but I was curious what had happened that night, the night Nathalie drowned. How fast was the case closed? She jumped, she fell—how long did it take them to make that decision? If they had no reason to talk to Sarah then, I think they did a year later after what Olivia had said. But they would have spoken to anyone who knew her back then…

In the dim glow of the bathroom, I let the water run until it ran too hot. I pulled away, and my red hands sank into the towel on the counter. I smiled at the plush quilted Christmas trees. What would the house be like after Christmas? I couldn't imagine it without dishes of candies and soap balls, the clay pot of cider in the kitchen, and the tiers of Christmas cookies and loaves tucked in foil. But I was sure Gina would transform it into a winter elegance, and then the house would see Valentine's Day, and then spring—Easter, and autumn—Halloween. What about 4th of July, would she decorate for that? But I could just imagine Halloween! Then another Christmas on Union. I headed back down toward the warmth, the aromas, the laughter. I would like to do this again.

I was enjoying the company, the ambiance, but it was nearing ten o'clock, and I felt the anticipation for the arrival of Jenna and Graham. Finally, I heard a car slow near Gina's place and then tires resisting against snow. The thumps of car doors, followed by *crunch, crunch, crunch* up the walk. I stood up before the doorbell, and all eyes around the room looked at me. Obviously, I had been the only one following the path of our guests to the front door. But then Kiki jumped up, and then Gina and everyone stood and moved to welcome the incoming visitors.

We all offered our greetings, and I made introductions as Harry and Joe eased Jenna and Graham out of their coats. Jenna extended a beautiful tin to Gina.

"Thank you, Jenna," Gina said and took an immediate peek under the lid. "Oh, oh, oh, I don't think I can wait. What do you say, we head right into the dining room for dessert?"

Again, the table was full. This time with pies, so many varieties—some open-faced, displaying candied sugar and pecans, others browned with bubbled thick pastry, cakes, loaves, tiers of Christmas cookies, including the additional ones from Jenna. I had my eye on the sugar pie since I had first got a glimpse of it—a *tarte au sucre*, another Acadian tradition. Jenna and Graham fit in nicely with the group. The conversation was light and lively, full of laughter—Graham was hilarious. At one point during a wave of laughter that Kiki joined, more than likely only out of her good nature and propensity to laugh easily, she ducked out of the room. Okay, she was getting the letter. That tickle ran up my neck, it was as though we were engaged in one of those murder mystery games and a possible suspect left unnoticed. I had noticed. Olivia was quiet, and I often caught her looking at me with her flat stone eyes, like shards of dull metal. It was as though she was waiting for something. I got it. I was waiting, too.

We transferred back to the living room, this time a little snugger in the space. The room seemed darker, as though the lights had been dimmed. I needn't look to the fire for the culprit—it blazed onto the faces around the room, and it seemed like there were more candles than before we went for dessert. I looked over my shoulder out into the snow. It was a perfect Christmas Eve—I imagined it looked the same from the outside, just from a different angle. An indoor and outdoor version of the ideal Christmas card. Joe rubbed my back. "You're awfully quiet," he whispered.

I leaned into his shoulder and smiled. It was enough, I knew he was enjoying the evening. There was plenty of conversation going around, allowing me to escape into quiet reflection. Kiki was quiet, too. I studied her face, her eyes seemed active, like she was checking off a list around the room. Our eyes met, and then we both dropped our gaze to the candles on the coffee table in the middle of the room. They were new—there were two clustered together that hadn't been there before. I think she must have placed them there when she left the dining room earlier. She had dimmed the lights. I thought I heard that click from the kitchen again, but I also knew where my mind was right now—actively trawling for fantasy. Then there was an unfamiliar straining noise, like cables pulling, and then from the hallway, a chime echoed. I had never heard that grandfather clock sound.

It continued to toll eleven more times as we all seemed to fall into its trance. The hum continued to reverberate into the quiet that had taken hold of the room.

"Kiki," Gina said. "You turned the grandfather clock on." She gave her a teasing, scolding look. I guess Kiki had been gunning to turn it on by that look Gina gave her.

"The letter," Kiki said. She sounded as though she was in a trance. She stood, handed the letter to Jenna. She returned to her seat.

I looked around the circle, establishing a baseline for everyone's expression. I wanted to see a before and after.

Jenna paused and then stood. She walked over to me. "You read it, Ali." She dropped the envelope on my lap and turned away from me and stumbled. Graham caught her hand. I reached between the cushion and the armrest for the envelope. She turned back to me. "Okay," she whispered as though there had been a protest. "I'll read it." I handed it to her. She removed it from the envelope. Graham took the envelope for her as she unfolded the letter. She stared at it, then looked over the white page at the faces. "It's a suicide note." She paused. Took a sweep around the circle. "Dated just over a year ago. It's signed, Nathalie." She shook her head. "No. No, I don't believe it!"

I kept scanning the circle, pausing at each guest.

Jenna stared at the page as though trying to take the blur out of the words. Graham reached up and held her hand. She looked down and through him for a moment and then released his hand to hold both sides of the letter. I still felt the grandfather clock's presence—I felt as though I'd never release those vibrations from the stroke of midnight that Christmas Eve. Jenna made a sound—a 'clearing the throat' sound? We all focused on her, all conversation suspended, and a few held breaths.

"It's dated just over a year ago," she repeated, her voice shook with the paper. I kept a slow scan going. "Just before…" She looked around the room and then back to the letter. She had the look of searching, wanting to move ahead too quickly. She finally looked up. "It's…not her…" She dropped the letter, and it drifted to the floor, white in the firelight. Graham stood and brought Jenna to her seat.

It was so quiet. Just the sound of the fire whispering hiss-pops as its glow dwindled. A log moved, and there was a whistle and then a louder pop as it repositioned. We all turned and fixed on it to detach from Jenna. Did anyone move closer to the edge of their chairs? Who had stared longer at the letter on the floor? Jenna followed our attention to the fire, moving her gaze onto the flames. And then suddenly, she picked up the letter. She moved to the fire and threw it onto the smoldering ashes, but with a flare, the fire woke and took hold of the paper; it licked at the sides, and they crumpled inward. Holes appeared at the creases, expanded, and then it was gone. "It wasn't Nathalie," she said, her voice a little stronger.

I looked at Harry, whom I hadn't even thought of before... I looked at his stony girlfriend, then to Gina…Mr. Brooks. And finally, Kiki. Innocent Kiki in the perfect position…with Nathalie's things…how long had that letter been there, in her room? Did anyone look happy the letter was gone? Who still wanted it?

Graham moved to Jenna, but she held up her hand. He stepped back and eased onto the edge of his chair, his eyes stuck, face motionless, as if looking out from a cut-out board people stick their heads through for a picture. Jenna looked at Kiki with a look I didn't think Kiki could handle. "Where did you get that letter?" Jenna released the words through her jaw.

"In her room," Kiki said. "She meant you read it."

"No." Jenna shook her head. She looked back to the fire. "I shouldn't have thrown it…" She turned her back to us and stared into the flames. "It's not her writing." She kept her back to us. "I was angry. I know she felt guilty. I wanted to get rid of those words she might have said. But she didn't. It's not her suicide note." She turned to the room. "Who wrote that letter?"

Hiss…pop. There was no other sound.

I moved around the circle to Gina. She looked like she was waiting for something, not looking at anyone or anything. Then she spoke, "Why do you say that, Jenna?"

"It wasn't her handwriting."

"What do you mean?" Mr. Brooks sounded irritated. I didn't like him sounding like that, I liked his ho, ho, ho's. But maybe the ho ho's were a cover. An undercover ho, ho.

Jenna turned to Mr. Brooks. "I know her handwriting."

"Well…I suppose it could have changed since the last time you saw it, no?"

"No." She twisted back to the fire. "I shouldn't have done that…" She shook her head and looked at Mr. Brooks again. "And she always signed her name with a small 'n' when she wrote notes, letters."

"Well…" Mr. Brooks said and looked to the room for support.

"I suppose…she might have stopped doing that as an adult?" Gina said. "I don't think I've seen her do that."

"And…did you know…" Jenna's eyes flickered.

"…Nathalie spelled her name without an 'h'?" She lifted her sinking stare from Mr. Brooks and let it anchor slowly around the room at all the…suspects.

I rode alongside her watching everyone. I believed the suspect was in the room…or on the street with my mittens. But how grave was it—what was the intent of the letter? When was it written? Not a year ago. I know these letters can be red herrings…but it could be evidence. I looked at Kiki. She had found it…a usual suspect. She hadn't known Nathalie, though. She moved in after it happened. Maybe she had known her…No. God, no. It was strange her interest in Nathalie, in holding onto the letter as though she held the answer. Then again, I had become interested in Nathalie…but I was known to get into things I wanted to solve.

Both spellings of Nathalie floated across my mind: one with an 'h,' one without. Stupid jokes of Natalie Wood, without an 'h,' who didn't float popped into my head. There really was something wrong with me. Did anyone look like they were going to protest that 'h'? If someone in the room wrote that letter…they would want to protest… But they couldn't stand up to it, that would reveal their guilt. I looked for their guilt. I knew. I think I knew…

I heard crunching on the snow outside.

The doorbell rang.

We looked at one another but didn't hesitate. It felt like a march heading to the door, everyone wanting to break away from the accusations. It was as though, yes, this is expected, something else added, someone new brought onto the scene. That's how I felt, anyway.

When I opened the door, the last person I expected to see stood in her shaky boots, her thin tights, staring at me out of the frame of her blue bomber. I kept one hand on the door and ran my fingers against the ribs in the wallpaper on the other side of me. I focused on Harry as he stepped in and introduced Sarah. He was the only one who knew her, I think. Harry had been close with Nathalie and Sarah was linked to Nathalie. But then I felt a stiff shoulder next to me. I looked sideways at Olivia. Sarah looked away from her, her gaze shot down, but I noticed the recognition, the stiff exchange. Although fleeting, it was palpable, tight in the foyer.

I searched Mr. Brooks' expression. He had met her—sort of. I waited for Gina's 'Come in, come in,' but maybe she was dumfounded for the first time, or knew Sarah wouldn't stay, or was having one of her 'vibes.'

And then there were ten.

"I saw cars and all the lights were on, so I figured it was safe to…" She looked up at me and faltered. I nodded, but I didn't know what to do with her, I couldn't imagine her coming in and sitting around with this letter in the balance.

Gina moved into gear. "Of course, of course. Come in, please." She squeezed in to get at Sarah. "I'm Gina." She held out her hand. She was like Mr. Brooks—she seemed to hug people right away, with one look, one beat of her heart. "We have lots of food. What can we get you to drink?"

Sarah shook her head. "I just wanted to say Merry Christmas." She turned back to the door.

"Please stay, Sarah," Gina said.

She shook her head again. "I have to go, really." She looked at me, paused, and pushed open the door.

I hung between the cold and the warmth. I looked down at my feet, in heels, looked back at the wide eyes, and then closed the door behind me, spikes sinking into the snow.

"Sarah…" I called and ran as best as I could up the path. "Wait."

She turned.

"You came here for a reason." I couldn't imagine why she came here.

She paused, looked over my shoulder at the house. I craned my neck back to see what she was looking at. Part of me wondered if she wanted to confess.

"What is it?" I asked.

She moved her hand into her pocket and looked again at the door behind me.

"I just miss her. I'm sorry. I have to go."

I stepped toward her and teetered in my stupid heels.

"I'd like to…" I reached for her and hugged her, my voice caught. "I don't know…" She was limp beneath my arms.

She pulled away from me, turned, and started to run.

I saw something shiny fly out of her coat.

"Wait!" I ran to where I saw it fall. "Sarah!" I stared down but couldn't see anything. I moved the snow back and forth with the toe of my shoe and saw it…that flip phone I'd seen her with. "Your phone!" I called. But she was gone. She didn't turn. She may have paused.

Gina and Joe were still in the foyer when I came back in. I looked at them as I rubbed my shoes back and forth on the mat like a bull, wanting to get back in at something. Gina waved at my shoes. "Just get in here." She put her arm around me, Joe following with his hand on my other shoulder.

"She dropped her phone." I shrugged and flipped open the cover without thinking. I closed it and reopened it. I pressed the side button for power, paused. Nothing. I flipped it back shut. I looked up. I felt stupid for prying into her life. "It's dead, I guess. I'll get it to her. I see her around town," I said, more to myself than to Gina and Joe.

"Is that Nathalie's phone?" Gina said, pulling my arm slightly before we entered back into the living room.

I looked at Gina, then the phone.

Gina touched it. "Yes, I think that's hers. She was the only person I knew with a flip phone." She shrugged. "Maybe she forgot it when she was last with Sarah…" She smiled a thin line. "Well, doesn't matter."

We moved back in, and I slid the phone onto the edge of the coffee table. I stared at the half-eaten pies on the plates, whipped cream puddled on the edges. What now? How would we segue into anything after all that? I just wanted to get to McCool. I still had the letter, of course. Remember the favor I asked Jenna at the Brik? It was to go along with the letter so I could read the faces in the group. I'd never thought she'd be so good at it!

If someone else had written the letter, the case had to be reopened. I was hoping someone would crack with the spelling of Nathalie's name. I had made that up, of course. I don't know what I hoped for. But I did get something through their expressions…but that wasn't evidence. I know I didn't have much, I knew these letters usually aren't anything. And I know, I know—I should have brought it to McCool right away. But I figured another day. I had everyone here for Christmas. And like I said, these letters usually don't amount to anything. But I had a feeling…

I stared at the flames. Maybe because it was Christmas Eve… Christmas Day…maybe everyone was holding onto words, keeping their thoughts silent. Wanting to move, get away, get out of the hot seat.

Mr. Brooks finally stood. "Well, it's late, guys. What do you say?"

Joe stood, then Jenna and Graham. I looked at Jenna, her face white and tight. "I'm sorry, everyone," Jenna said. She looked at Gina. I did feel bad about Gina.

I didn't have much. I'd pick it up again in the morning, it didn't matter it was Christmas Day.

"Wait," Gina said. "Please wait." She waved her hands for everyone to sit. "Just for another moment. It's Christmas Eve…it's Christmas. I don't want you to leave like this."

I scanned the room. Kiki looked the most relaxed. Her job was done. Harry and Olivia stared at the coffee table. I'd seen Mr. Brooks, Olivia's eyes on the phone a few times since I had placed it on the coffee table. I absently pushed it from its edge. Mr. Brooks finally made it back to his chair, as though he'd been waiting for all of us to sit before he followed suit. I couldn't see how we were going to get to a Christmas carol from here. The hiss of the fire rolled in the quiet.

"Okay, oh, what a night," Gina said, acknowledging everyone with a sweep of the circle, and then continued, "I think we have to let her go. I'm guilty. I know I've wanted to keep hanging on." She pulled her dress straight and looked back up. "Every Christmas Eve, Nathalie used to say, is for helping someone. I think this year it was for me…this here..." She pointed down with both hands. "I think this was all…you were all here to help me let her go." She looked at Jenna. "Maybe it was a two-for-one deal, what do you think?" She touched Jenna's arm. "Maybe for you as well?"

Jenna ceded a stiff smile.

"Okay, it's coming up to one. Can you believe it? But can we do one more thing before you go? Can we be really corny? We used to sing at the end of the night. It was another one of Nathalie's Christmas Eve traditions.

It never felt corny, then…but with all that's gone on here…" She clenched her teeth together and pulled back her lips, as though waiting to get an eye roll or two.

By God, we were going to get to a Christmas carol. I looked around the circle.

Gina continued, "I know it's not New Year's yet, but it's tradition…" She smiled. "…and it's fitting." Gina looked around the circle and then began, "Should auld acquaintance be forgot…"

And then the group joined… "and never brought to mind? Should auld acquaintance be forgot and auld lang syne?"

I thought of Gina's poem I had read earlier. What was the last line… 'step into the moment?' That's how I would sum up Gina: you always found her there, in the moment. Joe squeezed my hand. I was there—it had latched onto me. And that bass-baritone again from Johnny Cash… 'And then I *really* felt the Christmas Spirit.' But I still had a nag from another spirit. I looked at the two candles on the table that seemed to be flickering along with our song. I felt like I was saying good-bye to someone I never knew, would never forget. Maybe she was saying good-bye to Gina, to Mr. Brooks, Jenna…but not me. As I looked into the bobbing flames, it felt more like a wave. I was there for a reason.

"Join me in the den?" Gina asked after we finished drying the last pot, covering the leftover pies. "I know it's late, but you know me."

I was happy for the familiarity of the den, my cushion, her pipe. Plus, I was too aroused for sleep.

"Can we do it?" Gina let out a puff of smoke. I watched it swirl, I followed it as it stretched, floated by me.

"What's that?" I pulled my knees into my chest and hugged them.

"Let her go?"

I couldn't. "I *am* sorry, Gina. I guess I'm a digger. I push it too much…but I don't know…" No. I wouldn't tell her that I couldn't let it go. I could let Nathalie go, but I knew I'd be at the police station in the morning. I would have gone already, but there were no lives in danger. I didn't want to upset anyone, especially Gina.

"No, no," she interrupted.

I was grateful I didn't have to try to finish the sentence.

"Like I said, I know I said it as kind of a joke earlier, but there's truth to it. You brought her out for the good-bye. And Kiki, she had a big role there, too." She fanned her free hand. "For the grand finale." She laughed. "So, thank you. Really."

"That letter…sorry…" I pulled my dress lower down my legs. I had to know what Gina was thinking. "So, what do you think about it? It couldn't have been here a year ago…" I scrunched my nose and waited for Gina.

"I don't know." She tapped her pipe. "Maybe Kiki…for some strange reason. Maybe she really was helping me let her go in her way. I don't know. I think she will be okay now, though. I don't think she's going to hold on to that anymore."

Did she believe that? I had to wonder if Gina was trying to let something more go than Nathalie.

She tapped her pipe one more time and uncrossed her legs. "What do you say? It's after two."

I tiptoed up creak after creak, not wanting to wake Harry and Kiki. That was a first—going to bed after them. The moon shone along the bathroom tiles. I brushed my teeth, taking my time, waiting for the click of Gina's door. I pictured the letter. The handwriting. Did it look familiar? I headed up to my room, sat on the edge of my bed, and waited longer. I stared at the Christmas tree. My eyes blurred into the tiny lights…then blurred to the faces earlier by the firelight.

I jumped up. I did recognize the handwriting. I'd seen it on that card at the hospital. The person who wrote the note was the person who dropped off the flowers. That person had access to the house. I pictured Olivia that first day I saw her. Her gray eyes, like bullets firing up to the attic. And tonight, her flat stare across the dining room table as though she sensed I knew something. Mr. Brooks said he got a bad vibe from her. When was the last time Mr. Brooks had been at Gina's? His irritation about the letter…he did seem irritated. And Harry, who lived in this house. I shuddered. He had had a relationship with Nathalie. I pictured the N&H carved into the table in the break room at the diner. How often was it the person closest who was the murderer… And Kiki always scurrying in and out.

But what did I know? I didn't really know anything. I thought of Olivia accusing Sarah. But the flowers were sent to Sarah. Could Sarah have signed a blank card? Wow, that's a wild card! I kept zipping over everything I had compiled over the week. I had no real proof, but I knew there was something…

I tiptoed back down to the living room to retrieve the envelope out from between the cushion and the armrest. The original letter. I had planted the copy for Jenna to read when I lit the candles earlier before the guests arrived. I threw the cushion aside. I looked on the floor, and then I heard a creak on the floorboards behind me.

"Are you looking for this?"

Chapter Fourteen

"Gina!" I gasped.

"I saw that sleight of hand earlier with Jenna."

I sat on the edge of the sofa. "You nearly gave me a heart attack."

"Sorry. I knew you were up to something, Snoopy."

"I thought you were in bed?"

"I came back down to check the stove and remembered your little move. I thought I'd have a peek. I guess you're rubbing off on me." She smiled and wagged her brows. "So, tell me, what's going on?" She came and sat beside me and handed me the letter.

I gave her the short version. It sreas after two.

"So, what now?" she asked.

"The police will have someone who can analyze the handwriting. If it wasn't Nathalie…then they have to reopen the case." I didn't tell her I knew who it was. I was pretty sure. But I didn't want to upset her any further.

She put her arm around me and leaned her head against mine.

"So, what's up between you and Mr. Brooks? What was that exchange over his scar?" I asked.

She tapped her head against mine and pulled away. "Does that mind ever just rest up there? We were having a moment, were we not?" She laughed.

I giggled but nodded, waiting for her answer.

"He cut his arm badly after he left here years ago, the Christmas I had invited him as my guest. He took it as a sign. He wasn't ready to let go of Ella yet."

"Do you have room for him?" I remembered her swooning about her needing lots of room for a man in her life.

"I don't know, Snoopy. I don't know."

This time we walked the stairs together. She hugged me before turning into her room and said, "I guess you won't sleep, hey? But give it a try, Sweetie."

I sat back on the edge of the bed and stared at the letter. Yeah, I wouldn't sleep. I pulled my dress over my head and threw on jeans, a sweater.

I slipped out the front door and ran all the way to the station. My lungs hurt for the last few blocks, but I kept pushing, my gulps so thick in front of me, it felt as though it was trying to squeeze back into my chest. I bent over to catch my breath and pulled the letter out of my pocket. The lights in the hallway were dimmed, but the front office was bright with fluorescents. Detective McCool looked up at me as soon as I walked in, my breath audible. He stood right away, looked beyond me, out the glass doors. He must have thought I was in trouble. I put my hand up. "I'm okay," I managed to get out between breaths. I heard a phone ring in the distance. There was light from another bright office down the hall, then someone answered it.

"I couldn't wait until the morning," I said.

He looked at me, over me again, then stretched his arm out toward the office. "Have a seat."

I pulled off my hat, and he stared at my head and smirked. I looked back at him, he grinned and raised a finger to his head and then pointed to mine. "Cute." He chuckled.

I touched my head. "Oh." The candy cane. I pulled it out of my bun. Under any other circumstance, I would have handed it to him and said, 'Merry Christmas.' But I wasn't feeling it. And I wanted him to take me seriously. It was going to be hard enough with just a hunch and a letter in his office.

"So, you're okay?" He closed a file on his desk and moved it aside, picked up a pen, and started clicking the ballpoint in and out with his thumb. "I can relax?"

I nodded. I stared at the pen, willing him to stop the clicking. He took the hint and let it drop. "So, what's up that couldn't wait until Christmas morning?" I could tell he wasn't joking, but it seemed like something funny to say.

I placed the letter on the desk, and he looked down at it, then up at me. "What do you have there?"

I put my hand over it. I didn't want to start with that. I told him everything I thought was relevant. I was pretty good at getting to a punch line in those situations, mostly due to my experience with the CCCs. With our cases, I had interviewed a few witnesses, been at that station half a dozen times, sat in that seat I was sitting in.

As I wrapped up the latest, the events of the evening on Union, I started to hear it all play back to me. I didn't have much of anything. Although I stuck to all the bits and pieces I had, while keeping my delivery fast-paced, it did feel like I was meandering. Was his eyebrow always slightly raised as it was like that? I hadn't noticed it before. Maybe it was in my honor. Probably.

He picked up his pen, he clicked it once, then let it fall. Maybe he had noticed an eyebrow on me lift. "So, you have this letter here…" He looked at it, and I gave it a limp push across the desk. "And a box of hunches. Sorry, Ali, but…"

"I know. I know. But haven't you said sometimes you know. You just know and follow it. I am trying to do that here. Feel it in my gut…you've said that?" I paused. "Someone will take a look at that, won't they? Compare the handwriting?" My mind flashed to the card lying on the bedside table at the hospital. It had been crumpled and bent in half. I was sure Sarah hadn't saved it in a scrapbook. *Shoot.* I pulled on my scarf to let some heat rise out of my coat. It *was* a big box of hunches.

"Do you have the card, too?"

I shook my head. "But I could…maybe get it…" Maybe. My case was sounding weaker and weaker…my case.

"Even so…" He shrugged. He looked at me kindly. I think I recognized sympathy. "That's not much to go on, is it?" He picked up the letter and looked down at it. "You know it, Ali. You know these letters from your cold cases. They're usually nothing."

"I know." But I knew.

"Well." He paused. "We will take a look at it. There was no evidence of foul play, but we can look at it. We can talk to Sarah as well. See what she says about the flowers and if she knows …what's her name?"

"Olivia."

He took a pad, made a few notes. "I don't think there's anyone in danger here…" He looked at me.

I shook my head.

"I will set up a meeting, see if the department agrees to reopen the case based on what you've given me."

I bit my lip. I knew once a case was closed, no one got too excited about reopening it unless there was some hard evidence. I didn't have any. I pushed away from the desk. "Thank you. I appreciate it. I know I don't have much here, but I think it's worth a look."

He stood and met me on the other side of the desk. "Okay, Ali. If you think of anything else, don't hesitate."

We moved into the dim hallway, then walked to the front doors. The moon lit the sky. I turned and handed him the candy cane. "Merry Christmas." I know, pretty lame bribe.

Back in the attic, I left my Christmas tree lights on, as we used to do when I was a kid on Christmas Eve. Well, it wasn't Christmas Eve, anymore…it had been Christmas Day for hours. I went over my notes, over and over. Finally, I sank into my pillow and pulled the comforter up to my chin. The moon shone through the drapes as I waited for the sun. I would never sleep after all that. I flipped onto my side, and the moon caught the silver glint on my night table. I reached over and picked up the phone Sarah had dropped, flipped to my back again and jabbed the side in hopes for power. How long had the phone been dead and what was Sarah doing with Nathalie's phone? I slid it back onto my night table and sighed into the quiet. I had to let it go. I had nothing. I held on the silver in the moonlight, then stared at the desk. I threw off the covers.

The desk drawer jerked back and forth. I didn't think about being quiet. I stared at the box. The little keys glistened on the wood beside the desk lamp. I removed the box. A shot of adrenaline renewed my anticipation. Maybe I *was* meant to find that box, to find all I had found. I *was* meant to be here. Under the pictures, I felt for the battery. It had to be for the phone. That was the answer, that was why I was here, pulsed through my mind. I replaced the battery with the one in the desk.

Snap, click, hum. I paused. The phone vibrated in my hand. I held my breath, then flipped it open. The last caller had been Sarah. There were no phone messages. I scanned the texts. Nothing was recent it seemed. Again, I wondered how long the phone had been dead. I scrolled through the contacts, and I don't know why…the photos. There were only a few. Mostly of Nathalie and Harry…

There was a video. It was dark. Night. I peered at the jumping picture. It was too dark. But then I made out someone, and someone else bounced into the screen. I turned up the volume and squinted at the image. I recognized the coat. They were on the bank of the lake by the Red Rocks. I heard Olivia's voice. "Let's do a selfie." I recognized Nathalie from the pictures I had seen. Then a screech…then a scrambled shot of the lake. The video cut. Olivia had pushed her. Olivia had pushed her! I don't know how loud I screamed. It felt blocked like one of those frustrating screams in sleep-paralysis. My hands shook as I called 911 on my phone.

Chapter Fifteen

"Happy New Year!" I let the last customers out and flipped the closed sign on the door of the diner. I looked at the clock over the tree, just after three, then my gaze lay on the scatter of pine needles on the floor. It would come down the day after tomorrow. I felt a pang of sadness. It was all over for another year. It was all over. New Year's Eve would be quiet, due to the long week that had just passed. Gina was having a few people over, the usual suspects, except Jenna and Graham had finally headed back to their lives. Hopefully, Jenna would find some peace after learning that Nathalie was murdered. It would take a while for everyone to process that.

I started to clear the tables. It was my last shift. I was happy to have a few moments alone. I hummed along with Ella Fitzgerald to *What Are You Doing New Year's Eve*. I paused at one of the booths and stared out into the snow that kept coming, that seemed to have no end. I thought of Harry. He had been a sheet of white when I passed him the phone, and he watched the video that night…just a week ago. He had been in my room in under a minute after I screamed, Gina not far behind him. And Kiki, well, she slept through my scream, which didn't surprise me.

Harry hadn't been serious with Olivia, thankfully. But he was more than shocked, of course. Gina's anger surprised me—it rushed out of her like a mad banshee, but then she turned it over. I'm not sure what or whom she turned it over to, but it seemed effective. Harry took a few days off work, and all three of us had snuggled into the den each night. Gina with her pipe, Harry with his thoughts, all of us quiet, but there was a comfortable reliance we would all show up even if not much was said. Over those few days, Harry started to piece it all together as he shook his head, and Gina and I nodded. It seemed obvious to him, after the fact. Olivia's interest in him, her interest in the house…her access to the house through him and Gina. On the third evening, Harry seemed to have come back to himself for the most part. He surprised me, but Gina didn't seem all that surprised when he said, "What kind of a psychic are you, anyway?" That remark after Gina said she couldn't believe she hadn't picked up on Olivia. "I think I'm bound to the local fairs, that's all I have left," she had said. We all laughed, a little louder and a little longer than I think we thought possible. Even though I was prone to laughing in the wrong situations, it was in that moment I realized maybe we should take it when we can.

I helped Gina get Nathalie's old room ready for the new renter. "It's time," she said. I was glad I was with her. She had some moments, but she was ready. She was good at letting go, being in the moment. I was happy I would be able to have more of that being in the moment with her the year ahead…and who knows…maybe the year after.

We ran into Sarah at the police station. Everyone in and out having to make their statements. She had been there longer than anyone, I think. I hated to see her embarrassment for not giving up the phone to the police the year before. And a deep root that hadn't been touched in a long while it seemed when Gina hugged her with her eyes. Maybe the last person who had looked at her like that, who had wanted to help her, had been Nathalie. I pulled my arm out of my link with Gina's and touched Sarah's forearm. "I was thinking, I could ask Rick at the diner, I think they may need someone…I think you might start as a dishwasher…it would be a start…"

Sarah, who had been with Nathalie earlier on the night she was pushed off the bluff, had found the phone along the shore. Nathalie's phone. Sarah had been there before the police had had a chance to comb the area. She never looked at the phone until after she had heard that Nathalie had been found dead days later. She hadn't wanted to invade her privacy. And by then the phone was dead, so she never knew about the video. She had wanted to hang on to something of Nathalie's, always hoping she could get the phone working…to have something to keep her connected. She was devastated that she had held a clue and didn't know, that she never brought the phone to the police.

What motivated Olivia on that night is not entirely clear. She hadn't meant to take that video…she had meant to take a picture…to lure Nathalie into the right spot to easily fall…or to easily nudge. She had no idea there was that video, either. And she thought the phone had fallen into the lake. But after that evening, she had started to cover her tracks. The book, the letter. She planted them in case she ever needed them…in case anyone thought she had something to do with the 'fall.' She had known Nathalie felt guilty about her little sister drowning even though Nathalie had not pushed her into the river. I guess she had pushed her earlier and the push stuck to her, stuck to her forever. That came out in the end from a diary of Nathalie's that had seemed irrelevant a year ago but had become something to be looked at due to it being a case. A solved case. Olivia gave Nathalie the Ophelia book and at some point, had placed the letter in that box of Nathalie's things.

Sarah had said Olivia seemed jealous of Nathalie, that she had been interested in Harry before Nathalie came along. But the real reason, the sadness of it all was more than likely drug related. Nathalie, who had been Sarah's sponsor, also tried to help others at the detox center, including Olivia. Olivia had had a setback that night. Her sentence might be slightly reduced as they might plead it was a drug-induced homicide, but it's still Murder One, given the planning Olivia did. And a year later…how could anyone ever really know. I still don't believe in ghosts, but the house is quieter, and there was a reason I was meant to be there, to rent that room in the attic.

"Hey," Joe said.

I turned and smiled as he pulled off his white cap, and he smiled back with his teeter-smile, always teetering on a laugh.

"A last coffee together?" I asked and moved behind the counter.

He groaned, pretended to groan, and pulled me in, kissed my nose, my lips. "Guess you're made for sleuthing, hey? Can't convince you to stay?"

I kissed him back twice. "I'll still be in the 'hood." I wasn't going anywhere. I would look forward to the days when I'd be on Main, when I'd walk into the diner…I'd have a coffee from a different angle. I wouldn't look for anyone. Adam would just be there, Mr. Brooks, Boston, Sally. Maybe someone new. I'd see Sarah come out and take the tray of dirty dishes through the kitchen, her cheeks filled in, her eyes brighter. Joe would lean on the counter and lift his mug at me.

As I stared out into our winter wonderland, shoulder-to-shoulder with Joe, the snow whirling under the lamppost, I thought of our snow angels. My mind played tricks on me. I saw a woman crossing the street toward the diner, smiling up at the snow, and then the image was gone. The snow spiraled up toward the lamppost, I followed it up until I could no longer see it.

www.ingramcontent.com/pod-product-compliance
Lightning Source LLC
Chambersburg PA
CBHW070625100726
47907CB00007B/1865